Black Waters

"Every man approached in Flinthammock went off without question in any old boat. 'Di'nt get no further than Ramsgate. Owd boats fell ter pieces,' said Auburn spitefully."
(from *The Oaken Heart* by Margery Allingham)

Black Waters *is dedicated to Claudia Myatt, in gratitude for all the songs she has sung with my mother as well as all exquisite pictures she has drawn for me and all the good advice freely given.*

It is also dedicated to Nicci Gerrard in recognition of the extraordinary shared experience that is John's Campaign.

Black Waters

Julia Jones

VOLUME FIVE
OF THE *Strong Winds* SERIES

Illustrated by Claudia Myatt

GOLDEN DUCK

First published in 2015 by Golden Duck (UK) Ltd.,
Sokens,
Green Street,
Pleshey, near Chelmsford,
Essex.
CM3 1HT
www.golden-duck.co.uk

ISBN 9781899262267

www.claudiamyatt.co.uk

Title font (Old Rubber Stamp) by Rebecca Simpson
rebeccasimpsondesign@gmail.com

Design by Megan Trudell
www.emdash.me.uk

e-book conversion by Matti Gardner
matti@grammaticus.co.uk

Printed and bound in the UK
by Biddles Limited, King's Lynn, Norfolk

Contents

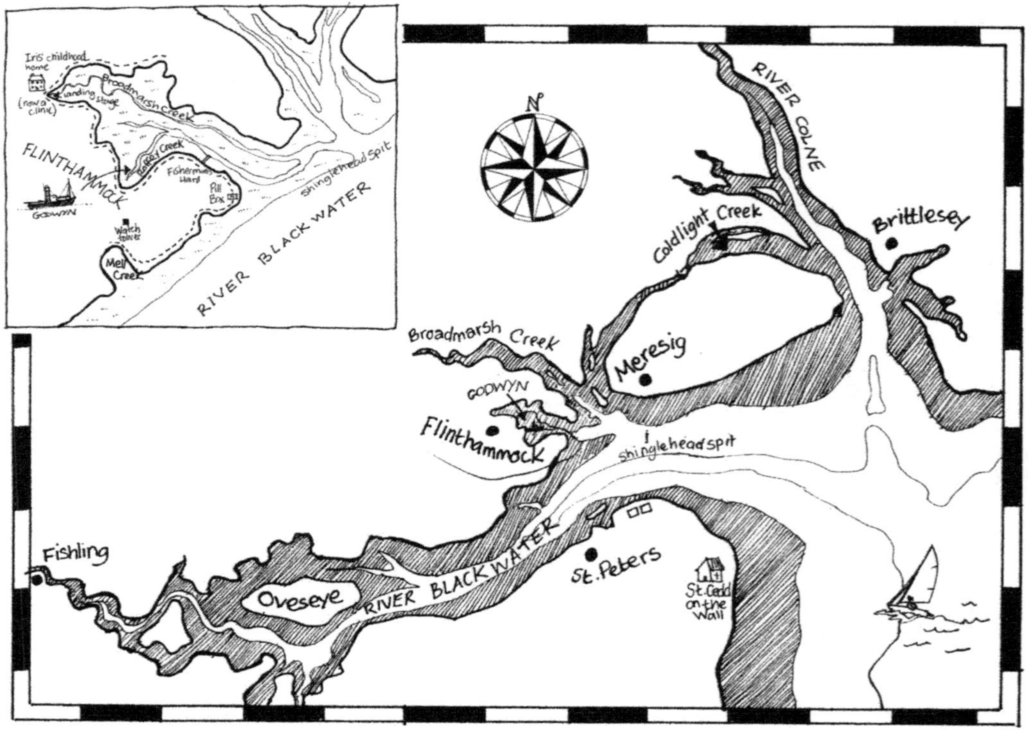

Iris' childhood home
(now a clinic)
landing stage
Broadmarsh Creek
FLINTHAMMOCK
GODWYN
Fisherman's Hard
Pill Box
Watch tower
Mell Creek
shingle head spit
RIVER BLACKWATER
RIVER COLNE
Brittlesey
Coldlight Creek
Broadmarsh Creek
Meresig
GODWYN
Flinthammock
shingleheadspit
St. Peters
St. Cedd on the Wall
RIVER BLACKWATER
Oveseye
Fishling

It was everything she could ever have hoped for! They were offering her their full, official sponsorship. It was public affirmation AND a new Laser dinghy. There'd be new kit as well and help with travel expenses if she was competing abroad. It meant she wouldn't need to keep asking her parents. She was sixteen now. It was time she began managing for herself.

She really wanted that new dinghy. She'd won the Area Championships using her younger sister's boat. It was okay but it had been getting old before they bought it. She was still in mourning for her own boat, Spray, *her wave-arrow, her foam-flyer – the dinghy she'd wrecked. If the sponsors brought her a new Laser she'd call it* Spray *as well –* Spray II *maybe – and the spirit would live on.*

The letter from the GB Racing committee had already arrived. The selectors had confirmed the offer they'd made earlier in the year. Xanthe was off their potentials list and into the squad. The letter said that she was expected to attend the Getting2Gold Easter training camp at the National Sailing Academy in Weymouth. By then she'd have the new dinghy and the new equipment which she'd sort of earned for herself.

Xanthe pledged that she would do whatever it took – she'd train harder, get up earlier, watch her diet and her weight, learn everything she could from the top coaches she'd be meeting there. They'd be medal-winners themselves, some of them. Her life of racing stretched before her. Maybe she wouldn't have to bother about exam results and university applications. The Olympics lay glimmering beyond her horizon like the gold at the end of the rainbow. She was on course. Her wave-arrow, her foam-flyer, her new Spray.

CHAPTER ONE

Rule 69

Xanthe was sailing badly and she knew it. She couldn't concentrate: couldn't get that sugar-sweet patronising voice out of her bad-tempered head. Their coach had ordered them to swap dinghies then race two-on-two. A dozen pairs of Laser Radials duelling in the clear blue waters of Weymouth Bay. She was in Madrigal Shryke's *Imperium*: Maddie had Xanthe's *Spray II*. The selectors were watching.

"If the helmsman's good enough, they can step into any boat and win," Griselda, their coach, had said. "Yes, when one of you reaches the final stages – when it's the Olympics and you're against the best in the world – then everything's going to matter. Now and here I don't need you to give yourselves the excuses that a team-mate has a richer sponsor or a better boat. Let's find your weak points now and get them sorted."

"What a treat this'll be for you!" Madrigal had said, smiling as if for camera, with her big, white, perfectly-even teeth. "The chance to take a peep at all those clever little tweaks and niggles my techies have dreamed up for me. Honestly, it's okay if you want to copy across. I mean we're all in this together, aren't we? For now."

Her golden tan was as smooth as if she'd paid for it – which of course she had, though not directly. Everyone knew that she was just home from the Antigua Classics where Daddeh had a Yacht. "The climate's so absolutely perfect for us fair-skinned types at this time of yeah. You must feel the cold terribly," she had added, turning to Xanthe. "I expect you need thermal undies even in our English summer!"

Xanthe hadn't bothered mentioning the years of childhood she and her sister Maggi had spent on the Canadian Great Lakes before their family returned to live in Suffolk. She knew Madrigal's comment was only one more way to draw attention to her colour. Yes, so Xanthe was the only black teenager competing in the Laser classes at this level – yes, *so*?

At least that's how easily she would have coped before this week at the Getting2Gold training camp. Now she was struggling. She was on her own and missing her family, Maggi especially. Maggi was a sailor too. They'd always competed together, since the days when they'd had little white Optimists and their old Mirror dinghy, *Lively Lady*. Maggi was good but she was in it for fun, not necessarily for winning. This week was only about winning.

Which should have been totally fine because Xanthe was desperate to win. She was capable of winning, she was determined to win. She just wasn't succeeding.

It had got harder and harder to keep her focus. She'd expected that it would have been easier without her sister always teasing her and setting her straight and their parents unobtrusively waiting in the background, watchful and ready to help. But it wasn't.

Xanthe had watched herself on the training video looking tense and uncertain and reacting too soon or too late. This afternoon was the worst yet. She knew she was a better sailor than Madrigal Shryke. Swapping dinghies shouldn't have made any real difference at all. So why couldn't she simply tune her out and win?

The course had started with a deceptively straightforward

down-wind leg, sending each pair of sailors directly away from the harbour and out to sea, giving them time and space to adjust to their borrowed boats and too much time to chat – or to 'sledge' as they'd probably say in cricket. It was almost the end of the week. Xanthe should have been accustomed to Madrigal's subtle put-downs, her fake compliments and the in-jokes, which she knew that Xanthe wouldn't get. Every other competitor was her 'bestie', it seemed, and she could lock Xanthe out of a conversation with a shrug of her shapely shoulders, a lift of plucked eyebrows or a flick of her honey-blonde hair.

Xanthe had mainly walked away. Sailed away. She'd spent all her free time either in the Academy library or out exploring Weymouth Bay – and trying to think. "Let's find your weak points," Griselda had said, "and get them sorted." First part done: second…not so obvious at all.

The water sparkled in the pale sun; the wind blew lightly off the land. It shifted with the swell and dip of the Jurassic coast and curved with the chalky outcrop of Portland Bill. It was tricksy and interesting. That's where her attention should be, not on Madrigal's continuous dissing of *Spray* and her over-excited cooings about how Xanthe'd simply *love* some particular feature of *Imperium*.

"Honestly, her high modulus ropes are to die for! Do get your sponsors to dig a little deeper. Most of the stuff they've given you is so twentieth century. Or did you deliberately down-grade for today?"

"It wouldn't have crossed my mind."

"Of *course* it wouldn't. You're so *refreshingly* straightforward. I expect you grew up with the lateen rig and rush-plaiting!"

"Huh?" Xanthe hadn't noticed how neatly Madrigal

had positioned herself and *Spray* to get maximum tow from *Imperium*'s quarter wave. When she understood what had been said, she lost concentration for a moment, shifted awkwardly and slipped sideways ahead of her rival.

"Ooops, careful," said Madrigal, fouling Xanthe's wind from behind, before luffing slightly and moving upsides.

"I've always imagined you being like those *amazing* footballers who learn in the dust without boots," she continued.

She had a high clear voice with perfect pronunciation. She turned her head to make certain Xanthe could catch every word, whilst simultaneously, expertly, adjusting her balance as *Spray* creamed ahead.

"You've done so well simply to get here – even with the help you've had from the quota system."

"I'm here," Xanthe snapped, "Because I'm the Eastern Area Champion. There is no quota in Suffolk."

"Ooops," said Madrigal again. "Sore spot? *So* sorry!"

With a huge effort Xanthe banished the conversation from her mind. She hung on grimly, inched *Imperium* forward and the two dinghies were almost together as they rounded the first mark. Now for the long up-wind beat.

"Oh *lovely*," called Madrigal, knowing that the assistant coach in the race boat could hear. "Oh well done! You're really starting to get the hang of *Imperium* now. Super!"

Xanthe saw her moment and luffed, seizing the windward position as brutally as she dared. Madrigal didn't seem fazed at all.

"You're sensing how good she is, aren't you?" she called again, not missing a beat as she eased *Spray*'s sheets, sailed through *Imperium*'s dirty wind and held her course smoothly as she waited for the first wind-shift to call for Water! and to tack across. "What an experience this must be for you!"

It was an experience – but not a good one. Madrigal was sailing her down as if the only thing that mattered was that Xanthe would do badly, not that either of them would do well. They made a hundred tacks where a dozen would have been normal. They pushed each other from side to side, they forced fouls and penalties on one another. Whatever Xanthe tried, she was blocked and she did everything she could to retaliate. It was a battle of tactics.

Her lack of flow and concentration made her sailing worse than it should have been. Slowly and surely Madrigal was getting the upper hand. On the final leg of the course, *Spray* began drawing away from *Imperium*. Madrigal was going to win by a distance.

Xanthe had nothing more to lose. She'd been out sailing at around this same time on the previous afternoon and she'd felt the wind grow stronger as it bent round the inner edge of Portland Bill. She'd take her own line and if she caught that same strengthening – well, at least she'd have had some fun. She was also gambling on the chance of an additional tidal boost.

It seemed to take forever to reach. The assistant coach followed anxiously as if she thought Xanthe'd forgotten the course. Xanthe gritted her teeth and carried on. She didn't even look at Madrigal and *Spray*.

Then she caught it – wind and tide powering her forward. She could feel *Imperium* shifting up a gear. There was more wave motion than she'd expected. That was joy. Xanthe loved sea-sailing. She steered up and surfed down, pumping the Laser's sail to increase her speed on every wave. It was absorbing and delicious. She was rushing on her way.

She didn't lose the race by much but she knew that she'd lost unnecessarily. If she hadn't allowed herself to be so angry and distracted for so long she would have gone up-wind earlier. She would have grabbed every knot of that extra speed – and she would have won. In the mind-games competition Madrigal had totally lapped her. Her moment of elation faded. She felt furious with herself.

"Not bad at all," said Madrigal as she passed *Spray*'s painter to Xanthe but made no move to fetch the launching trolley or help her take the dinghy from the water.

Her own team had been standing ready to wheel *Imperium* away and begin the careful washing-down process before removing the control lines and rolling the sail from head to foot.

"They've given you something quite solid there. It must have been such an unbelievable break for you when those Suffolk container people were forced into offering sponsorship. It was some sort of compensation wasn't it? Or do you think they were trying to make their image more multi-cultural?"

"I've no idea." Xanthe still couldn't credit what she was hearing. "If you're not going to fetch the trolley maybe you could hold the dinghy while I do? If it isn't too much trouble."

"Of *course* not," Madrigal smiled and stepped helpfully towards her.

Somehow this sent *Spray* swinging against the rough concrete of the landing slope. Suddenly there were two deep scratches scored along her hull.

"Oh, I'm *so* sorry! And you haven't any support, have you? Absol*utely* no need to worry, my team will patch her up. After all, it's us under the spotlight: our skills and not our boats – or so

Griselda claims. Between you and me, though, Daddy's certain that the selectors will be looking at the total package. They'll want to know who's bringing the most to the GBR party. He's made a *big* contribution to the Academy. And that's in addition to my sponsorship. He likes to give me what I want."

Madrigal's sponsors were some sort of property firm with a distinctive curved sword as their symbol. (Xanthe happened to know that it was called a seax.) Their spending was legendary. As well as the money that was lavished on *Imperium* they'd provided Madrigal with a different set of logoed clothing for almost every wind direction, let alone temperature change. The men on her support team were employed full-time and had her name and the logos on everything they wore. If Maggi had been here Xanthe would have taken a bet on there being seax patterns on their boxer shorts but she'd felt too much of an outsider to make jokes with anyone else.

Madrigal paused and smiled again. She got a lot of money from sportswear modelling contracts and always seemed to hold each pose those few seconds extra to give the cameras time to click.

She still didn't go for the trolley and Xanthe was definitely not going to leave her alone with *Spray* while she fetched it herself. She stood knee-deep in Portland Harbour wondering whether anyone else would offer help. A half dozen of Madrigal's besties were blocking her access to the ramp.

"Yeah, sure, waddever, but we need to get my dinghy out. The sooner we hit the training room, the sooner Griselda gets her post-mortem done and the sooner we all go to tea."

"Of *course* we must. Everyone's noticed your appetite! It's genetic, isn't it?"

Maggi always said that she didn't know when her sister was most likely to go ape: when she'd just lost a race or when she needed food. At the moment it was both.

"Can I share one teensie thought with you?" said Madrigal, her blonde hair haloed in a shaft of sun. "When I saw you struggling out there in *Imperium* I couldn't help wondering whether you'd ever thought how much it would mean to your own country if you elected to sail for them instead? Wherever it is in Africa that you originally came from…I'm so completely *hopeless* at geography. They probably haven't even got a sailing team! Rig a bathtub and you'd make it unopposed. It wouldn't be like country-shopping; you'd be a national heroine. Your own *tribe*!"

The afternoon breeze seemed to whistle with Madrigal's voice; her sight was full of Madrigal's pretty face and Madrigal's laughing friends; a whiff of Madrigal's flowery fragrance blew sweet in the sea-salt air.

Xanthe stepped up and punched her.

The other girl fell back. She lost her footing and missed the edge of the ramp. Her eyes were wide and her mouth an O of surprise as she tumbled backwards into the shallow water. Her primrose pull-ups were soaked. There was a rip in her lilac logoed windcheater.

Xanthe could not believe herself. How could she have done this? She was totally ashamed. She stepped forward to help her rival up with her hand held out and apologies pouring from her heart.

It was far too late. Madrigal was white with shock and fury. The luvvies were gasping. Griselda had been on her way out from the training room to hurry them along and had seen

Madrigal go down. She was told what had happened – and more – by all of Madrigal's friends.

Xanthe gave up trying. She pushed blindly past and heaved *Spray* onto the ramp. She fetched her trolley, loaded the dinghy and hauled it away.

Madrigal stood dripping and shaking as the sun went in. She refused to move until every single person had expressed their horror and she'd been given a phone to call her parents.

Her father, Sir Hubert Shryke, arrived within half an hour, threatening action for assault. Her mother was there even sooner, ringing Madrigal's orthodontist – despite the fact that Xanthe's punch had landed on her shoulder. Griselda did her best to pacify them. She summoned Xanthe and asked for her explanation but Xanthe found nothing she could say. Her shame at her own behaviour was too raw. Anything she could say would sound like an excuse. So she said nothing.

There was a disciplinary hearing at the Academy the next morning. It should have been informal as the incident hadn't happened in a race situation but the Shrykes had briefed a lawyer. He was a grey, fussy man who earned his fee by invoking International Sailing Federation Rule 69.1. Xanthe was charged with gross misconduct and bringing the sport into disrepute. *A competitor shall not commit gross misconduct including gross breach of a rule, good manners or sportsmanship, or conduct bringing the sport into disrepute. Throughout Rule 69 competitor means a member of the crew, or the owner, of a boat.*

Xanthe's mother, June, and her sister, Maggi, drove down from Suffolk but Xanthe made them wait outside the meeting room. She didn't want them to hear what would be said. The collapse of her dreams was so utter that she couldn't bear to share it. Not yet – probably not ever.

Inside the meeting she agreed that her punch had been deliberate. She listened dumbly as the assistant coach related the scraps of conversation that she'd heard and when Griselda asked her directly whether there had been provocation, she waited for a moment and then shook her head.

"I was just a sore loser."

The coach tried again to help her but Xanthe couldn't respond. It was too humiliating and too hard to explain – she wasn't ready to understand it herself. Let alone put Madrigal's insinuations into words in a room full of white, uncomprehending faces, however basically kind.

She was thrown off the squad and given a six month racing ban. The Shrykes demanded an injunction that she stay away from their daughter but were finally persuaded not to prosecute. The Ribieros drove home to Suffolk, trailing Xanthe's dinghy.

The first tweets had been posted before they reached the motorway.

CHAPTER TWO

#barbarianbehaviour

They didn't use as many characters as that. When you've only got 140 letters and spaces to slag off someone you've never met and you need to get all your friends and followers doing the same, you don't waste nineteen of them on the hashtag. Anyway it soon got objected to by the people in the senior bits of GB Racing.

So the Twitter campaign against Xanthe used #bbarbie instead. It was very neat. There'd been a new black doll brought out for Christmas and that was controversial. You could pretend it was nothing to do with racing: nothing personal against anyone. Once the mass outrage at Xanthe's 'barbarian behaviour' had made everyone aware what the tweets were really about, then #bbarbie could be used in any number of imaginative ways.

Some of them were plain threatening: photos of African-American Barbie dolls being held underwater, dolls with snapped limbs or their heads pulled off.

Others were more subtle. The new range of Barbie dolls were designed to have more 'realistic' African features and frizzy hair that could be straightened if the little customers required. Xanthe's hair was strong and wiry. She usually scraped it up onto the top of her head in a bunch but #bbarbie users posed their dolls underneath England flags and offered helpful advice on bleaching and extending. The results were grotesque.

These new dolls were still stick-thin and it was easy for even the dimmest of Madrigal's friends to start a social media thread with a remark about the naturally fuller hips or the heavier bones of racial stereotypes, then adding a sailing jacket or wet suit to make it clear who it was that they were talking about. There were pictures of black Barbies struggling in the water or Xanthe herself, snapped jogging or working out but with a doll's head superimposed. "Why do black people run faster than whites?" "Why don't they swim so well?" "Have they all got thicker skulls?"

Someone photo-shopped a Laser dinghy black and white and called it the Oreo. Then there were lots of good ideas for future Olympic competitions that would involve punching and running away and getting sponsorship to sail in hollowed-out tree trunks. It seemed this flood of creativity would never end. Old photos of Xanthe sailing for her club or receiving awards were discovered and manipulated. Then someone began using photos taken at her sixth form college.

"I can't," said Xanthe. "I'm sorry, but I can't."

"Can't, my big sis? I didn't know you knew that word."

They were finishing breakfast. Her father, Joshua, was about to leave for the hospital. Maggi would be catching the school bus to Gallister High and June, who was a magistrate, was due in court.

"Then don't," she said immediately, looking up from her newspaper. "You don't have to. I'm amazed that you've stuck it for so long. I'll ring the college and tell them that you're not coming in."

Xanthe didn't acknowledge her mother. She was staring

at her uneaten food while the words she'd been damming up began pouring out.

"Every time I hear a text arriving on someone's phone or someone boots up a computer I assume they're going to be reading something bad about me – 'Black Barbie'" Xanthe choked. "I ought to think it's funny but I can't."

"You can't because it isn't," said Maggi. "It's totally sick." Her normally sweet expression was fierce.

"Yet you don't let me lodge an appeal with the RYA," said Joshua. "There must have been some reason. You need to talk to us, Xanthe. Hashtag Black Barbie! It's beneath contempt."

Xanthe hadn't managed more than a mouthful of juice and a couple of spoons of yoghurt. She pushed her chair back and left the table. Next thing they heard her in the toilet, throwing up.

"If I could do one thing for my sister right now," stormed Maggi, "I'd banish the letter B from the alphabet. And I'd withdraw *all* those stupid dolls. I'd melt them back into chemical soup. And how can they be using photos of Xanth at college? It's completely creepy."

"Maggi," said her mother, still holding her newspaper and not answering the important question, "You loved your Barbies – you didn't care what colour they were. Did you?"

Maggi calmed down. She took a deep breath.

"I do remember using a felt tip to darken one of them once but it was more like a style statement. I was never political. I loved all my dolls and they needed to look good."

"Especially if they'd gone bald or lost a leg. It was a paralympic couture-fest. Oh, those poor families!"

Maggi gawped at her mother, then realised she'd glanced

back to the newspaper report of some gangland feud that was finally coming to trial. A young mother had been killed with her child beside her. It was foul but it wasn't for them. Xanthe was still out of the room so Maggi felt okay talking about her.

"Xanthe never really got it about dolls."

"Poor, poor Xanthe," said June. She'd put her newspaper down now and was really concentrating.

"Isn't there *anything* we can do?" Joshua spoke like someone who asked himself that question several times a day and hadn't come up with an answer yet.

"If there is, it seems unlikely that she'll let us. And I can't stay home with her today because I have to be in court."

"And I've got ward rounds this morning then a full operating list."

"I've a GCSE coursework assessment. It counts to my final grade."

"We're not much use, are we?" said Joshua. "Exactly when she needs us."

"No," said June with an angry sigh. "But it's time I talked to the college at least. I'll phone them now and tell them she's not coming in, then I'm going to arrange a meeting with her tutor – whether Xanthe likes it or not."

She brushed the last of her crispbread crumbs neatly from her mouth, checked there were none on her turquoise jacket and stood up. She folded the newspaper into her bag and walked briskly next door. Seconds later they could hear her on the land-line.

Maggi and her father looked at one another. There were frown lines deep in Joshua's forehead. He rubbed them with the soft heel of his hand.

"I can't understand why she won't talk about it. She must know who these people are. And it's bullying, however they dress it up. I would never have expected my Xanthe to put up with bullying."

"I wouldn't have expected her to punch Madrigal Shryke either. I don't get what went wrong in Weymouth. She wanted it so much. Being selected for that training camp, new dinghy, new kit, good sponsors. It was her big chance."

"Who is this girl? Couldn't we talk to her parents?"

"No way, Dad – you need to get real. Madrigal Shryke is a complete and utter hag but she's pretty and she's charming and she's actually incredibly talented (except not quite as good as my big sis) AND she's rich. Sir Daddeh and Mumsie Shryke are rolling in it. They're always sponsoring things – like they were major donors to the Sailing Academy. Maddie's at some amazingly posh school and she has this total gang of luvvies. They'll be the ones posting the tweets. She's way too clever. I wish I knew what she'd said to make sis flip."

She hadn't noticed Xanthe standing in the doorway looking like someone who'd just had to splash a bucket of cold water over her face.

"Leave it, can't you? I was completely out of order and I've probably messed up my entire life but I need you to STOP going on about it."

Xanthe flung herself down on her chair. The smoothie carton toppled and splashed thick mango across the bright tablecloth.

"I DON'T WANT SYMPATHY."

"Okay," said June, who had also come back into the kitchen.

"Then maybe you should stop feeling sorry for yourself and begin thinking about other people. You can start today. In a house with dreadful mobile phone reception where you don't have a password for the wi-fi – even if you had time to use it. Which you won't."

Xanthe stared at her mother. This didn't sound very loving or sympathetic. June stared back, challenging her. Xanthe shrugged and gave in.

"Yeah, okay, why not? I don't care what I do. I can't face college now. I'll probably never race again and if I stay here on my own I'll only go on the net."

Joshua looked enquiringly at his wife. She smiled across at him.

"After I rang Xanthe's tutor, I rang Rev Wendy at Erewhon Parva Vicarage. She's always needing help – especially now she's taken on the Shelter full-time as well as her six parishes and baby Ellen – and her husband Gerald's got a bad back. I thought you could drop Xanthe there on your way to work."

Joshua laughed. It made him look so much younger. "I thought I felt sorry for my older daughter. But now with you and Wendy joining forces…! I assume that by the end of today you'll have cooked up some other scheme to take her out of social circulation?"

"It's possible." June looked serious and even depressed. "There are so many people who are so very much worse off."

Did that mean particular people or people all over the world? It didn't feel the right moment to ask. Xanthe cleared the almost-empty smoothie cartoon onto the draining board and shoved the tablecloth in a bucket to soak.

"Ellen's not such a baby any more," said Maggi. "She's gorgeous but she's a total terror. Every time they try to leave her in a crèche she gets expelled. She has Gerald wrapped around her little finger. And Wendy."

"Exactly." June was her brisk and cheerful self again. "So there'll be no time for Xanthe to go checking Facebook or Twitter or reading nasty anonymous texts. You're to leave your mobile here," she instructed her older daughter. "If your father or I need to speak to you, we'll use the vicarage land-line."

Xanthe was meant to be in her third term of the IB at her local sixth form college but she didn't go back that week. Every morning either June or Joshua delivered her to Erewhon Parva Vicarage. Her job was to take care of little Ellen while Gerald went for physio and Wendy caught up with her paperwork. It sounded okay but Xanthe'd never had anything much to do with toddlers. She enacted endless pirate stories, mixed mud pies, changed nappies, mopped up mess, chatted to Ellen's canary and floated sticks down streams. By the end of every day she was exhausted.

It still was hard to keep herself off the internet in the evenings. Wi-fi was everywhere in the house, in her room, on her phone. It was such a habit to sign in, to read messages, even when she knew she wouldn't like them. She was dreading going back to college. Either she'd have to lie and say that she'd been sick all week or she'd tell the truth and then everyone would know that she was a coward as well as a loser. But those college photos that had been used – they were recent.

She wasn't talking much to her family. Not even to Maggi.

It was a good thing, really, that Gallister High had a new policy of putting people in for GCSEs early, especially top sets. Mags and their friend Anna were taking it really seriously and seemed totally focused on going to revision classes and stuff. Even Donny, the other member of the Allies, was mainly working in the evenings. She might have gone round to his otherwise. Donny and his mum lived on an old Chinese junk off beautiful, peaceful Gallister Creek. There wasn't any wi-fi there. And he had their old dinghy, *Lively Lady* – the one she and Maggi had sailed together when life hadn't seemed so complicated.

Xanthe was never going to go racing again. They'd left *Spray II* on her trailer at the Royal Orwell & Ancient Yacht Club, waiting for the sponsors to take her back. End of.

Then her mother announced that she'd arranged a month's placement for her as a volunteer sailing instructor somewhere on the Essex marshes.

"I've spoken to your tutor, Mrs Oakenheart, and to the college principal and they've both given their permission. They're pleased with your work but you're low on your IB community service hours. Also Mrs Oakenheart says you could get all the research done for your extended essay while you're in Flinthammock. And you should begin to think about what you're going to put on your UCAS form. Aim high, she says."

Before Getting2Gold Xanthe had been thinking about staying with her sport and not going to university at all. She had dreamed of making it to the Olympics and leaving any future after that to take care of itself. She was glad she hadn't shared that idea with anyone else. Not that she wanted to go to Uni either. The way she felt now, some dump in Essex would suit her fine.

"It's all arranged then? I notice that you didn't bother asking me. What's the matter with these children that I'm gonna be teaching? What have they done wrong?"

Her mother seemed stressed. She wasn't discussing at all.

"Listen, Xanthe. Or read my lips. I am unable to tell you anything at all about these young people. Except that they *are* young. I believe that the oldest girl may be thirteen or fourteen. There are five of them and their situation is quite unusually difficult. If Wendy hadn't vouched for you there would be no way at all you would have been considered."

"Rev Wendy? But you said I'm gonna be a sailing instructor. You made me fax off my certificates."

"The Flinthammock Project is run by a small group of Companions. They're based on a lightship and they're also linked to a peace camp. They're a charity that offers outdoor activity for children in need and they asked Wendy for an in-depth character reference. You need to thank her for this opportunity."

When June used that tone of voice her family knew there was no more argument.

"So what are Companions?" Xanthe asked Rev Wendy the next day. "I mean are they, like, religious?"

"Does it make a difference?" Wendy sounded tired.

"It would if they're going to want me to pray or anything. I don't do religion now I've left school. All those assemblies and stuff."

"If that's how you feel, you'll be perfectly safe on board *Godwyn*."

"*Godwyn*?" It sounded religious…

"It's a redundant lightship – from the Goodwin Sands. Where Earl Godwin lost to the Normans off the coast of Kent. You probably know more about that area than I do. I understand it's dangerous to shipping. The lightship has been converted to residential accommodation and the Companions are local volunteers with a paid administrator and a leader. They won't interfere with your…lack of conviction."

Maybe Wendy was bad-tempered as well as tired. Maybe she was fed up with trying to help Xanthe. Maybe she'd realised that Xanthe wasn't worth it.

"So you had to promise these people that I'm not going to punch anyone?"

"I couldn't promise anything. You're over sixteen. Your actions are your own responsibility. All I could do was tell them how long I've known you and in what capacity. I did my best to answer their questions about your suitability to undertake the specific duties they require."

What did Rev Wendy know about her 'suitability' to teach kids to sail? It should have been Griselda answering those questions. It was a good thing those Companions hadn't spoken to anyone at Weymouth. They'd never have accepted her then.

"Thanks anyway," she said.

Later Xanthe began to wonder whether the Companions had worked out that Wendy didn't know her gooseneck from her pintles. She discovered that she wasn't going to be allowed to stay on the lightship with everyone else. Apparently there was some big group of bird-watchers already booked in and she would have to start out as a lodger in a place called Rebow Cottage. She assumed someone had done a search on social media and they'd be issuing her with an orange hi-vis coverall so everyone would know to steer clear. Maybe she'd have done better to go back to college. Or jump in the river and go straight down.

CHAPTER THREE

Here be Monsters?

Saturday May 25, LW 1450 HW 2114

Rebow Cottage was a small plain house on the edge of Flinthammock village, just a short distance from the marshes and the creek. The old couple who lived there had some connection to the Project's Companion-in-Chief, the man who'd officially hired Xanthe. His name was Dominic Gold. She hadn't met him yet.

Rebow Cottage made Wendy and Gerald's grey Victorian vicarage look like an all-singing, all-dancing fun palace. And if it was possible to have *less* than no wi-fi, Rebow Cottage had it (or didn't). There wasn't even a phone.

She'd been delivered to Flinthammock the afternoon before she was due to start work. Mrs Farran, Xanthe's landlady, had tottered on her walking stick and looked as if she might faint when she opened the door and saw her and her mother and Maggi, all standing there together. They had experienced some difficulty convincing the old lady that Xanthe was the lodger she'd been expecting and that she was going to be working for Mr Gold on the lightship.

"But does he know…?"

"Dominic Gold and the Project administrator have seen all of my daughter's qualifications. They have spoken to her college principal and also to our vicar. My daughter is an extremely talented sailor and has experience instructing the younger children at our club and also on the local reservoir. I believe that the Flinthammock Project is lucky to get her. If your accommodation is unsuitable I will insist that they find her lodgings elsewhere."

Xanthe had looked at her mother in surprise. What was that all about? Then she noticed Mrs Farran cross herself as she stood aside to let them in.

The two girls had said nothing as they stood in the narrow hall and waited while Mrs Farran insisted on taking Mrs Ribiero upstairs and showing her the bedroom that would be Xanthe's. They heard their mother commenting politely on its cleanliness and its view of the village street and some piece of sewing or embroidery or something.

"But is this how she likes to sleep?" asked the old lady. "In a bed like this?"

Mrs Ribiero laughed. It was maybe not quite her usual warm chuckle. "I've heard my daughters begging to be marooned on a desert shore and to be allowed to bivouac in the bottom of a dinghy. I have sometimes wondered why I bother with the comfort of our home. I'm sure Xanthe will find this room perfectly acceptable until a cabin becomes available on the lightship and she moves to join her pupils there. Perhaps we should ask her to have a look for herself?"

It had carried on awkward. She'd gone upstairs, glanced round: the room was fine, everything immaculately clean and white. She had her own bathroom and was assured there'd be no need to share. Then Mrs Farran had invited her and her mother and Maggi into her tiny north-facing parlour and had tried to introduce them to her husband.

He was a grim-looking old man, wearing a threadbare fisherman's guernsey and a neckerchief and the sort of thick, dark, woollen trousers that you saw in nineteenth century photos. He could have stepped straight out of one of those photos except he wasn't smoking a pipe or wearing his fisherman's cap and, instead of boots, he had Poundland slippers.

Mr Farran wouldn't shake Mrs Ribiero's hand.

His wife might have been trying to cover up his rudeness. Except that her fussing had made it worse. She forgot to ask them to sit down and hobbled around removing the everyday tea-set that she'd already put out and replacing it with some translucently thin cups and saucers which were obviously for Special Occasions Only. Then she began searching through the drawers of a massive antique cabinet until she found a lace-edged cloth that she smoothed across the tiny table. She spent about five minutes rubbing a pierced silver cake stand, which was already completely shiny and didn't have any cakes on it anyway. Then, as they still stood there, feeling totally awkward, she brought out a fluted white porcelain teapot with a pattern of pink rosebuds.

"You do drink tea, don't you? Nobody said..!"

The moment you dropped one drip of tea on that snow-white cloth it was going to stain it brown forever. Xanthe and Maggi looked at each other and asked for glasses of tap water, if it wouldn't be too much trouble.

From the way Mr Farran glared you'd think they'd demanded his last two kegs of smuggled rum. Mrs Farran struggled back to the kitchen and they could hear cupboard doors opening and shutting before she came back with another tray, this time holding a cut glass jug of water and two matching crystal tumblers. Xanthe stepped forwards to offer help and knocked over a table. It was a spindly polished object with scalloped edges and tripod feet. A single plate of scones hit the floor.

"Hell, I'm sorry…" and then she remembered that she mustn't swear. How would she survive living here?

"Leave 'em," said the old man to his wife. "There'll be no more."

Finally they were all able to sit down. The tiny scones lay crumbled on the rug while June Ribiero made conversation into the silence. Mrs Farran offered more tea, which Mrs Ribiero declined. There was a general feeling of relief

"You need to watch yourself, Xanth," Maggi whispered as they hugged goodbye. "He was giving you the total evils."

"Mr and Mrs Farran are natives of Flinthammock," said June carefully. "And their families before them. They've lived here all their lives. Of course they will be insular. I don't know why I was surprised. They're museum pieces, I suppose."

Then she gave up. "My Xanthe, my darling, have I made a terrible mistake? The Project is good, I'm certain of that, but can you be happy in that very strange house?"

"I'm only expecting to sleep there. And you said yourself I've slept in worse."

She knew that wasn't what her mother had meant. Sleeping out on the hard floor of a dinghy – or onshore in a tent or a bivvy bag – was an experience that made you feel more alive and cleared your mind even when every bone in your body was aching. The atmosphere of Rebow Cottage felt oppressive and somehow dusty. Things didn't fit. All those random pieces of silver and grand furniture and stuff. Even that stupid little table had probably been some sort of antique.

"Nights in a museum…it'll be a new one. At least I can keep my history tutor sweet with recording wartime memories and that." She couldn't live with herself if she carried on being a coward about everything.

Her mother's face had brightened. She stood straight and glowing and confident again.

"This won't last for ever, my lovely one. You'll move to the main accommodation with the others. And we'll be always there for you if it doesn't work out. Don't hesitate. We're…so proud of you."

She had held Xanthe tight and for once Xanthe had been glad to let her.

"Don't panic, my mother, I'll hold a steady course and head for the horizon."

Maggi had turned on her then. "That's what you're always doing, sis. It's probably what got you in this mess. When are you gonna learn to keep a look-out for the half-tide rocks?"

Xanthe would have flared back but just in time she'd spotted that Mags was about to cry. Or she was getting a migraine or something.

"No rocks here, sis. It's the level wastes of sucking mud. I'm in Essex now. I need high-fives."

The sisters had done their full hand-slapping routine, only missing a couple because they were both maybe a bit blurry. Then June and Maggi drove away and Xanthe went back into Rebow Cottage.

"Should I go and unpack?" she asked. She didn't know when

they had supper or what was expected. Neither of the old people answered so she went upstairs and took a few things out of her case. Not many. Then she sat on her clean bed and scowled so hard that she could feel the halves of her head grinding together like tectonic plates.

About an hour later Mrs Farran rung a small brass gong and she guessed that meant it was supper. There were hard-boiled eggs, tinned potatoes, soft lettuce, pickled beetroot and salad cream but no conversation. Mr Farran ate his food, pushed back his chair and left and Mrs Farran very obviously couldn't think of anything except to ask Xanthe about her name and disregard the answer.

"It's not an English name then."

"No, it's Greek."

Xanthe carried on repeating the information as politely as she could and managed to force herself to eat the lettuce, three cubes of potato and a quarter of one egg. #bbarbie had found lots to say about the 'classic' West African figure and she hadn't been able to stop herself searching the net for ethnographic data to check whether they were right.

She had started to hate her body – her big, clumsy, genetically-determined body that had allowed her to behave like a maddened water buffalo – so she had decided to show it who was boss. Not eating when she was hungry had seemed like one good way. Then her body had got too clever and she found she couldn't eat even when she wanted to.

She had noticed her mother cooking her favourite dishes almost every night: heard Maggi's falsely casual "Hey, sis, get this down you!", saw her father looking grave and helpless, gazing at her with his deep brown eyes, his broad, wise forehead and the receding hair that was beginning to grizzle round the edges. She had felt his sadness most of all but it had done nothing for her ability to swallow.

She excused herself after her non-supper and walked down the short stretch of road that led to the wide, open saltings and to *Godwyn*. There was a signpost to the Project that pointed between a couple of storage sheds and along a straight gravelled path.

That signpost was so unnecessary! *Godwyn* outshone all the other boats in the area. She was the brightest red you could imagine and the high, round turret that contained her light was metres higher than the nearby masts. At sea she would have looked small and gallant and probably slightly shabby with salt-stains and incipient corrosion – and bird poo. Here, she was like a huge, in-your-face, positive statement.

Xanthe felt a tremor of anticipation and excitement. Except that this wasn't all about her. She was going to be responsible for five unknown kids. Was she up to it?

The lightship was moored off the edge of a narrow creek. The saltings that stretched inland were dotted with hulks and houseboats and with some of the smaller yachts and motorboats that could manoeuvre easily in and out of the mud-berths. Xanthe calculated that the tide had been flooding for about four hours. The smaller channels were filling and the boats were lifting from their individual hollows but there was still very little depth of water. It was obvious that access was going to be a problem.

She started up the gangway to introduce herself, then she changed her mind and walked further round to check out the dinghies. If she was going to make a success of this instructor job she'd best discover what she'd got to instruct with.

She found a half dozen Laser Picos and a rack of kayaks. They were all okay and there were a couple of RIBs moored in the creek that would be the safety boats. There were a few items of equipment scattered around but she guessed most of it would be kept in those former sail lofts at the far end of the path.

The Picos weren't very big. What if she stepped into one and sank it with her 'classic West African figure'? She'd got her body mass exactly right for *Spray* but she'd lost fitness since the training camp and there might be a kid or two sailing with her. What if she lurched and tipped them out?

Get a grip! She needn't lurch. She'd always had good balance and her muscles couldn't have gone completely to spaghetti. Not since Easter.

She was glad Madrigal and her five thousand Facebook friends couldn't see where she was or what she was doing. No one at college knew where she'd gone, except for Mrs Oakenheart and the principal. Her mother and Rev Wendy had been right to send her here.

She'd go for a run right now. Why not? *Godwyn* was moored between Roffey Creek – which led down to a much larger inlet called the Flete and then out into the main River Blackwater – and the Flinthammock saltings, a network of twisting channels and small mud islands. She'd seen a photo of the saltings taken from the air. They looked like the inside of a brain.

Xanthe didn't run like a sportswoman, checking her breathing and counting her paces against her stopwatch. She ran like a crazy little Pacman, trapped inside her own head. She pinged across the half-full streams and leapt along the wooden stagings and rickety bridges, jumping and splashing across the saltings until she reached the marsh wall on the furthest edge.

No one knew her. No one could see her. She took huge gulping breaths and flung out her arms to the evening sky.

Xanthe looked back at the lightship and sideways to the village. The flood tide was exploring the creeks with its silver fingers and the evening light was shining low and golden from the west. It lit up the white holiday homes and beach huts on the distant island of Meresig. There were shops and cars and civilisation over there. She'd raced *Spray* from Meresig. It seemed like a different world.

Between Meresig and Flinthammock lay a complicated network of drying channels and semi-submerged islands. Only fishermen and samphire-gatherers and wild-fowlers understood those secret ways, and they were all long gone. And so were the smugglers who had sculled ashore with muffled oars and felt their way to private landing places and hasty, whispered conversations. If these pools and runnels could speak they'd have some tales to tell.

Xanthe watched the water spreading inland, gleaming and serene, reflecting the colours of the evening sky as it faded from blue to pink and mauve and then to mother-of-pearl, glistening like the inside of a mussel. She looked at the chartlet that she'd printed from the internet when she still had access. This was Broad Marsh. It ran from the Flete to a private landing stage and what looked like a large house set back among trees. It wasn't a smugglers' haven; it was going to be the perfect sailing area for her young beginners.

"Cuck-oo."

A heavy greyish bird flew out from a distant wood and across the flat green meadow. The falcon plummeted from nowhere then gave chase with the agility of a Stuka pursuing a barrage balloon. The grey bird was struck and killed in minutes. The falcon landed in the field with its prey clenched in its talons. Xanthe was close enough to see its head bobbing up and down between its shoulders as it tore at its meal with a hungry beak.

"Hell," she said, aware that her breathing had quickened and her palms were slightly sweaty.

She looked around once more at the vast sky and the deserted marsh. Maybe it wasn't so deserted. Maybe it still had stories. Maybe some of them were the sort to twist your stomach with fear and keep your eyes open wide at night.

A small flat workboat had left the clear water of Broad Marsh and was winding its way through unmarked channels into no-man's land. She could hear the quiet popping of its outboard motor and could see a dark shape slouched beside the helm.

"Here be monsters," she whispered to herself.

Then she turned and jogged back along the wall with the controlled power of an athlete.

Mrs Farran was in the Rebow Cottage kitchen filling herself a hot water bottle. She gasped at the splashes of mud on Xanthe's jeans.

"They said you'd keep your work-clothes on the lightship. Mr Farran never brings his filth indoors."

Filth. That seemed like a strong word.

"And you'll need to come in earlier than this. I lock the house at nine."

No late evening sailing? On these beautiful early summer nights?

Where was Mr Farran now? Where did the old couple sleep? All she'd been shown was her own front bedroom and the cramped bathroom with nothing in it but a tablet of guest soap and a small white towel.

She was hungry that night. Her stomach rumbled and she couldn't sleep. She hadn't any snacks with her and couldn't exactly go raiding the kitchen. She kept thinking of those little scones, swept away into the bin. She read a bit and dozed. Then got up again soon after it was day.

CHAPTER FOUR

Fata Morgana

Sunday, May 26, LW 0330 HW 0958 LW 1610 HW 2220

Xanthe stood up in the unfamiliar dinghy and rocked it from side to side. She grabbed the mainsheet and heaved it across and back, across and back, to help create an air current. This wouldn't be allowed if she were racing but heck, she wasn't racing.

This was the first time she'd been on the water since Weymouth. After they'd unhitched *Spray* and left her in the dinghy park she'd written to tell her sponsors that she'd been sent home and banned. She apologised for letting them down but didn't – because she still couldn't – explain why she'd behaved as she had.

Their answer would be arriving any day. It would confirm that they had withdrawn their sponsorship. They would be reclaiming the dinghy and all its equipment. One good thing about hiding in Flinthammock was that she could put off that moment. Her parents had agreed that they wouldn't forward any mail and they wouldn't open anything.

"Or even put your glasses on and hold it up against the light or shine a torch from behind to check whether it's see-through?"

"No tricks, we promise." Her mother's voice was warm and relieved. "And you're suspending all your accounts and changing your passwords so you can't be hacked while you're away. New mobile – pay-as-you-go – new number, no internet. I'll lend you my camera and my Macbook. Solely for your essay research, you understand. And you'll only have wi-fi when you're on board *Godwyn*. You're not going to import your address book or any of your contacts except us – and Donny and Anna, of course. You are on your honour."

"And *you* are not to call me. I'm sixteen. I need to learn to survive on my own. That could have been...part of the trouble."

"Oh," said her parents.

"Okay," said Maggi. "That means I've got Only Child status. Could be very good indeed. I'll take a few tips from baby Ellen. No need to hurry home, big sis."

It had been soon after five in the morning when she'd given up any attempt to sleep in the unfamiliar Rebow Cottage bed. She'd crept down the narrow stairs, placing her feet to the outside of each step to make certain they didn't creak. She'd avoided a small, black, fluffy cat who stared knowingly from its basket but didn't meow or move, then she'd let herself out into the quiet street.

She knew she was expected to meet her crew on the lightship after breakfast but that still gave her a good couple of hours to begin to get familiar with the area. She mustn't mess up on her first day.

She'd found the kit alright but it had been a real issue getting the Pico away from *Godwyn* and down the shallow creek at this stage of the tide and she was beginning to wonder why she'd bothered. There wasn't a breath of wind. She'd paddled, pushed, punted and she'd made it to the main river but she still couldn't get the dinghy to sail. After a while she got fed up with standing up and pumping the mainsail and her shoulders began to ache.

As soon as she stopped working, the dinghy began drifting backwards with the tide so she made a loop with the painter and lassoed one of the furthest channel buoys. The sun was fully up now and the heat of the day was beginning to intensify.

The mouth of the River Blackwater stretched wide and blue ahead of her. Meresig shone glassily to port and to starboard the long flat line of the St Peter's peninsula curved away into haze. She ignored the redundant nuclear power station – it looked like it was a building site now – and she let her eyes follow the coastline until she managed to glimpse the tiny chapel of St Cedd looking eastwards out to sea as it had done for more than a thousand years.

It was possible that Xanthe dozed a while.

Was that a yacht smudged against the skyline? Wrong shape. Possibly a sailing barge? Not big enough. She'd been reading local histories; she knew there'd been a time when this river was home to fleets of fishing smacks. Tough livings for the men and boys of Flinthammock and Meresig. That was probably what it was – some sort of antique, sail-powered, fishing boat.

Then the boat began playing tricks. First the image grew, then it inverted. It was sailing upside down. Huh? Xanthe stood up and stared.

It righted itself as she tried to understand what was happening and seemed to sprout another mast. The outline distorted and grew fins and flippers. Xanthe pulled her mother's camera from its waterproof case and began taking photos.

The distant vessel rose from the surface of the sea as if it was floating on a grey-blue cloud. Enchanted fairy ship? Then, for a moment, she seemed to see it clearly in the golden morning light: it was a fishing smack, shapely and full of life and sailing like a dream.

The chapel of St Cedd had vanished into haze and now the concrete cubes of the former power station lifted up into the warm air, shimmered and disappeared. The straight stalks of the distant wind farm concertinaed like melting plastic.

Xanthe kept her eyes focused on the smack. She was heading in towards the river, her wide brown sail full out to starboard. Starboard? Xanthe took another photo then checked the water all round her dinghy. If she was going to get hit by a breeze like that she needed to be ready.

But there wasn't a ripple on the glassy surface. And when she looked out to sea again, the boat was gone. There was nothing except herself and her borrowed Pico and a sudden realisation that she was going to be late for breakfast.

She put the camera away, cast off in a hurry and dug into the water with her paddle. She'd got to get her fitness back. Must hurry. Never mind shoulders. Kids to teach. What a complete idiot. She hated herself for messing up.

A powerboat was slicing towards her, direct and definite as an arrow, spreading V-shaped ripples through the calm water. She recognised it as the RIB from *Godwyn* and that must be Dominic Gold.

Had he come to help her? That was so excellent. She really hadn't fancied much more paddling. Suddenly Xanthe felt ridiculously happy. Her appetite wouldn't be a problem today.

"Hi there," she called. "I don't take sugars in my tea but it's gotta be brown sauce if you're offering a fry-up."

He swirled alongside. "Pass me your painter. There's no time to waste." His blue eyes were cold and his bony face unsmiling. Her brief happiness congealed.

"In that case you should have let my egg go hard," she said. "I'd have been back in time for the washing-up."

He cleated her painter to the RIB and carried on without bothering to raise his icy voice. "You should have asked my permission before you borrowed the Pico. But I wouldn't have said yes. We don't go out alone."

She thought she had signed an agreement to work with this Project as a volunteer sailing instructor. She didn't think she'd sold herself into slavery.

"You're saying that I can't…take a dinghy out for a sail…by myself…in my own time?"

"Not a dinghy belonging to the Project. And there's nothing else for you to sail here."

He towed her back to the lightship as if she were a straying sheep.

"High-fives, sister," said a skinny black kid who seemed to be all arms and legs plus a total toothy smile. "Do you know why seagulls fly over the sea?"

"Because they're stupid-not-allowed to take a level one dinghy and have a couple of hours' peace in a flat calm on the river," Xanthe didn't say. This boy must be one of her students. Great start. Not.

The adult visitors had finished their breakfasts and gone. Her five kids – two girls, three boys – were left hanging around in the mess room while she vented her bad temper on the tables. She couldn't smile back at him but she forced herself to stop, squeeze out the cloth and answer. "Nope. Not sure I've heard that one – and your name is...?"

"Nelson. They'll have warned you off of me. I'm trouble. But you and me, sister – we'll do fine. About those seagulls..."

"Hold it there, Mr Midshipman."

If this Nelson was some sort of leader and if – as he claimed – he was trouble, she'd better start to regain some of the authority she'd lost being towed back up Roffey Creek like a failed escapee.

"Your sister, I am sure, is one lucky girl but I am your captain and my name is Xanthe Ribiero."

She didn't high-five him – that wasn't what a teacher did. She held out her hand and when he was slow, she took his and shook it. Then she did the same to all the others. Start formal, make eye-contact, try to dredge back some respect.

Nelson stuffed his shaken hand under his armpit and hopped around as if he'd been stung by a jelly. The others mumbled their names and looked away. The smaller girl put both her hands behind her back and shook her head.

"She's Siri, she don't ever speak," Nelson announced.

"She don't get a chance with you around," said a large, sulky-looking girl called Kelly-Jane.

"Waddever. But about them seagulls..." He'd taken his hand out from under his armpit and was holding it up in the air, flapping it like a single broken wing.

"And another thing," Kelly-Jane was fronting up Xanthe. "Sister's what they want you to say instead of Miss or Sir. Got more rules in this place than they have at bleedin' school."

"In my crew," Xanthe snapped back, "I make the rules. We'll all use our first names unless you get appointed officers."

Kelly-Jane shrugged and turned away.

"Cap'n Xanthe," said Nelson. He'd put himself between her and the door, desperate to gain her attention.

"Yes, Mr Midshipman Nelson."

"Why do seagulls fly over the sea?"

"I told you I don't know. Why *do* seagulls fly over the sea?"

"Because if they flew over the bay, they'd be bay-gulls – Bagels!! Geddit? It's a breakfast joke. Because you didn't get any…breakfast, that is…or jokes."

He jumped up and down waggling his elbows and grinning with delight. Maybe she didn't have to stay bad-tempered.

"Okay, very funny, helps to fill my empty tummy," she said as they set off to the on-deck training area.

Nelson was running beside her now.

"I've got another. It's a good one."

His eyes were wide, his face was eager. She had to smile.

"Give it to me, bro…"

"How do pirates know that they are pirates?"

Eh?

"They think, therefore they ARRRRRR!"

It made her laugh.

"Ok, here's one for you – any of you. Why do pirate children take so long to learn the alphabet?"

Kelly-Jane was dragging behind but the two other boys, David and Kieran, looked at Xanthe with the beginnings of interest. The quiet girl, Siri, seemed to be miles away. She had pale fair hair in two wispy plaits that tapered away into nothingness by the time they reached the thin rubber bands at the end. Her eyes were sweet-sky blue and her face didn't move at all.

Nelson was swinging from every metal handhold and rail as they made their way up the narrow stairways and onto the sunny deck. He was muttering as he swung.

"A, B, C, D, E, F, G…"

He really wanted to get the answer. He was trying so hard but he was missing it, totally. Maybe she should help him out?

"Think of those gulls, the ones that didn't fly over the bay."

"They were seagulls…oh, I geddit, **C**-gulls. Okay…okay…" But he was still stuck.

"So how many *seas* are there, in pirate books? We are talking storybook pirates here, not the real sort." She felt she had to keep saying that.

"Don't read a lotta books." He looked deflated. Stopped swinging.

"There's seven seas…seven **C**s?"

"Ok, I geddit – so the pirate kids mess up because there's only one C in the alphabet."

"Y'r there, bro."

It wasn't a great success. She didn't naturally do jokes. She'd better get on with what she'd been hired to do. Teach them sailing.

She led them off the lightship and round to the gravelled strip that had been constructed between *Godwyn* and the creek. It made a secure enclosed berth and provided a sort of artificial embankment that was almost like a miniature quay at high water. The Pico had been pulled out and left there, still semi-rigged. Maybe the dinghy was in disgrace as well.

Xanthe was aware of Jonjo, the children's youth worker, standing close and watchful. He was a tough-looking character with short hair and a South African accent. Probably in his late twenties? Xanthe had the oddest feeling that he could be armed. Martha, the Project administrator, was on the side deck, outside her office, looking down on them.

There was loads of water in the creek now. Blue sky, light, warm breeze. Best possible conditions.

"Okay, so here's our first dinghy and there's plenty more of them. Has anyone already sailed a Pico?"

The kids stood and looked. No one approached the Pico or looked like they were going to answer Xanthe.

"Why's it called a dinghy?" asked Nelson at last. "It's a tickly word. It makes me want to laugh."

He threw his head back and started giggling. It was obviously a put-on. Then he collapsed onto the pebbles and carried on laughing even more. The others stared at him and decided to join in. Zingy-wingy-dinghy. Now Kieran was rolling around and David and Kelly-Jane were doing fake laughs that were rude and silly.

Xanthe could feel Jonjo and Martha watching. In a moment one of them would yell at the kids to shut up and listen. But this was her class. This question was hers.

She sat down cross-legged on the pebbles.

"I don't believe this," she said to Nelson. "I've been sailing all my life and I've never thought about dinghy as a word. Respect to you."

He went quiet.

"It doesn't sound like an English word so we have to check out where it came from first. I haven't got internet where I'm lodging but I suppose there could be a dictionary on *Godwyn* or one of the adults might know. Let's give bonus points to whoever finds out the answer."

"Look, *sister,*" Kelly-Jane cut in. "Is this gonna be like school? Cos I don't *do* bonus points – or dictionaries. They told us this was for outdoor adventure – and Fun."

"But safe," added Kieran. "Not outdoor adventure where you might get hurt or nothing."

They must be related, thought Xanthe, looking up at the two Ks. Both a bit overweight and unhealthy-looking, as if they'd been spending most of their lives indoors. Sitting on sofas probably, eating junk food.

She stood up from the pebbles.

"No, it's not going to be like school. I'm here to teach you to sail. Is it not what you wanted? I mean obviously I'll also be helping you to keep safe."

There was silence. Nelson had turned getting up into a sort of breakdance routine – though not as if his heart was in it. The rest of them moved a bit too close to each other. Kelly-Jane took Siri's hand.

"We knew we gotta be kept out of the way," she said. "No-one asked us what we wanted."

Jonjo shifted slightly. Nothing much. Just enough to make them pay attention.

He looked at Kelly-Jane and shook his head. She stared back at him. Then her shoulders sagged.

Kelly-Jane had been trying to say something and had been silenced.

"Stuff the goons." Xanthe turned her back on Jonjo. "So do you or don't you want adventure? I'm not saying danger but do you want sailing? You need to tell me yes or no."

If they'd been forced into learning she wasn't going to do it.

No-one answered. The only sounds were the river noises: wavelets lapping against the bank, halyards against masts, the shake of a sail, seagulls calling…It looked as if she'd talked herself out of a job before she'd even started.

"Hell," she said, forgetting that she wasn't allowing herself to swear. "Look out there, won't you? There's sky, there's water, there's boats and distance and places to explore. Will you please just face away from me!"

One by one they turned towards the creek.

"Okay," she said. "Stick your eyes to your telescopes, Nelson-style, but make sure it's your good one."

Nelson flung up his arms in a shrug. Kelly-Jane sighed angrily. Kieran and David looked completely dumb and Siri stood like someone sealed into a vacuum.

Xanthe marched round all of them, making them do as she asked. Both hands cupped round and held up to one eye. The other eye shut.

"We are playing a game. I am calling it I-spy-glass. You don't have to stand still. You can swing yourself around and you can stop wherever you like. Then you focus through your telescope and you tell me what you see. You say 'I spy with my single eye something beginning with…?'"

If they thought she'd lost it, she didn't care. Lose now and she'd lost them anyway.

"Mr Midshipman Nelson, you go first."

He whirled wildly around, gazing up and peering down, hyping up his confusion and maybe aggravation. His choice came as no surprise, however; "I spy with my single eye something beginning with..D!"

He could hardly say for the giggles. And this time they were totally real ones.

"It's the D-D-DINGHY!" spluttered the awkward-looking boy called David. Then he giggled and Kieran giggled and Kelly-Jane giggled and even Siri almost smiled.

"You're good!" said Xanthe. "You're very good. So now we look closer at this rib-tickling object. There will be more weird words."

They forgot to hang back and clustered round her like any normal group of kids while she showed them all the different parts of the dinghy – hull, mast, rudder, tiller, hiking-strap, boom, sheets, halyards, dagger-board, gooseneck, pintle, painter, thwart, vang. She didn't explain what they were for, just gave them the words and checked each one for its giggle factor. Most of them scored high.

"Alternatively," she said, when they had no laughter left, "You could think of all these words as coming from a language that you haven't yet learned. You could let yourselves believe that this…dinghy…has the power to take you to a different world."

There was longing on the light, fresh breeze that was ruffling the sunny waters of the creek.

"Imagine that she has been stranded here. She is suffocating on this dry shore. We have to return this dinghy to her element. And I need you, Mr Midshipman, to hold her painter."

She handed him the flecked and braided length of rope and he held it as if it were the holy grail. Then they all watched the very ordinary plastic boat as she slid back into the creek and swung to the last of the flood.

Suddenly Jonjo was beside her ready to take away the trolley and Martha produced a half dozen buoyancy aids and began helping the kids to put them on. She was bustling around them, chatting and smiling.

"This morning," continued Xanthe, "We are gonna to keep it simple. All that I'm offering you to do is to take turns sitting in this dinghy. Then you can tell me whether you choose to go further. There is no pressure. If you don't want to learn to sail, I sure as hell won't force you."

They *did* want to – all of them – but she was still amazed how scared they were. It was as if she truly had been asking them to step into some alien dimension.

"Haven't you *ever* been on the water?" she asked Kieran. He was a sturdy, open-faced boy, the sort you'd expect to be outside fixing things or making some old go-kart or something – if he hadn't looked so pale and flabby.

"There ain't no water where we live…" He looked at Kelly-Jane. "Where we lived," he corrected himself.

"You didn't, like, go to the seaside on your holidays?"

"No, Miss. I don't remember no holidays."

Maybe she was the one who'd been living in a different world.

Kieran sat completely still, staring at the water, which was now so close to him. Then he relaxed and began watching some of the other boats that were moving up and down the creek on this sunny half-term morning.

Kelly-Jane gasped and froze when she felt the Pico shift

beneath her weight. It was an act of bravery when she allowed Xanthe to talk her gently down until she was sitting low in the centre of the dinghy and could trust that she was safe.

Nelson swung recklessly around the mast and nearly pulled the dinghy over while David tripped over his own feet even before she'd got him anywhere near the edge of the quay. Only the silent Siri stepped on board with the instinctive grace and balance of a bird.

"So have *you* been on the water before?"

The small girl looked up at her, directly, as if she was going to answer, but her face stayed motionless and her eyes seemed to bulge slightly as if there were words behind them that simply couldn't break out.

"Have you?"

"She's not able to reply." This was Jonjo. "But I'm guessing it would be a no. These are inner city kids and they won't have experienced water and boats unless someone's made the effort to take them."

"Not even their school?"

"In this case, no."

"Can they swim?"

"We're working on it. Flinthammock has an open air salt-water pool and we've been going there at least once each day."

"Ok," she said. "So let's learn steering."

Jonjo drove the RIB and towed each of them one at a time slowly to the end of the creek and into the Flete with Xanthe sitting with them in the dinghy, explaining how you pushed the tiller away from the direction you wanted to turn and how you could use your weight to help.

She left Siri until last and when she was as quick and as natural as Xanthe had guessed she would be, she called to Jonjo to cast them off. Then she got Siri pointing the dinghy into the wind while she ran up the mainsail. The little girl could obviously hear okay, whatever was the matter with her speech, and it was a matter of moments before she'd understood what was wanted and had the Pico reaching smoothly back up the creek in the kindly breeze.

Dominic Gold came out on the second RIB and prowled around them like a sheepdog on a motorbike. Xanthe did her best to ignore him. The tide had turned, the water in the creek was emptying fast and it was time for lunch.

Xanthe ate half a sandwich and a whole banana – then they spent the afternoon pushing little models of dinghies backwards and forwards while Jonjo sat near the gangplank, making out that he was reading the newspaper. They learned about 'dinghy' too. Martha had internet in her office and they discovered that the word had been borrowed from India about two hundred years ago.

"You're saying that we borrowed it – and we didn't never give it back?" Nelson looked serious.

"You said it, Mr Midshipman."

"So…what is this mid-ship-man, teacher-lady?"

"What Nelson would have been when he first joined the Navy."

"Who's Nelson?"

Huh?

"Admiral Lord Nelson – Horatio Nelson – national hero, born in Norfolk, died at Trafalgar 1805 – turned his blind eye to the telescope and saved England from Napoleon. Hey, you've got his name!"

The skinny boy shook his head. "Nah, don't think so. Maybe it was like borrowed from some other geezer."

"You mean Nelson Mandela, maybe? Oh, okay – great man. Still a great name."

"Or was it some boxer or someone? I dunno."

"You'll have to ask your mum and dad when you get home."

It was, thought Xanthe, possibly the worst silence she'd ever not heard. (Except maybe for that day when she and the others had been tapping a half-sunk container where there was only a single person left alive.)

Nelson's brown eyes filled. The rest of the crew stood like tombstones.

"You do understand," said Xanthe, after a while, "that they've sent me here to teach you and I don't know anything at all?"

"And we can't tell you nothing, neither," answered Kelly-Jane.

CHAPTER FIVE

Raising the *Igraine*

Sunday May 26, LW 0330 HW 0958 LW 1610 HW 2220

Mr and Mrs Farran were watching TV East when Xanthe came in. It was an early evening local news and country programme with an extended item about the anniversary of the World War Two evacuation of British forces from Dunkirk.

They didn't look at Xanthe or invite her to sit down – she wasn't certain that they'd seen her – but she stood in the doorway of the small dark sitting-room and she watched it anyway. Part of the arrangement her mother had made to allow Xanthe to have this month out of college was that she'd use her free time to research her IB extended essay. She'd chosen the title *1940: War on the East Coast of England* and the evacuation from Dunkirk was obviously going to be a major section. It could even make the whole essay if she discovered enough.

She knew the time line. Tomorrow was Monday, May 27th, when the government had stepped up the collection of little ships back in 1940. The TV East programme was focusing on some local Essex and Suffolk boats which were making commemorative trips. Some of them had started early today, taking the morning flood across the estuary to gather at Ramsgate.

Mrs Oakenheart had told her there'd been several boats from Flinthammock. She wondered whether Mr or Mrs Farran would remember any of them. And whether there was any chance she could get them to tell her if they did.

She was assuming not.

Now the focus had changed and the interviewer was talking to someone about an event planned next week for the historic vessels' return. It was a small black-and-white TV and the old people were both leaning forward so Xanthe couldn't see the picture properly. It was the opening of something on the River Blackwater and they were going to tow an artificial harbour into position and any genuine Dunkirk Little Ships that moored overnight on their way home would have their fuel and all the expenses of their crossing paid and a bounty for every member of their crew. There was possibly a museum for local historic craft? Xanthe wondered whether she should maybe find out more details and take a look.

"We are offering the tribute of the Saxon Shore to commemorate the men who brought our people home. And there will be more! St Peter's will become the greatest theme park devoted to national self-defence. We have repelled the invader for a thousand years of history. We shall not cease."

The person being interviewed had a pompous, plummy voice and it got louder as he went on.

"Y'r fancy man." Mr Farran growled to his wife. "Artie Fool's Gold."

"No..." Mrs Farran sounded tremulous, though not necessarily convincing. "Your brother."

"No more he ain't. I've had it with him and his big ideas and crooked ways. He'm yours – except I reckon I knows things that'd scuttle him."

"NO, Eli!" Mrs Farran pushed herself to her feet on her

ebony walking stick. "You wouldn't dare! You know there would be consequences."

The TV programme was dissolving into patriotic music and aerial shots of the Essex coast, panning away from a view of the sea where the boats were tiny dots. Neither of the old people were watching. Xanthe stepped back. It was obvious they were about to have a row and she wasn't certain whether she should walk in as if she'd just arrived or slip quietly upstairs to her bedroom.

"There's nothing left, woman." Mr Farran's voice was as low and bitter as breakers retreating from an unseen shoal. "Nothing that I care about no more. You've had me home and me living and me pride and now you've brought a darkie through the doors of me parents' house. I tell you there ain't nothing left for me – except that I might choose to bring that cuckoo down."

"You wouldn't dare," his wife repeated. She was angry but was there a note of doubt?

A darkie! Xanthe could hardly breathe.

Did the old man sense that he had made an impression on his wife? He sounded more cunning now. "I'm out o' credit at the Plough and Sail. Or I might've chose to go and have a pint an' leave my truth until another day."

"Sot!"

"Milky-face!"

"Killer!"

"That I never were!"

The fluffy cat shot out of the room and Xanthe leapt backwards in to the hall. A blow and a cry and she was legging it up the stairs.

As soon as she had made it to her bedroom she began to think again. This was domestic violence. You couldn't just ignore it. Whoever was right and whoever was wrong in the quarrel, the fact remained that Mrs Farran was small and shaky and Mr Farran was probably used to handling fisherman's anchors or beam trawls, although he was old.

She had to go down again. She didn't want to but she had to. She'd take her mobile phone with her and threaten to call the police. She was sure that she could get signal. Just because Rebow Cottage was time-warped it didn't mean the rest of Flinthammock wasn't living in the twenty-first century.

She found her phone and switched it on but then she heard the front door open. Her bedroom window was directly above and she watched Mr Farran leave.

He stamped to the end of the short front path, with his fists in the pockets of his jacket. Then he turned and stood for a moment looking back. He had a craggy face with his eyes sunk deep beneath his bushy brows. It was a harsh face, fierce and wild.

He took his left hand from his pocket and laid it against his cheek. There was something profound about the gesture but Xanthe could not read it. He stood a few seconds more and then he turned away.

Xanthe started downstairs to check on his wife. He might have hurt her, left her unconscious – or worse. She was angry. She didn't need any of this. She was only the lodger. The 'darkie' in his parents' house.

She heard Mrs Farran as soon as she reached the hallway. The old lady was singing – ding dong bell, pussy's in the well

– and when Xanthe peeped quietly round the door, she saw that the cat had been recaptured. Mrs Farran was clutching it against her and stroking it vigorously, not as if she was upset at all. In fact she sounded triumphant.

Xanthe went back to her room feeling fantastically relieved. Maybe she'd misheard the whole thing.

The village shop had still been open on her way back from *Godwyn* and she'd bought herself some Lucozade, cheese, apples and Hobnob biscuits. Now she found she couldn't eat them. Not here. Not in this house.

She couldn't settle to reading so she uploaded the photos she had taken that morning onto her mother's Macbook. There was no internet so she couldn't share them. Instead she sat and stared and tried to work out what it was, exactly, that she'd seen.

The sailing smack was real enough. She must have been well out to sea – over the horizon most likely – but the image had been lifted and refracted and distorted by freak atmospheric conditions. It was hot air layered on cold – or was it the other way round? Or maybe it was connected with ducts and down-draughts? It was definitely some sort of mirage and there was a special name for it that she couldn't remember. Anna would have known.

After a while there was a knock on her door. Mrs Farran had brought her a cup of cocoa and plain biscuits on a tray. She was hobbling and nervous and old again.

Xanthe's stomach clenched. She thought she might be sick. She took the tray with unnecessary thanks and placed it on the small table by the window where she'd propped the Macbook.

"You're welcome to sit down," she said. "I'm not that hungry though."

The old lady glanced out of the window, as if to reassure herself. Then she sat on the single chair and Xanthe pulled out the stool from beside the wardrobe, removed her pile of clothes and sat on that.

Neither of them could think what to say.

"They didn't tell us you were foreign," the old lady whispered after a while. "I don't know what food you like."

"But I'm not...foreign. And that's not why I'm not eating. That's...something else. I hope I'll be moving to the lightship soon."

Mrs Farran stared at Xanthe with her faded blue eyes. She must need reassurance or to talk or something. Xanthe wished that she was Maggi or her mother. They'd have known what to say. All Xanthe knew was that she didn't want to get into a conversation about what she might have heard downstairs.

"I took some amazing photos this morning," she said, waking the Macbook, "You can see them really well on here."

Xanthe ran the photos as a slideshow. The brown-sailed boat appeared clearly in the middle of the screen. It gyrated, sprouted bits, wafted along the cushioning cloud then turned and came straight towards them as if it would burst out into the third dimension. It was impressive every time.

Mrs Farran gripped the sides of her chair with her wrinkled hands. She leaned forward, peering.

"The *Igraine*..." she sort of breathed.

"You recognise her?"

"Show me again. I must be sure."

Xanthe ran the slideshow a second time. And once more. And again.

Mrs Farran stretched out an arthritic finger and touched the screen as if she thought it might dissolve. Her face was transformed as if she'd seen a vision.

After about the seventh showing Xanthe had had enough. She switched off the Macbook and began to describe the appearance of the Project safety boat and how she'd been towed back to *Godwyn* for breakfast.

She was hoping it would help her to say it aloud. If she was going to carry on working for Dominic Gold she had to try to see this morning's events from his point of view. He must have thought he was right in some way– though she knew she'd never find a justification for his ban on her using any of the dinghies to go sailing in her own time.

She might as well have been talking to the cat. Mrs Farran wasn't even pretending to listen. She was shaking her head and muttering to herself.

"How did you do that?" she asked at last. "How could you know?"

"Do what? Know what?"

"You have raised the *Igraine*. You showed me on your magic book."

"No, Mrs Farran – it's a Macbook, not a magic book. It's just a new sort of computer." Xanthe felt like some sort of missionary explaining modern consumer goods to a forgotten tribe. "I went sailing very early this morning. I didn't want to disturb you – or Mr Farran. Then it got hot and I saw this mirage and my mother had lent me her camera so I took some photos. I think they've come out really well – but it was only a mirage. You see them sometimes over the water. It's to do with air at different temperatures."

"She has returned to take him. Soon, very soon, I will be free!"

Mrs Farran's breathing was starting to sound fast and shallow. Xanthe didn't like it.

"I'm sorry Mrs Farran. I don't know what you're talking about but I think you might be tired. Should I help you to bed? I'll clear up the tray and everything."

The cocoa had skimmed over. It was greyish and wrinkled. Her stomach heaved. She had to get Mrs Farran out of her room.

"And would you lock the house?"

"Yeah, sure, anything." She was certain she was about to be sick. "But what about your husband?"

"He's gone out. We had…words."

Mrs Farran raised her hand to her face, touched her own cheek and cowered slightly. There was something about Mrs Farran that didn't ring true – it was more like she was a child, acting out.

But Xanthe's nausea wouldn't let her think.

"Won't he lock up when he comes home?" she asked.

"This house is locked at nine. Those are the rules. He knows the rules."

Xanthe checked her watch. She forced the sickness down.

"It's only half past seven."

"But I've waited for so long!"

Mrs Farran tottered and Xanthe lunged to catch her before she fell. She put her arm round the old lady's thin chest and half-carried her into the room next door.

"Look here's your bed," She did her best to sound reassuring as she eased her onto it. One side of the floral bedspread was already turned down. "Do you take pills at night or anything?"

"Nothing. Unless you can give me peace."

Xanthe took off the old lady's slippers and pulled the bed covers up. Should she have offered to undress her?

No, she couldn't. Totally no way.

"Do you want me to call a doctor?" she asked.

"Of course not." Mrs Farran's voice was suddenly sharp. "It was a shock. To experience your sorcery. That was all. You can fetch me my hot water bottle now. They're in the kitchen cupboard."

Xanthe went to her room first and got rid of that revolting cocoa by flushing it down the toilet. Then she hurried downstairs and threw away the smooth, beige biscuits. She didn't care that she was being wasteful; she began to feel better as soon as they were gone.

She washed her hands and drank some cold water and splashed her face lavishly under the tap.

By the time Xanthe had found the hot water bottle, filled it and carried it upstairs, the old lady was in her nightdress. She had brushed her white curls and looked up at Xanthe with a face full of sweetness.

"It must be our secret that you have raised the *Igraine*. Mr Farran mustn't know."

"Okay. No worries. I can keep the photos to myself."

"Girl! Girl!"

Xanthe put down her book. The old woman was calling from her bedroom. She was never going to learn her name. Xanthe had spelled it out for her, she'd written it down; she had explained that it was Greek, not African. That it meant daughter of the sea god, or an Amazon, both of which were good. It also meant blonde-haired which had been her parents' idea of irony or something.

"Yes?" she answered wearily, getting up and crossing the landing.

"I'm frightened, girl. I need to know you've locked the doors."

"But your husband's still out."

"If he comes home tonight, he'll be drunk. I'm frightened of him coming home. You must lock the doors and attach the chains. It's after nine o'clock."

"Is there somewhere else that he can sleep?" she asked. "Does he have friends who'll put him up?"

"He can sleep in the boot-room with all his dirt. He has a truckle."

Boot-room? Truckle?

"He knows the rules," Mrs Farran said again.

"Oh okay, I'll lock up if you want me to. But you ought to talk to someone official if you're frightened. A policemen or a social worker or…a vicar. You could have a panic button."

"You have raised the *Igraine*. It must be time."

The old lady was off her trolley.

"Okay, okay. But if the *Igraine* doesn't sort things out, do you promise you'll get yourself some help?"

"How little you know. She is his death-ship. Please lock the house and close my door and let me have some peace."

Then as Xanthe was trudging downstairs again, Mrs Farran called after her, "Both bolts and chains to be on and the cat flap must only open out. If the cat wanders in to the garden at night he must wait until I call him in the morning."

He knows the rules, Xanthe mimicked to herself.

Something woke her an hour or so after she'd fallen asleep but she wasn't sure whether she'd actually heard it. She thought it was a single sound – a deliberate angry smash. Then there was silence in the house and silence from the street outside.

She didn't like this house. She didn't like the feelings in it. This silence wasn't peaceful: it was a tense and angry silence. She wished she'd bought some music with her so she could put on headphones and blot it out. She was also hungry but she felt strangely prevented from getting out of bed and crossing the room to fetch herself an apple or a biscuit. Was she afraid that there was something that would hear her?

Xanthe lay there in the dark needing the sound of something identifiably normal and external: a car engine or a night-bird would be equally okay; the hum of a fridge or Mrs Farran snoring.

Her wish was finally granted. She heard the kitchen cat-flap click.

CHAPTER SIX

In Broad Marsh Creek

Monday May 27, LW 0430 HW 1052 LW 1700 HW 2309

The cat's basket had been empty when she came down the stairs and once she'd walked into the kitchen it didn't take a detective to work out why.

Mrs Farran's special rosebud teapot lay shattered on the floor. The animal must have knocked it down from somewhere then scarpered into the night. The locks and chains were all in place and the cat flap shut. She didn't reset the catch until she'd swept all the broken china into a newspaper. It was only a local paper but even so it had something about that gangland trial that had been all over the news before she left home. It was odd not catching headlines on the internet. Maybe she should ask if they took newspapers on *Godwyn*.

She wrapped the remains and put them beside the waste bin. She couldn't see a china cupboard open and didn't recall noticing the teapot when she'd been filling the hot water bottle last night. It must have come from somewhere. Right now she needed to get down to her crew, grab herself some breakfast and make the most of the early tide.

The youth worker, Jonjo, told her that he was a kayak instructor with lifesaving and rescue qualifications from the Lea Valley Centre in East London. Xanthe wasn't sure why she didn't entirely believe him. Jonjo was quick and efficient and muscular. He obviously had the qualifications but he didn't seem big on fun. His shoulders were broad and his neck seemed almost as wide as his head. He looked like Action Man.

She guessed that Maggi would accuse her of prejudice at this point and would ask whether there was any reason for her to assume that youth workers shouldn't look like Action Man.

She banished her sister from her head and asked Jonjo to wait in the centre of the creek with the safety boat. She wanted him a little way away from the lightship, idling his engine and keeping his bows pointed to the flood. They had three Picos today, two kids in each one and herself with David. The wind was light, conditions good.

Xanthe waded in to the water with each dinghy, holding them steady while she supervised the letting down of centreboards and rudders and gave detailed instructions about mainsheets. A smooth start, a breath of wind, that brilliant mix of pulling and gliding and both of the first two dinghies reached the safety boat.

Then it was her and David's turn. A neat spring to get herself on board: the dinghy had scarcely lurched.

David startled. He flung his arms up, dropped the mainsheet and sort of dived across the centreboard case. He turned a somersault into the shallow creek and splashed like a stranding porpoise before he realised that all he needed to do was to put his feet down and stand upright.

"You ok?" she asked in amazement once she'd got the dinghy back on the ramp and was in the water herself, standing beside him.

He hadn't shouted. The water was pouring off him and he

was breathing pretty fast. He blinked at her and rubbed the side of his head but he didn't answer.

"Anyone there? Hullo. Earth to David. This is Captain Xanthe, mission control, are you receiving me?"

Anyone else would have laughed, or apologised or, quite possibly, stormed off.

"Blink once for yes. Blink twice for yes. Blink any the heck number of times. Or stand on one leg and scratch the middle of your back with the other big toe if you're not hearing my signals."

David was still breathing like he'd run a marathon. He was blinking though, blinking like crazy.

He wasn't signalling, poor little shrimp, he was struggling not to cry.

She lowered her voice. "David, it's Xanthe. Did I scare you?"

A gulp, more blinking and a nod.

"Then I'm truly sorry."

It hadn't been her weight that had catapulted him overboard: it had been his own extraordinary nervousness. She needed to learn from that. She made him keep on watching her: she made herself keep reassuring him. Together they slithered cautiously back into the Pico and she gave him the tiller while she managed everything else.

"Keep steady," she said, "Keep her pointing to the stern of Jonjo's boat. That's excellent. When we get there you leave me to do the work. You don't move until we're alongside. You're our skipper now. Solid."

"Good feeling?" she asked everyone when they were all clustered together around the RIB and Jonjo was towing them down the creek towards the wider space of the Flete. Nods from

Nelson and Kieran. Uncertainty from Kelly-Jane and David. No response from Siri.

She'd asked Jonjo if there was anything she needed to know about the little girl. Was English maybe not her first language?

"Look," he'd said. "I'd like to be able to talk to you about these children but I have to tell you thet I can't."

She must have looked as irritated as she felt.

He carried on, "We're not looking for you to turn them into the next generation of Olympic sailors." (That hurt.) "Just try to build their confidence, let them hev some fun." (Could be a tough one.) "And there's another thing," he added. "I didn't agree with the way Dominic handled your sailing without permission thet first day but you need to know thet he has reasons to be cautious. Don't ever organise an activity thet would involve any of them being alone or out of sight of the rest of the group."

"I don't think they'd let me."

The sun was shining, waves were dancing, the Flete was filling with the flood tide and if anyone had a total capsize situation they'd only drift upstream into the shallow water of the marshes. Not that anyone was going to go over. The wind was so light it wouldn't capsize a paper bag.

They floated together in a three-dinghy raft and Xanthe set them simple beam reach courses across to the RIB. When this had been achieved several times by everyone, she used herself and David as demonstrators and taught them how to tack. Then she added a jib to the mainsail on Kerry-Jane and Siri's boat.

Broad Marsh Creek led north-westwards from the Flete. The tide was almost at its full height; the breeze was southerly.

"Time for a cruise in company," she told them. "We'll ask Jonjo to go on ahead. All the way to the top of the creek, with luck. Then we follow. No stress and it's NOT a race. You heard it here first."

Except that the dinghy that had Siri at the helm appeared to have grown wings. Xanthe could see the younger girl leaning forward to touch the older one on her shoulder. Kelly-Jane eased the jib sheet then, as the dinghy gathered speed, another sign from Siri had her moving forward and inward. That was communicating. No need for speech.

Xanthe continued to watch as Siri shifted her weight to allow the dinghy's slim transom to lift and pull away. The temptation to give chase was almost overwhelming. She forced herself to stay behind, to sail at David's pace, to be a teacher.

But she wasn't a teacher yet. She was a racer. She wasn't going to give up. She understood that now.

Nelson and Kieran were larking about, their line wavering and peals of laughter suggesting that Nelson was spouting his usual dreadful jokes. They'd hauled their sheet too tight. They'd be over in a moment.

"Steer to them, would you Skip?" Xanthe asked David, trimming the Pico for maximum speed. "Let's see if we can steal their wind."

"Let the dinghy settle," she called across to the boys. "She's designed to sail flat."

"Let go of your mainsheet!" she yelled more urgently.

David's steering lurched violently. They'd be over themselves in a moment. She made herself stay steady and quiet. She spoke – didn't shout – across the water to Kieran. He understood her and no one fell in.

By the end of the simple course Siri and Kelly-Jane had reached the top of the creek, not far from the landing stage. They'd tacked through 180 degrees without being asked and were lying neatly moored alongside the RIB.

"That was impressive," said Xanthe.

Kelly-Jane looked really pleased. She couldn't read Siri's expression at all.

"What goes Quick-Quick?" called Nelson.

"A duck with hiccups," Kieran supplied and they both rocked wildly with laughter.

Xanthe dug out the oldest joke in the entire book. "So what goes ha ha bonk?"

The engine of the RIB was humming gently; small wavelets splashed against the sides of the dinghies as Jonjo began towing them in a wide circle, turning for home. Sails were furled, rudders and centreboards up. They were skimming the furthest edge of the narrow creek. Xanthe was scanning the water surface as she always did. It had become habit with her and Maggi.

"David," she said urgently, forgetting his amazing clumsiness, forgetting he wasn't her sister, "Look there, your side, quick! Can you get it?"

Their dinghy was on the outside of the raft, closest to the marsh wall and the landing stage. She'd seen something protruding from the surface of the water. Not a broken withy, nor the periscope of a submarine.

He listened, reached out, nearly tipped over. Gasped for breath, reached a bit further. She kept the dinghy balanced and hung on to his legs. It wasn't graceful.

Jonjo slowed the RIB to nothing and everyone watched as

David stretched impossibly far from the side of the dinghy.

"I c-can. I know I c-can."

He did and Xanthe hauled him back and the two of them collapsed. There was bewilderment and applause from the others.

"Ha ha bonk," said Jonjo, unexpectedly. "It's us laughing our heads off. So what was thet about?"

Now that Xanthe considered the matter she wasn't entirely sure.

"Let's call it a challenge for my young apprentice. Think Sword in the Stone – Excalibur – Lady of the Lake. Could have been an arm in white samite under all that."

She didn't know what samite was but she'd always assumed it was some sort of silky material. Ultra-clean, expensive stuff which would probably have gone nicely in the main bedroom at Rebow Cottage. So that was quite appropriate because the object that David had just handed to her was Mrs Farran's ebony walking stick.

The kids were hugely chatty and happy after their sail. Siri didn't speak but once they'd unrigged the Picos and carried the sails and foils back to the lofts and were walking back along the path to the lightship, she turned her face to the breeze and spread her arms on either side. Then she stretched out her fingers as if they were flight feathers and did the smallest skip.

Xanthe had hoped to catch Dominic Gold at lunch. She wanted to talk to him about Mr and Mrs Farran and the situation at Rebow Cottage but he never showed up. She'd left the stick in the sail lofts and was planning to take it back to Mrs Farran later.

She thought she'd better check first whether the old lady really had lost it and also make totally sure it was clear of 'filth'.

She saw a search-and-rescue helicopter heading out to sea and she found herself telling the kids about Maydays and coastguards and the time her friend Donny's great-aunt had a heart attack at sea and had to be winched up into a helicopter which was like a flying ambulance. Kieran and David seemed interested in what Xanthe was telling them about the rescue and radioing for help but then she started to explain about the attack by modern-day pirates and Kelly-Jane began to look uncomfortable and Siri withdrew completely.

Xanthe found herself staring at the little girl's blue eyes. They were pretty eyes but there was something about them that made her think of a transparent, toughened screen – soundproof, bulletproof even. Sometimes Siri was right up against this invisible barrier, close and intense as if she was trying to get through. More often she was some way back in the dim light, existing in a life that seemed entirely disconnected from whatever else was going on around her.

"Where do you take a sick ship, teacher-lady?"

She was still thinking about Maydays and Pan-pans. She wasn't quick enough.

"To the doc, of course. Gimme high-fives!" Nelson jumped up and went palm to palm with her before she had a chance to remember her dignity. "So what lies at the bottom of the sea and shivers?"

"Nelson, my bruvver, even I know that one – it's a nervous wreck."

They took a couple of the kayaks to the salt-water swimming pool and messed about constructively until it was the end of the afternoon and Martha was hurrying the kids off to her mother's to learn to cook a barbecue tea and then play board games. Xanthe should have been heading back to Rebow Cottage but she couldn't face it. She searched again for Dominic but someone told her he'd been called away. The lightship was filling up with birdwatchers looking forward to their supper. She felt awkward and out of place.

She went down to the sail lofts and set herself up a trestle and a loop of rope so she could begin to get back her fitness for hiking out. At least exercise took your mind off your problems. She had her arms crossed over her chest and was arched horizontally backwards feeling the strain – and the pain – in her lower back muscles, stomach muscles and thighs. She was moving her head from side to side and she was breathing deeply and counting seconds to see how long she could hold still.

"You okay there, Xanthe?"

Jonjo had come in with his arms full of gear.

She drew herself upwards towards vertical very, very slowly. It hurt.

"Thet was impressive," he said. "I hope your landlady provides you with a handsome supper if you're working out like thet."

"She doesn't know what darkies eat."

"Say thet agen?"

His voice was sharp. Suddenly he was so South African. She wished she'd kept her mouth shut.

"You heard what I said and it isn't your problem."

"I think it is." He stood there frowning. "Hev you spoken to Dominic?"

"Couldn't find him."

"Then I'll come to your lodgings with you. How old are these people? Even if they're ignorant, it's not acceptable."

He took no notice of her protests and walked up to Rebow Cottage with her. But Mr Farran wasn't there and Mrs Farran had already gone to bed. They found a note on the kitchen table. It had been written in pencil first then gone over very carefully in pen. The handwriting was extremely old-fashioned.

"I have visited the shop and hope there is something here that is suitable. Please lock the house at 9pm. Yours sincerely, Iris Farran."

There was a tin of lychees, some boil-in-the-bag Uncle Remus rice, a small jar of mango chutney, a packet of peanuts and a single banana.

Xanthe and Jonjo looked at each other and burst out laughing.

CHAPTER SEVEN

Grey Shapes

Tuesday May 28, LW 0500 HW 1140 LW 1740 HW 2354

A morning mist had spread across the saltings like a duvet. Rebow Cottage and the other small houses in the village street were lit by pale sunshine but wafts of wet air came reaching up to Xanthe as soon as she turned downhill. By the time she reached creek level she could only see ten metres in front of her. It was hard to find the gap between the sail lofts that led her onto the main pathway to *Godwyn*. Even the blazing scarlet of the lightship couldn't struggle though this damp greyness.

Then she smelled breakfast and hurried up the gangway.

"Hey, Cap'n Xanthe, teacher-lady, what comes after the Stone Age and the Bronze Age and all them?" Nelson didn't wait for her to try to answer. "It's the Saus-Age…sausage, geddit? And what did the space-pirate find in his pan? Un-identified frying objects!"

David asked her very quietly whether they would be going in the dinghies today.

"Do you want to?"

"I think I d-do."

"We might need to wait a bit. It's foggy outside."

"I hate fog," said Kelly-Jane. "Anyone could creep up in it."

"Giant orcs," Kieran agreed, "Or dementors."

"Yeah and loadsa zombies too. We are the living dead…"

Nelson got up and began to prowl around making sudden grabbing movements.

"Stop it," said Kelly-Jane. "It ain't funny. Siri don't like it and neither do I."

"You're right," said Xanthe. "Let's leave out the orcs and zombies. They don't belong here. Does anyone know what *Godwyn* used to do during the years she was at sea?"

"Big Dom told us that before he even offered us a toilet-stop. She was like a floating lighthouse so if ships saw her in the dark they wouldn't run on the sands or whatever." Kelly-Jane sounded bored by the idea.

That annoyed Xanthe.

"What about in fog? You wouldn't see a light in fog but all the dangers of the shallow waters would still be there. Do you know what the lightships did then?"

"Made a noise or something? They could have been programmed."

"No computers. There were men on board who lived there for months. They didn't see their families and couldn't phone them or message them or anything. When it was dark they had to look after the light and if it was foggy they'd be blasting a hooter for hours at a time."

"Does *Godwyn* have one of them hooters?" Nelson jumped up.

"Unless it's been taken out."

"Could we work it? Make the noise. Keep them dementors off of us?"

She so wanted to say yes.

"I wish! But best not. Those foghorns were really loud. The birders would go mental. You guys get ready and I'll teach you small boat fog signals on our way to the sail lofts."

The kids were soon back with their outdoor kit but when she got them off the lightship, they completely froze. They only needed to walk together down the path that led across the saltings. Then they could collect their sails and come back to start rigging dinghies so they'd be ready as soon as the sun came out.

She explained all that. But they wouldn't do it.

"We'll stick to the path," she said. "It's straight. It's gravel. And we've got Jonjo as our total safety man."

"It wouldn't hurt if we were to wait a while, maybe?" He was agreeing with the kids.

"But if we have everything ready we won't miss too much of the tide and there's so little time until high water."

She was wasting her breath. "What don't you like?" she asked them.

"Sorry miss, I shouldn't have said nothing about dementors or zombies."

"There's bits of that mud that can suck you in," said Kelly-Jane.

"I watched a film once and there was a big man come out of the fog on a marsh like this and he had chains round his legs."

"I saw that one too and the boy couldn't get away. And the man caught him and bullied him and made him go nicking stuff."

"He was well hard. He'd been inside. My dad knows blokes like him."

The crew went quiet and looked at one another.

Then they heard footsteps.

The kids fled and Jonjo hurried after them. Xanthe stood where she was. There were no orcs, dementors, escaped convicts or zombies on this solid stretch of man-made path. There was nothing to be scared of.

She watched the grey shapes materialising through the mist. They wore flat official caps with badges and chequered hat-bands. Their dark, belted jackets were dusted with tiny drops of moisture and their silver buttons were dulled by condensation.

These were policemen.

"Miss Xanthe Ribiero?"

"Yes?"

"We need to ask you some questions, miss."

She felt herself go hot and cold at the same time. Something terrible must have happened to her family!

"We'll use my office on the lightship." Dominic Gold was walking with them. "My secretary can take charge of the students."

Her tongue felt too big for her mouth. She needed to force her voice to push it out of her throat.

"You have to tell me what this is about," she managed.

"It would be better if we went inside, miss."

The policeman's voice was kind. Policemen were trained to be kind on occasions like this. They'd want to sit her down. Offer her a cup of tea.

"YOU HAVE to tell me NOW! What's HAPPENED to my FAMILY?"

Why had she let herself be exiled to this dead-end swamp when she could have stayed at home with her mother and father and Maggi? 'We need to ask you some questions,' he'd said. What if the accident – or whatever disaster had occurred – had been somehow her fault?

Orcs and dementors and zombies!

"Nothing at all, miss. This is nothing to do with your family at all."

The gravel steadied beneath her feet. Her vision cleared. She saw the policeman's faces now, as well as their caps and uniforms: one a bit fat and middle-aged, the other one younger, probably quite new. Two ordinary people doing a job.

"We need you to give us some information and we have to record it with a witness present. We were hoping to use Mr Gold, if you've no objection."

The summer sun was breaking through at speed. It was about to be a glorious day. Get this over – whatever it was – and she'd still have time to get the kids into the dinghies before lunch.

Unless Madrigal's parents had decided to press charges? They couldn't, could they? Not after this amount of time. What would she need to do? Get a lawyer or something? Dominic would sack her anyway.

"Okay," she said, when they were settled in the Companion-in-Chief's small office. "How can I help you?" She was trying to sound more confident than she felt.

"It's Mr Farran from Rebow Cottage. I regret to inform you that he's met with an accident."

"I'm sorry."

That was such a lie. She wasn't sorry at all. She was sort of dazed with relief and struggling not to show it.

"Was it serious? Is he in hospital?"

"Not exactly, miss. I'm afraid Mr Farran has been found dead."

Dead.

It was a good thing that Martha had brought them tea and

coffee. The handing round and the warmth of the mugs lessened the impact of that bleak word.

Dead.

Martha was offering her sugar. Xanthe loathed sugar in coffee but she took some anyway and noticed that her hand was shaking as she tried to stir it in. She hadn't even liked Mr Farran. He'd called her a darkie and she thought he might have hit his wife. There was the way he'd looked back at the house when he'd left it that evening. She'd never know what he'd been thinking then.

Dominic told Martha that she should go and help Jonjo with the kids. The policemen gave Xanthe a moment or two while they took a few swigs from their own hot drinks. Then they carried on.

"Officially it's an unexplained death. The doctors will be taking a look and then there'll be an inquest. Our duty is to collect any relevant information and prepare a report for the coroner. So we have to ask you when you last saw Mr Farran and whether there's anything you can tell us that might help us to ascertain his state of health. Or, indeed, his state of mind."

Xanthe swallowed and nodded. Her tongue had gone big in her mouth again. One of policemen had a notebook and was checking for his questions: the other would be watching her as she gave her answers.

"We understand that you're currently a volunteer sailing instructor with the Project and that you're lodging with the Farrans at Rebow Cottage. We'd like you to confirm that, on Sunday May 26th, you returned to Rebow Cottage in the early evening."

She could do this, if she was careful and if she thought about each question before she spoke.

"I called at the shop first," she said.

"What sort of time would that make it?"

"Maybe half past six? Mr and Mrs Farran were watching TV East. There was an item about Dunkirk. They were quite… involved with the programme. I didn't actually speak to them. I'm not sure they knew that I was there."

You have brought a darkie into my parents' house.

"So, as far as you were able to ascertain, Mr Farran was alive and well at half past six on Sunday evening. That's very useful, miss. And what happened next?"

That was it, she had no idea.

"He went out after the programme. I'm not sure where. He might have said something about the Plough and Sail…?"

She rubbed her face. She was trying to remember. The shock of death seemed to have blotted out everything else. Except for that overpowering impression of mutual hatred. And possible violence?

"Did you see Mr Farran again? Or hear him come home?"

"No, I didn't. After he had gone out Mrs Farran went to bed. She came to my room first but she wasn't feeling well. Then, later, she asked me to lock up. She said her husband would sleep… somewhere else. It sounded like it was normal. I didn't see him before I left in the morning and I don't think he was there last night."

The policemen nodded as if this fitted with what they already knew.

"Am I allowed to ask what happened? Was it a heart attack or a road accident or something? Where was he?"

"How old are you miss?"

"I'm sixteen."

"You might want to phone your family after we've gone. Or we can give you the number of our youth support team. We can't discuss any details at this point. There'll be a statement later to the local press and the coroner's report will be on the public record. We may need you to repeat your statement at the inquest. That'll be in a week or two if there are no complications. If the cause of death isn't clear, however, we may be directed to take it further."

"Okay."

She'd told her family she could cope on her own. Now she was going to.

Martha had left her a glass of water as well as the coffee. Xanthe took a mouthful and got ready to begin answering their questions again. Her memory was better now. She didn't have to tell them the word he'd used about her but possibly she should say something about the Farrans maybe having a row? It wasn't that sinister. Plenty of married people had rows.

Except that one of them didn't necessarily die soon after.

And there was the hitting. Which she hadn't seen and totally wasn't sure about.

And the stick? Which might not even be the same one.

Could she possibly explain the weird things Mrs Farran had said about the *Igraine* 'coming for' her husband? Should she even try?

She had heard nothing in the night except the cat breaking a teapot and exiting through its flap. And the next day Mrs Farran had left out her supper and a note and had gone to bed.

She hadn't left any food for Mr Farran. Maybe she already knew he was dead? When had he died?

One of the officers showed her that he had an audio

recorder. As he put it on the desk between them, Dominic Gold leaned forward, shuffled, cleared his throat.

"Miss Ribiero has only been with us for three days. She may not be aware that Mrs Farran is my aunt."

The blue eyes, the cheek bones. Square, determined faces – delicate in her case, stern in his. Probably Mrs Farran had had fair hair when she was younger. Mags would have spotted it at once.

Look out for the half-tide rocks.

"So Mr Farran was your uncle…?"

"She married him."

There was something odd and angry about the way he said that. Xanthe made up her mind to repeat exactly the words she'd already used and not add anything at all. Then Dominic could fetch her stuff and she'd never have to step inside Rebow Cottage again.

"My aunt wants you to stay with her."

The police had gone. She and the Companion-in-Chief were still in the office on board the lightship. She hadn't had a chance to tell him what was on her mind.

"I offered to sleep in Rebow Cottage myself," said Dominic. "During the day my presence is necessary on *Godwyn* but I would have sent Martha to sit with her."

Martha seemed like his answer to everything. Watch out for the kids, run the office, sit with the aunt. Did Martha have a life?

Did *she* have a life, come to that?

"Sorry, but I'm a sailing instructor not an aunt-minder. I'm not comfortable in Rebow Cottage. I'd prefer to move onto *Godwyn* straight away. I was going to ask you before any of this happened."

"There isn't any space."

"I'll stay somewhere else then. There were bed-and breakfast adverts in the shop. I'll sleep in the sail lofts if I have to."

"My aunt tells me that she needs you. That she hopes you like the special food that she bought you and you're not to worry about breaking the teapot. I couldn't understand what she was saying."

"It was the cat."

He looked at her and frowned.

"The cat broke the teapot. I'd locked all the doors as she'd asked and they were all still locked in the morning. The cat flap opened outwards so once the cat had gone out it couldn't come back in again until I released the catch. I swept up first."

He wasn't listening.

"She must be in shock. I can't think why else she wants you to stay. He's gone now."

Then he realised what he'd said.

"I'm sorry. I didn't put that very well. I'm going to have to ask you, out of kindness...to continue living in Rebow Cottage."

He wasn't finding this easy. Good. Because she hadn't yet forgiven him for the way he'd towed her back to *Godwyn* on her first day and banned her from sailing alone.

"My aunt is a very private person. There's no-one else I can ask."

"No-one at all?"

Neighbours? Friends? Other family members? *Martha*?

He'd been going to 'send' Martha – not 'ask' her. She didn't like Dominic Gold. She didn't see any reason she should help him out. Mrs Farran wasn't *her* aunt.

"There's...no-one."

There was a hesitation in his voice.

"I don't believe you."

She had nothing to lose by challenging him. Did she?

There was her job. Xanthe didn't want to get sacked. She liked her crew – those awkward, frightened kids. She'd promised to teach them to sail.

There was her personal pride as well. She'd been chucked off the training camp. Now she imagined herself going home, telling her parents and her teachers and Maggi that she'd been sacked for refusing to help care for some bereaved old lady who hadn't any friends.

"I'm not completely saying no."

Dominic looked smug too soon.

"But I definitely haven't said yes. I don't understand why your aunt wants me when she can't even remember my name. She calls me 'girl'. It's as if she thinks I'm the parlour maid or something. That's when she's not treating me like something from another planet because of the colour of my skin."

Dominic opened his mouth. And shut it again. Xanthe carried on.

"Also I may as well say that I'm still incredibly angry about not being allowed to go sailing on my own in my own time with no good reason given."

The Chief Companion's office was in the deckhouse of the former lightship. Only the light was above them. The tide was high and it was perfect weather – sunshine and a light but steady southerly breeze. She should be out there with the kids.

They were surrounded by strong, square windows. Xanthe glimpsed white sails on the Flete, birds wheeling above the marshes, boats rocking with delight at being lifted from their dreary mud-holes. She could see across the main river to St Peter's and all along that pale gold coast to the chapel and the open sea. She caught her breath with longing.

"In fact that one's non-negotiable. If I'm not allowed to go sailing by myself in my own time, I'm not staying any longer anyway." It was her life. "I heard your aunt say that Mr Farran had a brother. I don't think you're being straight with me."

His face went slack with surprise. Then he was climbing down the twisting metal stairs as if he couldn't care less.

"There's a community support worker waiting with my aunt," he called back. "And I'm expecting the doctor to visit. Collect whatever you have here in your locker and walk with me to the cottage. We can talk as we go. My aunt has asked you to remain but if you're not able to help her, then I'll get Martha to ring your parents or call a taxi while you pack the rest of your possessions."

"She can call them right now if you're not letting me have the use of a dinghy to go sailing in my own time."

"Please," he said, "Allow me to explain as we walk."

He had – finally – said please.

CHAPTER EIGHT

Little Miss Iris

Tuesday May 28, LW 0500 HW 1140 LW 1740 HW 2354

So now she was sitting with old Mrs Farran in the same back room where Mrs Farran had been sitting with her husband watching TV East only two days ago.

She'd agreed to carry on lodging at Rebow Cottage until the end of the week when there would be cabins available on *Godwyn*. That would give Dominic time to sort out longer-term care for his aunt. He'd asked Xanthe to have supper with Mrs Farran and keep her company in the evenings. She'd work with the kids whenever the tide was good – and she could choose what she did beyond that.

"I have to be able to sail by myself. I can't be trapped every day. I've made a decision while I've been here and I'm going to get back to racing as soon as I can. So I need to think about my fitness."

He had tried to tell her that it wasn't possible. That she couldn't use the Project boats and there wasn't anything else. She'd kept her face completely stony and shrugged her shoulders. He'd sighed and given in.

"I'm going to introduce you to my cousin. I don't like him and he doesn't like me but he'll lend you a dinghy and you can moor it in the Flete off Fisherman's Hard. Go where you like in your own time but please, stay safe."

That was twice – the p-word twice.

"My mother left me here after my father died at Dunkirk."

Mrs Farran sat gazing in front of her, her hands folded on her lap, a slight crease, not quite a frown, between her faded eyebrows. She moved one hand and shifted slightly. She didn't look at Xanthe as she talked.

"One of the maids told me afterwards how she waited in the drawing room of our big house on Broad Marsh for all of that terrible week. We had officers billeted indoors and troops camped in the grounds. I was placed here, in this cottage, with the Farrans, to keep me out of the way. Then, when he came and told her that my father was dead, they left for Scotland. It was safer there."

Mrs Farran's voice was without emotion. Xanthe couldn't work her out at all: one moment she was calling her 'girl' and explaining that she must put the milk in the teacup before she poured the tea – or was it after? One was 'drawing- room' and the other was 'nursery', apparently. Then, moments later, she'd be treating her like some sort of freak.

Xanthe was doing her best to get across that she was a volunteer sailing instructor with an interest in local history. She was asking the easiest, most obvious, questions.

"How old were you when your father died?"

"I was ten. Eleven a few weeks later. That was when my mother wrote to Mrs Farran."

"But you're Mrs Farran…"

"Old Mrs Farran was my nanny. Her husband was a fisherman and there were the three boys. But then she discovered there would be only two of them left and her husband was dead and the *Igraine* had sunk so I suppose she needed money."

Xanthe wasn't quite sure she was following all this.

"What happened to them – any of them?"

The old lady shrugged. "The *Igraine* hit a mine off Flinthammock pier. They'd been to try and help with the evacuation but they weren't needed. That was when Fisherman Farran died. I expect they would have carried on fishing otherwise. Eli was there but he didn't drown."

The word 'unfortunately' seemed to hover in the dim air as Mrs Farran returned to her own story.

"It was Nanny Farran who told me that my father had died. She was crying when she told me. It was either because she loved him or she was worried about her wages."

Mrs Farran's voice was horribly snobbish but her blue eyes were wide and frightened and her thin chest was heaving like a trapped bird.

"Mother's letter explained that they'd gone to live in Scotland and it wasn't convenient to have me with them." Her fingers convulsed as she gripped her honeycomb rug but her voice stayed as steady as if she was reciting. "She didn't expect to be returning to Flinthammock so she offered to carry on paying Nanny Farran to look after me. People were making all sorts of private arrangements for their children then. Though it was usually to get them away from the danger zones, not leave them there."

OMG! How could her mother do that? Xanthe didn't know what to say. She'd best stick with the history questions.

"Um, so, was Flinthammock a danger zone?"

"That was why the army had taken over our big house. The Navy were on Oversee – my father's island. They didn't seem to mind who they dispossessed."

Mrs Farran was bitter, she was angry and abandoned but this was genuine World War Two reminiscence. It was exactly what Xanthe wanted. She wished she could run and fetch her dictaphone but that didn't seem appropriate.

"Did you go back when the war was over?"

"To our house? No. Mother had sold it as soon as she could."

Xanthe didn't really want to follow up on that one either so she asked Mrs Farran what she could remember about local defences.

"There were the minefields and then they built the watchtower. They had a big gun down by the pier. Eli used to go there selling fish. He said he was watching the grave."

Xanthe didn't understand what this meant but it could be a clue that Mrs Farran needed to talk about her dead husband. Xanthe hoped the old lady wasn't going to cry. Maybe they'd been childhood sweethearts.

"Was Mr Farran quite young then?" she asked, as gently as she could.

"Eli never seemed young to me. He was the oldest and he was already a bully. I kept out of his way as much as I could."

Oh.

"He was exactly like his father. I was glad when the *Igraine* took Fisherman Farran and so was Nanny. Though we still had Eli. Then I had to marry him so he could salvage that boat and go fishing again. Until she took Joe too. Then they drowned the *Igraine* and I thought I'd be burdened with Eli for the rest of my life. Until you came."

She grabbed Xanthe's dark hand in both of her own and kissed it. There were tears pouring down her face now – liberation tears.

"When you showed me that you had summoned the *Igraine* I knew that I would soon be free!"

"Mrs Farran!"

"Surely I can be Iris now?"

"Mrs Farran...Iris...you have to be more careful what you say. Your husband's death was unexpected so the police are investigating. They could think that you *wanted* him dead. You know there's going to be an inquest."

The old lady put Xanthe's hand down carefully and sat up. She dabbed her cheeks with her lacy handkerchief and stared at her wide-eyed.

"But it was you who revealed the death-ship to me. And you who locked the doors of the house and loosed the poltergeist. Everything has happened has been caused by your dark power."

"Iris! You must listen! What I showed you was a mirage, an atmospheric illusion – layers of warm air over layers of cold – or something. I was on the river. There was a boat out to sea. I saw it. I took some photos. THAT WAS ALL! It was you who told me to lock the doors because you and your husband had had an argument and you said you were afraid. And it was your cat that smashed the teapot. NOT ME!"

Xanthe was completely shaking. As soon as Iris had gone to bed she would be ringing Dominic Gold. His aunt. His problem.

Something she had said had made the old lady listen. Iris was visibly switching back into drawing-room mode. She crossed her ankles and clasped her hands in her lap and arranged her lips into a smile. Then the cat padded in to join them.

"Puss, puss, puddums," said Iris and he jumped into her lap and perched there kneading her leg with his front paws.

"His name is Joe. I called him after Eli's youngest brother. It's a reminder of the things that he might have wanted to forget."

Was Iris completely mental?

"You didn't think that could have been unfair on the cat?" Xanthe asked. "If Mr Farran didn't like him, mightn't he have, um, neglected him?"

She meant kicked him but she still couldn't say it. With her cat sitting purring on her lap Mrs Farran looked like such a sweet old lady.

"I told Eli that there would be Consequences if anything ever happened to Joe. We've always had a Joe since Joe died. I forget how many now."

She offered Xanthe another cup of pale, cold tea.

"You say that you're interested in the war. Joe was the only one of them who crossed to Dunkirk and returned. He went seven times! And he was the third son. He should have been lucky."

Xanthe breathed again. "Please do carry on about Dunkirk," she said. World War Two felt like a good safe subject. "Did many people set off from here?"

"Most of the fishermen had already left the village. The yachts were laid up and the yacht crews had gone. The bargemen went. Of course *my* father was already there."

She'd revealed earlier that her father had died, so Xanthe decided to stay away from that one.

"And did you say that Mr Farran and *his* father went as well?"

"Only as far as Ramsgate. The *Igraine* was too small." She sounded contemptuous.

"Oh," said Xanthe, "I had thought that was the point of

Dunkirk – Operation Dynamo – using lots of little ships?"

"Little ships with engines. *Igraine* was a sailing smack. They wanted motorboats to ferry soldiers off the beaches and out to the bigger ships in the deeper water. Joe explained it to me later. Joe and I were always friends. Until that boat and Eli killed him."

Had she heard right? Xanthe asked the first alternative question that came into her head.

"Did Joe see your father at Dunkirk?"

That was a dumb-ass one. She'd studied photos of Dunkirk, columns of black smoke, ships burning, buildings burning, continuous hail of bombs and shelling, air attack, fires, men packed together, machine guns and drownings. It wasn't exactly Friends Reunited.

Mrs Farran stared at Xanthe. Crossed herself.

"*Joe* didn't see my father. There was only him and the cook on board a paddle steamer. After the first boatload came alongside he never left the galley. The paddle steamer made seven crossings with a thousand men each time. The cook made stew and Joe made tea and sandwiches. And most of the men were sick and some were wounded and all of them were filthy and they smoked everywhere and dropped their cigarette butts. So by the time Joe and the cook had cleared up and got fresh stores they were on their way back to collect another thousand men. *Joe* couldn't have seen anyone."

Xanthe nodded. "Sounds tough."

"Artie saw…"

"Artie?"

Mrs Farran didn't speak. Couldn't speak?

"Where was Artie?"

Xanthe had meant to ask *who* was Artie but it came out wrong. There was such a weird atmosphere in Rebow Cottage. It was as if she'd lost control of her questions.

"Artie was in the middle, with the light."

Iris stopped stroking the cat and he stopped purring. She'd shut her eyes. Her face had gone grey. Xanthe's heart went out to her. She must be way into her eighties. Her husband had died. Of course she was upset.

"I'm sorry. I shouldn't have asked all that. You need to get some rest. Joe looks like a nice puss. I'll feed him if you like. I don't suppose he'll want tea and sandwiches!"

Iris got slowly out of the chair and onto her feet. Xanthe ought to fetch her back her walking stick, though the way she was looking, she'd be better with one of those frames.

"You'll find his dinner in a single portion sachet near the sink."

Xanthe helped the old lady up the stairs and into her bedroom. She fetched a hot water bottle from the kitchen without being asked and breathed a sigh of relief when she found that Iris was already in bed when she returned. She was wearing a brushed pink nightdress with a high lacy collar and small pearl buttons. Some sort of knitted pink bed jacket with broad satin ribbons and a hairnet to keep her white curls smooth. There was a box of tissues by the bed in a quilted floral cover and Xanthe could see the edge of another embroidered hanky peeping from Iris's long sleeve. You would expect that the first night alone after your husband had died would be seriously upsetting.

"Do you want to speak to your nephew before you go to

sleep? He left me his mobile number and I could bring my phone in to you."

"There's no need for that. Perhaps you'd like to telephone him yourself? You can tell him that I'm perfectly alright – as far as is possible. I must get accustomed to my new situation."

Iris gave a brave little smile and pulled out the hanky to dab at her eyes. Maggi would have managed so much better but Maggi was revising for her GCSEs and they'd agreed that they weren't going to phone or text except at weekends. Dominic had told her he had sedatives if his aunt became distressed. There wasn't much sign of that.

Xanthe glanced around the pretty room. The chintz curtains were already shut, though it would be hours before it was properly dark. The bedside lamp was in the shape of a china shepherdess and there was a china pony and trap that held Iris's flesh-pink hearing aids. It was a completely feminine space, girly even. There was no feeling of loss in the room because there was no evidence Mr Farran had ever lived in it.

"Do close the door. I could ring a little bell if I need you."

Like heck you could, thought Xanthe, feeling annoyed all over again that she'd been pushed into this situation. That dinghy Dominic's cousin was going to lend her; all those free afternoons – they'd better be good.

She fed Joe the cat and left a message on Dominic's voicemail, then she stood around in the kitchen wondering what to do next. She washed and dried the supper plates while Joe ate hungrily. She should have been hungry herself but her stomach was clenched tight and she knew that if she ate she'd be sick.

She watched the cat as he sat and cleaned his whiskers before hopping neatly into the back garden. She'd released the catch that morning so the flap swung easily to and fro. Then, just because she'd nothing else to do, she bent down and relocked it so that the flap would only open from the inside. She tried to prise it open it from the outside but it was tight-fitting and magnetised. Must have been expensive. Even when she took out her rigging knife and wiggled it into the cracks, she couldn't make it flip. Not even the cat could have got back indoors once everything had been locked last night.

There was a bamboo pole propped outside the door. It had a piece of wire reinforcing the top and a large removable screw inserted down into the hollow centre. The wood was dark with age. Xanthe ran her fingers up and down its smooth, weathered surface. It reminded her of something. Lots of people used bamboo in their gardens, for stakes and things. She knew that. But why the groove and screw and that twist of tarnished wire? What was it saying to her?

Objects didn't speak. And she didn't believe in poltergeists. This atmosphere was beginning to make her paranoid. There had been no one apart from herself and Mrs Farran in Rebow Cottage last night. The cat had broken the rosebud teapot and the pole was just a pole.

Xanthe didn't want to go back indoors. There were summer evening noises and the smell of barbecues in the air. This garden was a hidden space squeezed between dark hedges. There was a paved path running down the centre and there should have been flowerbeds except that the hedges had blocked the light and were leaching the goodness from the ground.

The cat flattened himself onto his stomach and disappeared beneath the evergreens. Xanthe walked along the path. She could see the dry remains of shrubs and roses that had suffocated. If there had been flowers they were long gone. The hedges seemed to close behind her until she could no longer see the house.

Soon she found herself in a wider space where there'd been a bit of kitchen garden with clippings and a compost heap and a small stable. Both the top and bottom halves of the door were closed and there were no windows. She noticed a boot-scraper and a tap, a metal bucket and a brush. Was this where Eli Farran had been made to leave his 'filth', she wondered?

Xanthe tried the stable door and was glad that it was locked. She wasn't even tempted to look for the key. She was certain that she didn't want to know Mr Farran's secrets. There was a gate beside the stable that led out into an empty field. She opened the gate with a feeling of relief and potential escape. She could see that it ran all along the backs of the Flinthammock houses and there was a track straight across which would take her to the tangle of bushes that lay inland of the river wall.

Yes! She stepped out. And then she stopped. She had been about to tread on splinters and icicles of glass, edges of wood, bent nails and a picture, smashed and trampled on the ground.

She felt sudden goose-bumps as she bent down to look.

The picture was a sampler – a careful type of sewing that olden days children did to practise different stitches. Or maybe a loving adult would make one as a gift for a baby. Then they would be framed and hung above the mantelpiece. Had she noticed it even?

This sampler had been thrown face down and stamped on – heavily, repeatedly, until it was ground into the earth and pierced through and through with broken glass.

Xanthe found some old newspaper beside the compost heap and took her time pincering up the shards of glass with a handy couple of twigs until she'd removed as much as she could. She'd found herself getting rather fond of Joe the cat. She wouldn't want him getting splinters in his paws. Then, finally, she managed to spread out the sampler and read what it said.

IRIS AUGUSTINE GOLD
BROAD MARSH HALL & OVESEYE
JUNE 19TH 1929
FROM ABRAHAM & ANN FARRAN
ELIJAH, ARTHUR & JOSEPH
WITH OUR RESPECTS

It must have been a present from 'Nanny' Farran to the little Iris. There was an embroidered rainbow, which was the meaning of Iris's name, and other small, personal decorations. Even in its ripped and dirtied state it was obvious that the stitching had been exquisite.

Xanthe was going to have to start believing in poltergeists because the alternative message of this destruction was terrible human violence and anger. And grief. She was certain that there was grief in here.

She put all the remains in the metal bucket by the boot-scraper and spread a thick layer of compost over the place where the violence had occurred. It was the best she could do to protect any small creature from the last crumbs of glass. Then she turned back towards Rebow Cottage.

The light was fading and when she walked through the kitchen she noticed that the hallway was almost completely dark. She hesitated by the door to the sitting room and then made herself go in.

Just as she'd thought. There was an empty space above the mantelpiece and even in the gloom she could see the rectangular mark where a picture had been covering the wallpaper. There was a small hole in the plaster where a picture hook had been wrenched out.

Xanthe stood and thought about the family who'd lived here long ago: Abraham – that was 'Fisherman Farran' and his wife, Ann, was 'Nanny'. Then there had been three boys. Had one of them died, or something? Something Iris had said about the family after Dunkirk…

Rebow Cottage was quiet but not silent now. There were breathings in the thick air that could almost have grown into voices.

"My name means rainbow." The child was speaking clearly, confident in her right to be heard. "Mother says I must be careful that I'm not too pretty for my own good but Father says it means that I'm his e-lu-sive treasure."

"It's from a story." This speaker was an older boy, pleasant enough but patronising. "First you have to catch yourself a leprechaun."

"Little Miss Oy-ris," said a much older, heavier voice as threatening as distant thunder. "Our own personal Crock of Gold. I hope you're a-listenin, Eli, me boy."

"Nanny?" said the child. She didn't sound so certain now.

Xanthe forced herself to go upstairs to her bedroom: to sip some of her Lucozade and eat a Hobnob and an apple – then keep them down. She didn't need her hunger to be giving her hallucinations.

CHAPTER NINE

Fritha

Wednesday May 29, LW 0600 HW 1220 LW 1820 HW 0034

Xanthe didn't meet Dominic's cousin that afternoon. She wasn't quite clear why he didn't show up but it couldn't have been less of an issue. All she wanted from him was a dinghy.

"So how do I find this dinghy?" she'd asked Dominic when she'd finished the morning's lesson and returned the kids to *Godwyn.* She'd tried to talk to him about the odd things Mrs Farran had been saying and the breakages and the generally weird atmosphere in Rebow Cottage but he wouldn't listen. Now she was going to enforce her side of the deal. She was going sailing.

"You follow the wall on the south side of Roffey Creek and skirt the marshes as if you're heading for Shinglehead Spit."

"Where's Shinglehead Spit?"

"End of the Flete, where the south channel curves towards the Nass. You passed it on your first…outing."

She hadn't noticed. On the way down she'd been looking ahead to the open river and the sea and on the way back she'd been too angry to care.

"The wall swings right where the creek meets the Flete and then you look to your left for Fishermen's Hard. You'll see a fence and some steps going down."

A hard? Xanthe imagined a nice concrete slipway where you could wheel your dinghy to the water. Or a good solid slope of hardcore and pebbles. She could really use that – and not just for herself. It would help her give the kids more time as well. They could only launch the dinghies from *Godwyn* two hours before and after high water. After that the creek shrunk away to a trickle, winding between the ramparts of mud. She couldn't believe how much mud there was in Essex. Shiny dark flatlands and craggy, pock-marked boulders of the stuff.

The session this morning had been much too short. They'd listened to everything she said: their progress had been spectacular. They were happy and noisy and glowing with achievement and they wanted more. They wanted her to come into lunch with them and then do something – anything – out of doors this afternoon. But the wind had freshened and she was desperate to stop being a teacher and go sailing on her own. Especially with another evening with Mrs Farran ahead of her.

"Aren't you going to eat anything, Xanthe?" Martha asked.

If she went in to lunch with them, they'd never let her out.

"I'm okay," she lied. You don't have to worry about me. I get supper where I'm lodging."

She was going to have to make sure that was true in future – even if it meant eating peanuts and tinned lychees with boil-in-the-bag rice.

Kelly-Jane had turned grumpy and was slouching at the end of the companionway with her arms folded. Her brother, Kieran, had taken no for an answer and was heading into lunch. David and Siri were looking at Xanthe like puppy dogs pleading for a walk. Both of their faces were pink instead of pale.

"You were so good today," she told David once again. "You were solid. And you've got a real gift," she added to Siri.

The little girl's eyes were open wider than most people's; whatever was behind them remained a mystery.

"What's wrong with someone who's got jelly in one of her ears and sponge cake and custard in the other?" Nelson asked. He'd lost his smile.

"Huh? Don't know." He wasn't telling the joke as if it was funny.

Xanthe felt annoyed with him. "Siri isn't deaf."

"He didn't *say* it were Siri," said Kelly-Jane.

Martha had fetched Xanthe a wrapped sausage roll, a satsuma and a drink. "You need to let Xanthe go," she told the kids. "She's earned some time to herself. You'll get your sailing lessons."

"Didn't get 'em yesterday."

Yesterday?

Fog. Death. Dominic – and the long grim evening in Rebow Cottage.

"Yesterday wasn't exactly my choice," she said.

"But this is, innit. You could make it up to us."

NO! She had to be back there again tonight. She'd done a deal. She needed me-time.

"You're a hard woman, Kelly-Jane, but I am in a rocky place. I'll see you tomorrow. Okay?"

She turned away and felt the breeze on her face. Oh please let this dinghy be fast.

Dominic had told her that the dinghy was moored in the middle of the channel but that the hard wasn't marked.

"Will your cousin meet me there?"

"I told you – we don't get on."

Xanthe had clenched her hands into fists so her nails dug

into her palms. She clamped her jaw so she couldn't speak. She wanted to tell him to go stuff his cousin and his cousin's dinghy and his aunt and his pathetic family feuds because she'd had it up to the brim with Flinthammock and she was ringing her mother and going home where she'd got a dinghy of her own to sail.

Except she couldn't go home because she'd promised the kids. And anyway the sponsors would surely have repossessed *Spray* by now.

Maybe some of her frustration showed because Dominic had stopped his obsessive polishing of *Godwyn*'s already gleaming handrail and looked at her directly.

"I told my cousin who you were, Xanthe, and he said as he 'reckoned you'd understand why the dinghy were for you'."

It was obvious that he was quoting exact words. It didn't mean that Xanthe understood them.

She reached the wall on the opposite side of the creek. Now she could see a whole new landscape. A wide green expanse of marshland stretching between the creek and the main river. Lush grass and reed-fringed ponds and fat cattle grazing. And in the distance, across the far side of the Blackwater, was the St Peter's power station with its cranes high above it.

Xanthe gulped in a lungful of fresh air, resisted the urge to fling her arms wide and shout aloud with happiness. Yes! She said to the open sunlit world. And she ran.

She almost overran the hard.

Hard? What were these Essex people *like?* This so-called 'hard' was no more than a line of fat cement-filled bags laid down to make stepping stones across the mud. The water was dense with silt and she had to stretch out her foot and feel for each step as she waded out to the dinghy across the ebbing tide.

Dominic's cousin's dinghy was an old wooden Firefly called *Fritha*. Xanthe'd seen the GRP version at rallies – they were robust, two-person dinghies and some of the universities had them but *Fritha* was like their great-granny. Her varnished hull had darkened and streaked with age and there were signs of water seepage around the base of her centreboard case. Her ropes were greyish and stiff with salt and her mast was some weird part-metal construction that could only have looked modern on Noah's ark.

He said as he reckoned you'd understand why the dinghy were for you.

Well, thanks a lot. Xanthe pulled the mainsail and jib out of a mildewed canvas bag and set them without enthusiasm. The sail number shocked her – 486 – just three figures. *Fritha* must be seriously old, even for a Firefly. Madrigal would have wanted her humanely destroyed! Or sent to the Third World.

Fritha was quick, though. As soon as she was out of the Flete and into the main river she was heeling to the breeze and Xanthe was hiking out over the varnished side-deck with her feet hitched under the toe-straps and sending up a serious prayer that the ancient webbing was sound. Never mind the classic West African figure: she was a lightweight in a two-person dinghy. She hardened her sheets, set a course even closer to the wind, tensed her thigh and stomach muscles and stretched out flat as she could go. She was going to ache later. It was *so* going to be worth it.

The Blackwater was a wide river but she was across in minutes and the ugly bulk of the former power station was fouling her wind. She bore away on a broad reach. The afternoon sun was sparkling on the wavelets, the wind and tide were hurrying them along and *Fritha* seemed to skitter with delight as they headed out to sea.

I could sail myself back into college. Or home. I could make the River Orwell before nightfall if I chose.

But I don't choose, she added quickly to herself.

She took one long look down the curving coast that ran north towards her home river and the people she loved; then she glanced south to the chapel of St Cedd-on-the-Wall. Someone had said there was a peace camp there. She couldn't imagine a more special place for it to be.

Then she rounded up into the wind again and put in a couple of tacks. Plus a 720 degree turn, simply to divert herself and because she could. *Fritha* was amazing for such an old boat. Xanthe put the Firefly through a private dance: tacking, turning, gybing, heeling. She made her sail sideways and backwards. Maybe one day they'd make dinghy-dancing an Olympic event.

But Xanthe wouldn't be there.

And she was a racer, not a dancer.

She *had* been a racer.

If she wanted to get back into the GBR squad – ever – she was going to have to show that she'd changed her attitude.

Except that she hadn't

changed

at all.

Had she?

Her thoughts returned to the private meeting room and to the group of a dozen people seated more or less unhappily round the long table.

She knew what she'd done.

Yes, she had punched Madrigal Shryke.

Could she tell them why?

I couldn't help wondering whether you'd ever thought how much it would mean to your own country if you elected to sail for them? Wherever it is in Africa that you originally came from…They probably haven't even got a sailing team! Rig a bathtub and you'd make it unopposed…Your own tribe!

Would she ever get Madrigal's words out of her head?

She was British. This was her country. But Madrigal had made her feel like a total outsider. And then she'd behaved exactly like the barbarian they were saying she was.

The chairman had asked her whether she could express any regret for what she'd done. She wanted to say yes. She knew that there were people round that table who liked her and had believed in her talent. She could have found supporters if she'd said the right words.

Madrigal had made her punch: she wasn't going to make her lie as well. So she told them no, she couldn't. Not entirely.

"Oh come along, Xanthe!" Griselda, the head coach, had burst out. "You're academically gifted, you're musical, you're an exceptionally talented sailor. Your family are backing you, your sponsors believe in you. If you and Madrigal have a personality clash, can you not deal with it in some more…civilised manner?"

Xanthe jerked at the mainsheet. *Fritha* luffed, resentfully. She stalled and lost way. This was like kicking the cat for your own mistake. Totally unacceptable.

It had been that single word. If the coach – a former three-times medallist and a decent person who Xanthe utterly admired – hadn't chosen that particular word, 'civilised', she might have had a go at explaining.

But then she had happened to look round the room. Everyone there – male and female, young and old, grizzled and weather-beaten, pink-cheeked, brunette or blonde – every one, with the exception of herself, was 'white'. All of them, at that moment, seemed to Xanthe to possess that comfortable assurance, that kindliness even, that unquestioned assumption that they knew what 'civilised' was and, whatever it was, they had it.

There was so much she could have said that Xanthe had said nothing at all.

So now she apologised – wordlessly – to *Fritha;* hardened her sheets again and prepared to come about.

The Romans had defended this shoreline against the Saxons: the Vikings had sailed up this river to win one of the most invasive battles in English history. Her pre-research on the internet had told her that this was one of the last remaining stretches of coast where she could get an idea what the World War Two sea-defences had been like: 'From Sales Point to Bradwell Waterside there are twelve pillboxes in less than three miles.' As long as she kept an eye on the tide she wouldn't risk being late for Iris and she would have made a proper start on her extended essay.

She dropped anchor just off the edge of a bathing area on the seaward side of the former power station. The ground here was hard – as much sand as mud. There were cranes angular against the skyline, scaffolding, men in hard hats, the noise of machinery: heavy hammers, pneumatic drills, the clang of metal girders. Xanthe took her time stowing *Fritha*'s mainsail and jib. She needed to be sure that the anchor would hold.

Then she slipped over the side and waded ashore feeling quite unreasonably excited. She had left an area of saltings, grey sticky mud and tiny twisting channels: she had arrived at a long, pale golden beach. The sort of beach that made you want to walk for miles. Her canvas sailing shoes dripped and squelched but she was glad she was wearing them. Once she neared the top of the tideline the beach seemed of be made almost entirely of shell. Humps and swathes of shell – cockles, mussels, whelks and big rock oysters. She didn't have names for them all. They were crunchy beneath her feet, empty and dry and dead.

She looked back at *Fritha*. The dinghy was riding securely to her anchor. No worries there. Then she looked both ways along the beach. To the right the ex-power station. To the left that long, seductive stretch into blueness. She could see the chapel standing quiet against the distant sky. The word 'fritha' meant peace – how did she know that? – she just did.

Then she climbed the river wall and discovered that there was a deep ditch preventing her from exploring further inland. She could see a small, low, tough-looking building set well back in the flat fields. It was her first World War Two pillbox but it was on the wrong side of the dyke and it also looked as if it might be private.

She had to make a choice: left or right? If she set off towards the chapel it would be hard to make herself turn back.

The ex-power station was huge and distracting. What could

you do with something like that which was past its sell-by? There were loads of workers, some of them virtually of sight, so high on the scaffolding. Xanthe gazed upwards and felt giddy. People who worked that far from the ground were amazing. They'd have hard hats and harnesses and safety procedures, lights and cameras – but all the same…

She dragged her eyes away and turned right. She hadn't gone more than about twenty metres before she walked straight over her second pillbox. Its roof was constructed of slabs, level with the height of the river wall and there was some sort of lush green plant doing its best to act as camouflage. She got out her camera and took a few photos then she jumped down onto the beach and did her best to peer inside. She felt repelled by the darkness: frustrated by the impossibility of pushing more than her head through the small square gaps. Why was there no door? And why did she automatically assume that people would have peed in there?

"Has anyone been left on anchor watch while you're busy spying?"

She jumped backwards, scraping her head, and stared towards the river again. *Fritha* was fine. So who was fretting?

There was an elderly man standing, legs astride, on the concrete top of the pillbox, arms folded, staring down at her. His hair was long and thick and bleached like the dead shells. It was parted in the middle and flowed strong and wavy down below his shoulders. She guessed it must have been golden once.

"Manners please. You haven't answered me."

There was a moustache as well, combed and lavish and drooping either side of his mouth like a well-groomed walrus.

Not that he looked like a walrus. He was a strong-looking old man, energetic and upright and with those bright blue Nordic eyes that seemed to be surrounding her here. He could have been auditioning to play Thor or some Hollywood Viking chief. The rest of him was pretty standard – if your standard was some 'By Appointment' county outfitter: waxed jacket, check shirt, cavalry twill trousers and highly polished brown leather shoes.

"I checked the anchor myself before I left. The holding ground seems good and I'm not expecting to be here long."

"Purpose of visit?"

"I'm looking at what I think is a World War Two pillbox. Is that a problem?"

"It's a problem to me if I observe neglect of a historic dinghy."

Xanthe thought about *Fritha*'s condition. Yes, fair point, she could probably use some attention. But how did he know?

"This is the first afternoon I've sailed her."

"And it's obvious you don't appreciate what has been entrusted to you," he snapped. "I'll need your proof of identification now."

There was a startlingly clean Polaris all-terrain vehicle parked on the broad track that ran between the river wall and the dyke. Did this man see himself as some kind of border guard? She took a deep breath and struggled with her anger.

"My name is Xanthe Ribiero. I'm a volunteer sailing instructor at the Flinthammock Project and I have permission from the dinghy's owner. I don't know what you mean by identification but I'm sure that Dominic Gold will vouch for me. He's the Companion-in-Chief at the lightship."

"But I am the Commander of the Saxon Shore. I know

Dominic." He almost spat the word. "I know his penchant for degenerates but I had no idea that even Dominic would stoop as low as this. I recognise you, Miss Ribiero and you are not welcome here. You should never have been allowed to sail that dinghy."

Xanthe's confidence drained into the sand. She'd almost forgotten her outcast status.

She wasn't intending to back off, however. "I don't believe I'm trespassing," she said.

"Technically, as long as you remain outside the dyke, you are permitted. Everything else belongs to me. Look far and wide. This is the Saxon Shore."

He made a big gesture. He was claiming the flat meadows and the curving river wall, the scattered inland buildings and the ancient chapel.

"So do you ever allow access for research?"

She didn't know why she was wasting her breath but she carried on anyway. "I'm doing a World War Two history project for my IB and I noticed another pillbox in one of your fields. Also I think some of those buildings might have been aircraft hangers. I have a letter of support from my college tutor."

"The airfield is now closed. Later there will be interactive air raids, combat training and the memorabilia market. Currently I'm arranging a major commemorative event and I don't like spies. Hand me that camera and I'll check its contents."

"Sorry," she said, though she wasn't, "My camera's *my* property. To be precise, it's my mother's. She's lent it to me so I can photograph any World War Two remains."

She wondered whether he was one – a World War Two

remain. His face didn't have many lines but he could maybe have had them wiped. He looked rich enough.

She'd worked out who he was now. He was plummy voice: the man who'd been speaking on TV East that night. He surely couldn't be Mr Farran's *brother*?

"You're accommodated on the lightship, I assume?"

Why was he still talking to her when he'd already told her that she wasn't welcome?

"No. I'm lodging in the village."

"At what address?"

"With Mrs Farran at Rebow Cottage."

She watched him carefully for his reaction but his face was as expressionless as if it had been carved.

"With Iris Farran! Do, please, remember me to Iris."

He pulled a business card from an expensive-looking wallet and held it out to her. He couldn't be the brother – she must have heard that wrong. His eyes were peculiarly level and direct, 20:20 vision she guessed. She didn't take the card.

It was stand-off. But anything else that either might have said was drowned by a wailing from the construction site. An alarm, harsh and clamorous. The cranes ceased moving and the clattering of power-tools stopped. She thought she glimpsed a flashing light. The old man threw down his card. He hurried back to the Polaris and drove fast in the direction of the emergency.

There was no way she was going to pick up the card. She didn't even care that it was litter. In fact she hoped that he'd come back and find it abandoned in the dirt. She took a photo and headed back to the Firefly.

She checked the image as she went. Commander of the Saxon Shore A.F. Gold was in bold across the centre. Then there was smaller type with contact details and a job title: Chief Executive, Saxon Holdings.

Gold, not Farran. The more she thought of that half-heard quarrel between the two old people watching TV East, the more confused she became.

This man had the same surname as Dominic and he'd appeared to know a lot about the dinghy. Could he possibly be the owner?

Sails up, anchor up and an easy course across the river to the Flete.

It wasn't enjoyable. Xanthe was struggling to remember exactly what had been said and by whom and when. She was hoping desperately that the wannabe Viking didn't turn out to be Dominic's cousin. Otherwise she was going to be giving *Fritha* back even before she was asked.

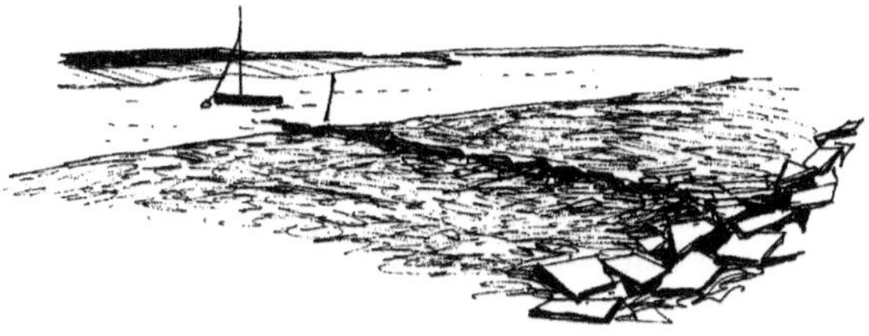

CHAPTER TEN

Gareth

Wednesday May 29, LW 0600 HW 1220 LW 1820 HW 0034

Xanthe had planned to do a more formal interview with Iris that evening, record it and then write it up. It seemed the safest way to keep her off the subject of Mr Farran's death – or the magical appearance of the *Igraine*. She probably shouldn't ask her anything about Dunkirk either.

"Could you maybe tell me about your childhood," she asked Iris, once she'd shown her the dictaphone and tried explaining how it worked. "And about your family and wherever it was that you lived before you moved into Rebow Cottage?"

It was slow to start with. Iris wasn't at all worried by the dictaphone. She obviously enjoyed talking about Broad Marsh Hall, the house her father had brought for her mother. She talked for ages about its gardens and the staff who had worked there and what perfect parents she'd had. She seemed to blame the war for everything that had gone wrong with her life: she blamed it for her father's death and her mother's desertion, then the sale of her home and her marriage to Eli.

"What else was I to do?" she asked plaintively.

Xanthe did her best to bite back the obvious answers: like, do some training or get a job?

"Didn't you hope to find someone you could love?" she asked as gently as she could.

Suddenly Iris was staring as if she thought Xanthe had the Evil Eye.

"But…there was *Dunkirk*!" she gasped. "How could I?"

Hadn't Iris been only about ten or eleven then?

"And I'm *not* going to talk about it. Ever," she added.

Xanthe took a deep breath and reminded herself that she needed to be really sensitive.

"That's okay. You don't have to talk about anything at all. We can stop this session any time. Maybe you'd like to go to bed now?"

Joe was sitting on the old lady's lap. He kneaded her leg with his paw and purred. This seemed to help her relax. She waved to Xanthe to carry on.

It was a mistake.

"So, you married Mr Farran. You must still have been very young."

"I was sixteen after the end of the war and Eli wanted my money to rebuild the *Igraine*. Fisherman Farran was dead and Joe was clearing minefields. Nanny was glad enough to be kept on."

Kept on?

"What did your mother think of your decision?"

Xanthe wasn't sure she should have asked that one, but she did want to know.

"I've no idea what my mother thought. We managed everything through trustees. They put this house in my name. Eli got his money. Then I set the rules to make sure he never… bothered me."

She couldn't imagine a sixteen-year-old behaving like that.

"And I bought myself a pony."

That made more sense.

"You didn't…want a family?"

"That would have been *disgusting*!" she said.

Xanthe should have stopped the session there. Instead she tried what she thought was a different subject. "Could you tell me more about your father, Augustus Gold? He sounds very… dashing."

God knows where she'd dredged that word from but it worked for Iris.

"My father was better than dashing: he was famous. When he came back from abroad – that was in the first war – he built top-secret boats on Oveseye. They were his own design and faster than anything else, and the government used him to rescue people out of Russia."

This sounded amazing. Except that it turned out that Iris didn't know anything about the top-secret boats and who her father had rescued from Russia. She did know that he'd invented some process that had made him very rich, but by the time he married her mother he wasn't inventing any more, he was mainly just spending the money.

Her mother was from some ridiculously posh family and sounded a complete pain in the butt. In fact she made Xanthe feel almost warm towards Madrigal Shryke. At least Maddie was ambitious and determined and trying to achieve something – by whatever foul means. Iris's mother only seemed to want to give dinner parties and spend money and whinge about her servants. Before abandoning her child in the middle of a war.

"My mother wouldn't live on Oveseye – she couldn't stand being cut off by the tide – so my father bought Broad Marsh Hall. The previous people had lived there for centuries but they'd let it go awfully. My parents were rebuilding and making everything the best – stables and tennis courts and big garages and a landing strip. There were walks all the way to the creek. But the war spoiled everything."

"And you were their only child. You didn't have any older brothers or sisters?"

"I really don't want to talk about my family. Who gave you permission to ask all these questions? I'm not interrogating *you*."

Mrs Farran pushed the cat violently off her lap, flapped her hands and kicked out to shoo it away.

"I'm s-sorry," Xanthe stuttered. "Maybe we've gone off topic. I was interested in hearing about your father."

"Well he wouldn't have thought much of you. He'd spent time in the colonies. He knew you needed to keep the natives in their place."

It took a moment before Xanthe got it.

Then she pressed save and stood up.

"I'll say good night then, Mrs Farran. I hope you can get yourself upstairs without my help. It's a pity, isn't it, that you've lost your ebony walking stick."

"Oh…" a soft, deflated, moaning sound. "Oh no, no…don't leave me here. I can't manage by myself. I never exactly wanted him to *die*…"

"What did you do?" Xanthe was horrified, shocked, bewildered, fascinated.

"Nothing. I did nothing. What could I do? I allowed you to do it all."

Iris was clutching her chest now.

"Oh, oh, oh!"

She'd fallen backwards in her chair and was staring up at Xanthe with her little girl's eyes.

"It was you who locked him out into the night."

"You said that you were frightened. You said he had somewhere else to sleep."

"But you had summoned the *Igraine*!"

Xanthe felt like chucking a jug of water over her.

"I'm phoning your nephew. Now!"

Dominic's phone rang and rang. Then it went to voicemail.

"It's about your aunt," was all Xanthe said.

Mrs Farran was hyperventilating and rocking herself from side to side. She supposed she should call the number she'd been given for the out-of-hours doctor.

Then Dominic's number rang back. It was Martha.

"I'm sorry Xanthe, Dom's not here." She called him Dom – did that mean they were an item? "One of the kids has gone walkabout. He's out looking."

"OMG! Who?"

"Siri, the little girl with mutism. But what about you? You weren't just ringing for a gossip?"

"It's his aunt. She might not be well."

"Can you explain a bit more? Does she need a doctor?"

Iris was listening and shaking her head.

"We've just had a really bad conversation. She keeps telling me I've got dark powers – like I'm some sort of alien. But it's more than that. There's other things. I even think I ought to talk to the police again. But she's Dominic's aunt, not mine."

She heard Martha sigh. "That's all we need."

Iris had gone quiet now. She looked small and frail and

was sort of mumbling at the knuckle of her thumb as if it was a comfort mechanism. For no reason Xanthe remembered the child's voice she'd heard – or imagined – last night. The child who'd been left with people who were not her own.

Little Miss Oy-ris. Our own personal Crock of Gold. I hope you're a-listenin, Eli, me boy.

There were undercurrents and deep troubles here that she didn't understand.

Joe was rubbing against the old lady's ankles – which was forgiving of him considering how she'd been kicking out just a few moments ago.

Martha continued talking. "I didn't think it was fair to ask you to stay there in the first place. Dom likes to send her occasional lodgers to help her earn some money. It's okay if it's birders. She keeps the house immaculate and she can look quite sweet. I'm so sorry Xanthe. I'd come and take over but I can't leave here. Jonjo's out looking too, so I'm responsible for the kids."

"That's okay. I'll cope. It's probably my fault – Siri, I mean – I shouldn't have left her earlier." The moment she said that she knew it was the truth. "I suppose you've looked round by the dinghies and in the rigging store," she added.

"The boys were there all afternoon with Jonjo. They were just hanging about, fiddling with bits of equipment, trying things. You've started something with those children, Xanthe."

"I hope that's good – but where were K-J and Siri then?"

"They'd gone to their cabin. I don't think Kelly-Jane's well. I was in the office and we took our eyes off them. We were negligent."

"So do you think I should call the doctor for Mrs Farran?"

Iris was watching her intently. "Though she does seem to have quietened down."

"I'll ring the pub," said Martha. "Gareth'll be there. They can send him over. You don't want to have to deal with that old witch."

Iris Farran might have had had the last hot water bottle she was going to be getting from Xanthe. Result!

"That would be totally excellent. But who's Gareth?"

"My brother. He and Dom don't hit it off but he's okay. Rough diamond, possibly."

"And he knows Iris?"

"Everyone knows everyone in Flinthammock. Anyway we're Farrans too. Leave it with me. Give the old bat a glass of water. Or use your 'dark powers' and magic her into a toad or something."

Suddenly Xanthe wanted to laugh. She felt about a squillion times better. That was the first time she'd talked to Martha without Dominic or Jonjo there.

"That's so good. You will update me about Siri won't you?"

"Yeah, will do."

Martha sounded sombre now. What was it with those kids?

Xanthe settled the old lady back on the sofa with a glass of water within reach, tucked a rug round her, then took out a notebook to begin her activity log. Joe the cat hopped neatly up and pushed himself next to Iris.

"I don't know what I said to upset her," Iris began whispering in the cat's attentive ear. "She's very changeable. I suppose it's because she isn't English."

But it had been Iris who had flipped.

Xanthe couldn't remember which question had triggered her sudden hostility. It would be on the dictaphone somewhere…

Then Gareth Farran arrived: short and dark and smelling of diesel. He nodded to Xanthe and held out his hand. It wasn't especially clean.

"Thanks for coming," she said, shaking it.

He was maybe later thirties, forties? His hand felt leathery and strong. He'd got a half a finger missing.

"I don't think she's really ill. It was mainly that we had a falling-out."

"Don't you worry, lass. She's got quite a tongue on her, has Auntie Iris. Have you had your tea yet? I was about to go up the chipper when I'd finished my pint."

"No, I haven't eaten anything this evening."

The apple and the sausage roll seemed a long time ago.

"And she's never got much in her larder."

He pulled a crumpled £10 note and some coins from the back pocket of his jeans. "Why don't you pop along to the Happy Haddock and fetch us a couple of portions of cod and chips and I'll have her tucked up in bed by the time you're back."

He gave the money to Xanthe and turned to Iris. "I hear you're not so good tonight, Auntie. Let's get you upstairs and you can have your bite of supper on a tray. Off you go, lass," he said over his shoulder to Xanthe. "It's up the hill and left past the Plough and Sail. You'd better ask for two large portions between the three of us – and the cat'll want his share. I'll have mushy peas and curry sauce with mine. You're not on a diet or anything are you?"

"No," she said. "No, I'm definitely not."

She couldn't imagine how she'd ever not wanted food.

They ate the fish and chips with their fingers, directly from the paper – though Gareth shifted Iris's portion onto a fluted china plate with a dancing shepherd and shepherdess. He seemed to know his way around the Rebow Cottage kitchen because he also produced a couple of sturdy blue-striped mugs into which he poured their tea.

"Eli's," he said. "She didn't usually offer him porcelain – and I reckon he preferred these anyway. All right for you – or do you want the feminine variety?"

Xanthe's mouth was full. She held out her hand for the large, warm mug. It made her feel as secure as if she was sitting in the cockpit of *Snow Goose*.

"You don't know," she said later, "how good that was."

Each succulent white flake had lingered on her tongue and then been swallowed with a golden crunch of perfect batter or the slight saltiness of a floury chip. She hadn't binged; she knew she wouldn't throw up. She'd simply eaten her first completely normal meal for weeks.

"I will admit that I don't exactly feel like doing aerobics at the moment but I'll be totally cool looking after Mrs Farran if you need to leave. She's an old lady and she's lost her husband. I'm sort of struggling to understand her attitude…but that could well be me. My sister says I've got the emotional intelligence of a World War Two landing craft."

"Funny girl, your sister, then."

Gareth crumpled his paper into a salty, faintly greasy

ball and left it on one of Iris's fragile occasional tables. He stretched himself out in the plain leather armchair that Xanthe assumed had been Eli's. Joe was straight onto his lap, cleaning his whiskers.

"Martha told me what Auntie Iris said to you," he continued "and there's no call for them sorta comments."

That was a relief. She'd been worrying that she'd overreacted. She felt safe to think aloud. "I haven't figured what set her off. I was going to check on the recording. We were mainly talking about her father and she seemed okay with that – until I asked her whether she was the only child. Then she flipped. I wondered whether somebody'd died? You know – an extra sibling or a twin or something?"

"Ahhhh," said Gareth.

There was a silence. Then he sighed. "If you're all at the end of the line in a village like Flinthammock, there's things you might decide it'd be better if you didn't know. That-a-ways you can still say a civil good morning to folk or accept if they want to buy you a pint in the pub."

"You're all one big happy family, then?"

So far she'd been struggling to find anyone who seemed even normally affectionate, except possibly the cat.

And Kelly-Jane, she was good. But godssakes, Siri was lost! They should all be out searching for her. Not sitting here, eating chips.

"We rub along, most of us," Gareth was frowning as he answered her question. "The main thing you need to know about Uncle Eli and Auntie Iris is that he's a Farran and she's a Gold and it weren't never a love match to start with."

If only she knew that Siri was okay she might try to talk to Gareth. Tell him what Iris had said about Eli. Maybe she needed to play it back first? Sort it out a bit better in her head.

"Yeah, except that you and Martha are Farrans (I think) and Dominic's surname is Gold but he and Martha seem okay together."

"She's a good girl, is Martha. And she's always been fond of Dom. Pity he's her cousin really. Though he don't deserve her. Thing is, in a place like Flinthammock you can have a feud that's run so long it's turned into a tradition. Farrans and Golds don't get on. End of story. That's what it were like when we grew up. Martha wants to make it different."

"It doesn't make any sense to me," said Xanthe.

"It's probably a neighbour thing. Next-door villages fight each other and so do next-door families. Next-door countries do too – if you're thinking wars. Usually no one can quite remember what started the trouble except, in the case of the Farrans and the Golds, it was the building and the owning of a fishing smack."

"*Igraine?*"

"However did you come ter know that?"

"It doesn't matter. I'm sorry I interrupted."

"It were the Golds who had her built. Golds always had a bit more of adventure about them. Sometimes they got rich for a while: other times they was flat broke. The Farrans were close, they hung on tight as barnacles and they kept their money tight as well. I won't say that either of them was necessarily admirable."

"What did they do?"

"Fishin', mainly. That made for rivalry. You'd want to know where the others had found their catch and you wouldn't want them to know where you'd found yours. You didn't show a light at night – no more than you could help anyways."

"That's dangerous."

"Of course it were but those old fishermen had great night vision. You should have seen my Uncle Eli. Or my dad. But even with a smack like the *Igraine,* it weren't necessarily profitable. Rumour had it that the Golds had put too much into having her built and that they'd needed to start supplementing their income with a little light smuggling."

It never took long before someone started telling you smugglers' tales in these East Coast villages.

"That's old history," said Xanthe. "And it's so not important. We should be out there helping to find Siri."

"Siri?"

"She's one of the kids that I'm teaching on the lightship. She sails like a bird. It's like she's a complete natural but she can't speak and I don't know why. And now she's gone missing."

"That's bad. Martha said they had a problem but she ain't allowed to talk a lot about her work."

"Would it be okay if I rung *Godwyn?* It's not that I'm not interested in the *Igraine* and smuggling and all that…"

"Call 'em up lass, settle your mind."

"I don't know what those kids are doing on there."

"No more do I."

"Oh." She'd hoped he might have told her something. "I'll ring Dominic."

It was Martha who answered and she had no news. Suddenly

Xanthe felt completely appalled that she'd been guzzling while Siri was lost.

"I want to look for her," she said to Gareth.

"Course yer do. I'll bide here and I've got me phone with me though I don't advertise the fact. You can take my number and I'll have yourn."

"I don't know where I'll start."

"Follow yer instincts, lass. She loved the sailing, you say. Well, you love it too. Imagine it's you there, cooped up on the lightship of a summer's arternoon and the river's a-calling to yer…"

Yes, Xanthe could do that.

CHAPTER ELEVEN

Miranda

Wednesday May 29, LW 0600 HW 1220 LW 1820 HW 0034

Xanthe went straight back down the river wall where she'd been that afternoon. She called Martha to say what she was doing but she didn't bother stopping at *Godwyn*. Martha had told her that Jonjo and Dominic were mainly watching the exit roads. Local police were out too.

Follow yer instincts.

Everything in her – if she was Siri – would be leading away from the creek and the lightship and the houses and the businesses. Siri could have slipped out from *Godwyn* and crossed the Broad Marsh saltings. She could have gone for miles, picking her way around the reaching, fingering inlets.

But Xanthe didn't think Siri would have gone that way. She'd been frightened of the saltings. All the kids had. They were too complex, too ensnaring.

"Hi Siri!" she shouted into the quiet evening, "Wait for me!"

She ran along the marsh wall, heading towards the river, just as she had done earlier. There was a pony in among the grazing cattle, a white pony. It flung up its head, ears pricked and alert in response to her shout. Some of the ducks scuttered as if they were about to fly up, then decided not to bother. She passed *Fritha,* moored off the end of the Fisherman's Hard. The dinghy had tried to swing with the flood in the narrow channel and had stuck on the mud's edge.

Xanthe ran on. She was getting a stitch. She began to wish she hadn't eaten all that supper. The wall turned right-handed, 90 degrees when it reached the Blackwater. If you carried on along the wall you would be going upstream.

Xanthe stopped. If Siri had gone that way she could have travelled miles – past Oveseye and Goldenhind, all the way to Fishling. Maybe this was hopeless.

There was a pillbox on the corner. A much more obvious in-your-face structure than the one she'd photographed this morning. This one jutted from the wall, positioned to defend access both to the Flete and the northern shore of the river. Some one had chalked a big CND disarmament slogan on it. Maybe it had been a protest against the power station? Maybe it was those peace campers? Xanthe would protest against anything even remotely connected with that 'Commander of the Saxon Shore' – but it probably wasn't.

She climbed onto the top of the pillbox and stood staring in all directions. There were a few late sailors coming back into the river with the flood and a distant motor launch emerging from the inlet beside the power station. The cranes were still working over there. Did they carry on all night? The light was low across the water. She wished she had binoculars.

"Siri?" she shouted, but without much hope. Some white birds flew up from the long, shallow spit that reached down towards the sea and formed the outer edge of Flinthammock Flete, separating it from the main river.

"Siri!" she called again, turning to look up along the length of wall that stretched upstream. She could see all the way to the first of the small inlets where her map told her there had once been a pier. Beyond that, and looking down the length of the Blackwater, was the bleak outline of a tower, dark against the setting sun.

No child in sight.

Xanthe climbed down and walked carefully round the outside of the pillbox. If you had wanted to be somewhere you could watch the river in secret, this would be a good place to be.

"Siri?" she spoke quietly now, "Siri, are you here?"

There was a place on the outer edge where the dry grass was flat and where the afternoon sun would have been warm and where Xanthe herself might have sat if she had been a silent ten-year-old tormented by feelings which she couldn't express.

The motor launch was rounding Shinglehead Spit and cruising quietly up the Flete.

This pillbox had a wider opening. Xanthe leaned through as far as she could go, which wasn't far. She tried to use a torch but she couldn't reach in to see what the torch might be showing.

"Siri, please, if you're here, please come out. It's Xanthe, your sailing teacher. We can go sailing again. Every day, I promise."

But there was no movement, no sound and why would Siri squeeze herself into that small, smelly space?

Follow your instincts, Gareth had said. They had brought her along this edge of the Flete and towards the river where Xanthe herself had gone. But not into the pillbox.

She hadn't asked Martha when exactly Siri had gone. It must have been some time after lunch if the boys were in the sail lofts and Siri and Kelly-Jane had been left.

So where was Kelly-Jane in all of this? Not well, Martha had said. Maybe she had fallen asleep. Then, if Siri had left quite soon after, and if she'd followed the way that Xanthe herself had led – if – if – if – then she could have been here, crouched against the outside wall, watching, while Xanthe had been out on the river in *Fritha*.

If she had been here, sheltered by the pillbox, pale arms wrapped around her skinny legs, head hunched down between her shoulders, motionless as a nesting bird, she would have seen Xanthe and the dinghy return to the Flete and to Fisherman's Hard, even if she hadn't seen her go.

And *Fritha* had stuck when she had swung to the flood.

Xanthe left the pillbox with a gasp of relief and set off running back along the wall to the hard. Siri must be hiding in the dinghy now, weighing her down very, very slightly.

Thank heaven the kid hadn't tried to go anywhere. All Xanthe had to do now was persuade her to come out. She could maybe offer to let Siri sail them both back up the creek to *Godwyn*?

She wouldn't have noticed the motor launch at all if it hadn't been so extreme. Impeccably varnished, probably old, definitely fast. It had the longest foredeck Xanthe had ever seen. *Miranda*. Good name for such an amazing-looking boat.

The launch had passed her several moments earlier, sliding quietly up the Flete. But Xanthe wasn't all that interested in classic motor launches, not tonight anyway.

She changed her mind when she saw *Miranda* humming lazily back. Towing *Fritha*.

It was the wannabe Viking at the wheel.

"No," she shouted. "No, you can't have her!"

His surname was Gold: he was Dominic's relation. *Fritha* was his and he was repossessing her.

It's obvious you don't appreciate what has been entrusted to you… You should never have been allowed to sail that dinghy.

That's what he'd said. But Dominic had said…something else. Which somehow didn't seem to fit?

The Firefly *so* didn't matter: the point was that he was stealing Siri.

"Hey, Commander Gold!"

Miranda turned away from Xanthe as the Flete swung eastwards towards the main river and the sea.

"Commander Gold! Stop! Please."

Miranda was towing faster now. She and *Fritha* were disappearing steadily into the dusk. Xanthe was running to keep her in sight. She was pulling her mobile out and calling Dominic.

"Hi, Martha! That's still you? Siri's being hijacked but it's a mistake. It's *Fritha*'s owner and he's towing her towards the river."

"*Fritha?*"

"You know, the Firefly…that I sailed this afternoon? I mean maybe that's okay – maybe he wants her back, whatever. It's all cool with me. My point is that I'm certain Siri's hiding on board and I'm stuck here on the wall. I've shouted but he's not listening. We need the RIB."

There was hesitation at the other end. Martha was great but maybe she wasn't quick?

"Martha, I know you've got the others to look after and I know I could be wrong. But please. Get K-J to keep them safe. It's getting dark."

"But…"

"Siri will be frightened. *Please!*"

"Okay. I'm totally confused but okay, Xanthe, I'm on it. You keep watching."

"Yeah, sure."

"What's he using to tow with?" Martha still sounded uncertain.

"Some sort of uber-launch. She's called *Miranda*."

"*Miranda*! Oh shit! Artie Gold! I'm there Xanthe, I'm there!"

The Commander and his launch rounded the point and began forging their way up the river. Up, not across. That was good. And they were towing *Fritha* on their starboard side and it was cramping their speed.

Xanthe was running and twisting and watching them all of the time. She was straining her eyes through the gloom and she was texting Martha as she went.

She saw the small person slip over the side. She watched her begin doggy-paddling for the shore with her pale face up-turned and the smallest trace of phosphorescence trailing like chiffon behind her.

Siri wasn't a strong swimmer. Once she was away from the safety of *Fritha* the shore would seem a long way off. The hijacker hadn't noticed her – he was continuing steadily on his way – but Siri would soon begin to feel the pull of the tide and the salt splashing in her mouth and her eyes and her legs might already be tired and her small white paws would be doing their best but their best might not be quite enough.

Xanthe's phone was back in its waterproof case and she was in the river swimming fast towards the little girl. She could hear the Project RIB approaching but she didn't even look. Just kept her eyes on the small white face and the silvery gleam in the river.

"Okay Siri. You're okay now," she said as she reached the child.

Siri stretched her cold hands to Xanthe's shoulders and clung on tight.

By the time they were in their depth and wading, Martha had challenged the Commander and he'd dumped the dinghy and was hydroplaning towards Oveseye.

But the two girls weren't looking that way. They were trudging out of the shallows and towards the wall. The mud tugged at their tired feet and small tussocks of marsh grass stubbed their toes and tried to trip them.

Xanthe put her arm around Siri. "I have to tell you straight off that I'm sorry. I should have stayed with you this afternoon. I should have understood what it had meant. That was a bad mistake. But can you tell me if there's anything else? Is anyone unkind to you on *Godwyn*?"

She felt Siri's headshake like a shiver in the rushes.

"You're okay to come back there now? I won't force you if you're not."

Her nod as slight as a water-skimmer's footfall.

Xanthe felt her mobile starting to vibrate.

"I've got the dinghy but Siri's not on board." Martha sounded desolate.

"I am so sorry, Martha. I should have called. Siri's not there because she's here with me. Can you get in close enough to give us a lift home?"

Iris was long asleep and Gareth was nodding over a newspaper. He'd taken off his shoes and put his feet up. You could see he wasn't really reading. Joe was a perfect circle of soft blackness, with his eyes tight shut and his small pink nose pushed against his own underwbelly and covered by his strong front leg.

His head came up when Xanthe walked in. Gareth blinked and grunted. Then the cat hopped down and Gareth groped around for the newspaper, which he'd dropped.

"I found her," Xanthe told them.

"Didn't expect yer'd have come back if yer hadn't." Gareth's speech was a bit slurry. "And she were presumably alright? I'd best be off. Early start tomorrow. It was an early one today an' all."

"What's your job?" She forgot she'd only just met him this evening.

"Oysterman. It ain't a bad way of life but there's times when it gets a bit long. Eli used to help me out. Poor grumpy old git."

"Get on arright with *Fritha,* did you?" he asked as he was leaving.

"*Fritha?*"

"Little old Firefly. Cousin Dominic said you needed some'at to sail and he wouldn't let you take one of his."

"*Fritha*'s yours? OMG, that is *such* a relief."

"Whose did you think she were?"

"I can't believe I even thought anything! I love her. She's magic."

"A-course she is. I'll tell you her story someday. Tell you about the *Igraine* an' all."

He left by the back door and Xanthe locked it after him.

Then she went upstairs and fell into bed. *He said as he reckoned you'd understand why the dinghy was for you.* She'd identified the voice now but she still didn't understand what Gareth had meant.

As of this moment, it totally didn't seem to matter.

CHAPTER TWELVE

Whales and Beetles

Thursday May 30, LW 0634 HW 1256 LW 1856 HW 0111

Martha woke her with milky coffee and brioche. You could see she was Gareth's sister when you knew. She had wavy dark hair and red cheeks, was wearing jeans and a dark blue polo shirt with the Project logo. So why wasn't she in her office on board *Godwyn*?

"I'm sorry," Xanthe said, "I wasn't expecting room service. I must have slept though my alarm. Is everything okay? Iris? Siri? And have you noticed that their names work backwards?"

Martha looked a bit surprised. Then she laughed.

"Probably not the only backwards things around here. Gareth called in last night, after he left you. He and I had a bit of a go at Dom. Told him that you shouldn't be up here on your own. That it's our job as family and if we can't look after her we should get carers in."

"I don't know what carers cost."

"That's totally not your problem. Dominic's got too used to letting Iris have whatever she wants. Apparently she wanted you because of some sort of vision or something. Then she ends up using you as if you're her household staff!"

"But she didn't exactly know she was going to get widowed."

Or had she?

It was weird how she'd called the *Igraine* a death-ship – and then Mr Farran had died. But Iris was pretty weird anyway.

"And she was insulting," Martha went on. "I'd almost say that's typical Gold but Dom does try, bless him. It's excruciating, sometimes, to listen to him blundering around trying to remember what he should and shouldn't say."

"About race?"

"Yeah. Sorry."

"It's okay," Xanthe repeated.

She got up and began looking around for her clothes. She could have told Martha about #bbarbie but it wasn't an issue any more.

"I need to get down to the kids."

"Jonjo's getting them ready – and rigging the dinghies. He says he's learned a lot from you. He agrees you should be living on *Godwyn*. He thinks it'll be safer."

"There's danger?"

"We're supposed to call it security. But that's Jonjo's department mainly."

"He's a youth worker."

"You might want to add 'plus plus' to that . Our problem is that there genuinely isn't a spare cabin on *Godwyn* right now. But when the current flock of birdwatchers leave – which is Saturday – then there will be. So we were hoping that you might be prepared to hang on here for just two more nights if Gareth and I do *all* the oldie-care? Gareth says he'll shift his things and sleep in the boot-room so you know you've got someone on call."

That was where Eli had been supposed to sleep wasn't it? The night that he died. On a 'truckle'.

"What is this boot-room? Is it that shed down the garden?"

"One of Auntie Iris's less appealing ideas. It used to be a stable when she had the pony but as soon as Granny Farran died – and Iris actually had to do some housework for herself – she decided that she couldn't bear mud. Calls it 'filth'. She'd given up on the pony by then so she made her husband use the stable."

"That's where he had to sleep if he went to the pub? Where did he sleep if he didn't?"

"In the attic. C'mon Xanthe, you need to get going. Gareth won't mind a couple of nights. Eli made it quite snug. We think he liked it in the end. He didn't get nagged so badly."

"It didn't seem like that to me," said Xanthe, swinging her legs out of bed and grabbing her washing things. "I thought he could have stuck up for himself. And he might have hit her. Did he kill someone once?"

Martha stopped. Her busy confidence seemed to leave her for a moment.

"He's gone now," she said at last.

"We shouldn't speak badly of the dead?"

"Not if you want to carry on living together for the next few hundred years."

"That's what your brother told me."

"Okay. I'll tell you: it was our dad who died."

Xanthe stopped. Stared. Opened her mouth to ask when? How?

Martha blocked her. "It was a sailing accident with no other witness. So we'll leave it there, if you don't mind."

Xanthe remembered once again that she was an outsider

here. Martha and Gareth seemed normal and friendly but there was too much that was hidden under the surface of their lives. Thick and dark like the stagnant water trapped across the saltings.

"Hi," said Jonjo, as soon as he spotted her coming up the *Godwyn* gangplank. He sounded relieved. "We've a situation on our hands this morning. Young Siri has decided thet she won't leave the ship."

"Why is anyone surprised about that? Think about it – she was hidden inside *Fritha*. Maybe she was even asleep and then she finds herself being towed away!"

"Do we know why?" Jonjo asked. "Why the boat was being removed, I mean."

"I thought I did. I thought that *Fritha* was his dinghy and he didn't like me using her so he was taking her away. But now I'm told I have that wrong. And I'm still not certain who he is."

"He's a property developer. Bit of a megalomaniac. He's organising some promotional Dunkirk event at the weekend and he was pressuring Dominic to bring *Godwyn* across. I mean seriously!"

"What does Dominic say? They've got the same surname so I'm assuming they're related – but I might be wrong about that as well."

"No comment. Pulls down the iron curtain. I tell you, Xanthe, the attitudes round here aren't making my job any easier. I'm not sure I wouldn't hev been better keeping these kids in London."

She didn't want to stop him opening up like this but she was late already.

"Okay – so we've pooled our ignorance. Let's get back to boats. Where are you at this morning?"

"I've only worked with the boys. We think we've got two of the Picos rigged but obviously you'll need to check. Dominic has offered to drive the safety boat so I'll stay back here. It could be Siri just wants a lie-in. She looks exhausted and Kelly-Jane's not much better."

"Tell them I said hi. I'm doing capsizes this morning. I'll try to think of something peaceful we could do this afternoon. I'm not leaving them again."

Another perfect morning, sunshine and light wind and the tides were getting later. There was a real difference in David today. He was still quiet but he seemed much more relaxed in himself. When she asked him how he'd feel about sailing with Kieran, instead of with her, he said yes straight off.

That gave her Nelson. He wasn't too bad when they were actually sailing. She tucked herself down as low as she could in front of the centreplate and left him to do all the work. Down the channel inside Shinglehead Spit, then round between the last two port hand buoys and up the River Blackwater with the tide and a fair beam wind. The two Pico dinghies scampered easily along and Dominic had the sense to keep a comfortable distance away.

She was tempted to go on round Oveseye – she wanted to see where the Viking had been heading last night – but she oughtn't let the kids get too tired if they were going to be practising capsize drills. She led them in to beach the dinghies on a flattish area of sand just near where the old pier and the railway line had been at the entrance to Mell Creek. This was where Flinthammock had once hoped to have a seaside resort. It seemed a bit deluded – the sea was miles away. Then the war had come and the pier had had to be dismantled so it couldn't be used by invaders.

It was hard to imagine invasion on a sunny summer's day up a river. But you needed calm seas if you were going to go invading. Or calm nights, anyway.

They'd built a gun emplacement here – she could see its remains – and teenage Eli Farran had hung around, trying to sell his fish to the soldiers.

He said he was watching the grave.

What had Iris Farran meant?

The tide was coming up and round the ruined structure. It was like an abandoned castle on a tiny, ugly block. The river was its moat.

"What is it about this place?" she asked Dominic.

He startled as if he'd been miles away. And for once he answered straight. "Eli Farran and his father had sailed to Ramsgate in their smack, *Igraine*. They were offering to cross to Dunkirk but they weren't needed. They came all the way back and struck a mine, just here, in their home river, off this pier. The *Igraine* went down and Abraham Farran died."

For the first time ever she felt sorry for Eli.

"He'd have been about my age then. His father and his boat were gone. He must have been traumatised."

Watching the grave.

"Possibly. Eli was certainly obsessed. As soon as the war was over he bullied Iris until she married him, then he used her money to raise the *Igraine* and rebuild."

Little Miss Oy-ris, our own personal Crock of Gold. I hope you're a-listenin, Eli, me boy.

"Except there wasn't as much money as they'd thought," added Dominic, almost to himself.

The naval watchtower looked down on them and along the river with its blank, dark windows. The boys were larking about, daring each other to climb on the ruined gun emplacement and wave imaginary flags from the top.

"Come on, guys," Xanthe shouted. "We're not here for fun, we're here for you to learn capsize drills. Life and death, you know!"

She hoped with all her heart that these ten or eleven year-olds would never get any closer to danger than tipping over a small plastic dinghy on a sunny river in controlled conditions.

"What goes up when the rain comes down, teacher-lady?"

"It's an umbrella," Kieran interrupted him. "You told us that one earlier."

"But you never got my breakfast joke – the one about the butter."

Did Nelson ever stop?

"Don't let's spread it, Mr Midshipman."

He grinned his irresistible wide grin and she took him off in the first of the dinghies to spill themselves into the river and scramble round the hull, loosening the sheets then standing on the centreplate to pull her upright and sail on again.

"What did the earwig say when he capsized his dinghy the second time?" He wasn't giving her a chance to answer. "He said earwig go again!"

It was splashy. It was fun. It was even a little bit silly – except it was all in the cause of being safe. Both the other boys managed fine and she swapped them round again to begin the sail home. She told David and Nelson they could sail single-handed then persuaded Dominic to hand over control of the RIB to Kieran and begin teaching him some powerboat skills.

"You're okay, aren't you Kieran? You can do this if Dominic shows you how."

They were concentrating. They were busy. Kieran was almost breathless with suppressed excitement at being allowed to take the wheel of the RIB and it was a lovely sight – so Xanthe thought – to see Nelson and David helming their two small dinghies a little distance ahead of the safety boat. And these were kids who'd never been near water just four days earlier.

People who live in an island country should all get a chance to sail, thought Xanthe suddenly, fiercely.

The Picos were neat and colourful in the midday sun. The breeze was blowing gently from the St Peter's Shore. Everyone was focused on the distant marker where they would meet and reorganise before entering the Flinthammock Flete.

Xanthe checked astern. There was some enormous structure, emerging from behind Oveseye. It was dark against the sky and being towed by two small tugs. She tensed and stared. Then came other tugs towing smaller, equally unidentifiable objects. There weren't oil rigs round here, were there? Would this be something for the offshore wind farm they were building on the Gunfleet Sands?

She tapped Dominic on the shoulder to ask.

He didn't answer or explain. He ordered Kieran to change places then he gunned up the RIB and began a wide fast circle that would put him ahead of the dinghies. Xanthe shrugged at Kieran. She had thought she was meant to be the teacher here. Kieran grinned and shrugged back

Dominic swung the RIB in front of the Picos. Gestured violently to the boys to order them alongside.

David's response was wobbly but it worked.

"Well done," she said, as she took his painter.

Nelson sailed straight past.

It was no good Dominic attempting to swirl onwards and give chase now he had David's dinghy attached to the RIB with David still on board. *Miranda* was streaking towards them, a red flag streaming from her varnished flagstaff.

"What is this, Dominic? That's the man who tried to steal *Fritha*. What is his problem?"

Miranda wasn't going for them; she was heading for Nelson.

They were getting closer, too. David had clambered carefully on board the RIB and Dominic was accelerating. The Viking seemed to be ordering Nelson back to the shore.

Nelson didn't seem to have heard him. He was sailing merrily on. Had the Pico going nicely. Good straight wake.

Now they, too, were within shouting distance.

"Leave the boy alone!"

"Tell him, Dominic!"

"His name's Nelson and he's one of mine. Get back to your own side of the river. You've no business here."

Miranda curved gracefully alongside the RIB.

"Rubber and plastic!" The old man spoke with utmost disdain. "And what right do *they* have to be here?"

He could have been talking about the boats – or he might

have meant Xanthe and Nelson and the other two kids.

"You can't talk about rights. You tried to steal *Fritha*."

"All's fair in war, Miss Ribiero."

"But in peacetime, that's theft. Because she's not your dinghy."

"You should never have been allowed to sail her." He looked at her with disdain. "You have disgraced British Racing."

"Get away from us," Dominic hissed through clenched teeth. He was white with anger.

The Viking laughed and sped away to where the tugs had arrived in front of the former power station. They all had SAXON painted on their sides in large white letters.

Nelson tacked for the RIB once *Miranda* was gone. He was a bit slow releasing his mainsheet but Kieran and David reached out and grabbed him as he passed. He was all legs and elbows as he scrambled on board to join them and his face was vivid with excitement.

"Why do bees hum?" he asked at once.

"Because they don't know the words. Gimmee high fives, Mr Midshipman."

He grinned his most enormous grin yet. "I was puttin' my deaf ear to the telescope, teacher-lady. That other Nelson, he was some cool dude. Martha's mum told us 'bout him."

"That man mustn't be allowed to think he's scared us," she said to Dominic. "We should stay and watch. I know we'll lose the tide but we can leave the dinghies in the Flete and use the Fisherman's Hard. The kids and I don't mind mud."

He managed a nod, though he didn't answer her directly. Then he turned the RIB and motored carefully out into the river – though not beyond halfway. He held them there, steadily breasting the tide as they watched the tugs manoeuvring their loads into position.

The first and largest structure was pulled to a standstill some way out from the shoreline. It had cylindrical legs at each corner and Xanthe guessed that it was being anchored into place and would then slide up and down its legs with the tide. The second group of tugs delivered lengths of pontoon that were positioned between the platform and the beach. Then a complex process was begun to heave other metal structures on top of them.

"Blind eyes or not, I wish we *had* a telescope," said Xanthe. "Or even a camera with a really serious zoom lens."

"Mmmm."

Dominic was agreeing. That must be a first!

The boys, even Nelson, were fascinated. *Miranda* was constantly busy. It was clear that this entire operation was under the personal direction of the self-styled Commander of the Saxon Shore.

"I know what those things are," she realised suddenly. "They're beetles and whales and..." she searched in her memory, "a Spud Pier."

"You know *that*?" said Dominic.

"I told you I'm studying history. Those are the components – except I suppose these are more likely to be replicas – that were used at the D-Day landings to build the Mulberry Harbour."

"Give it to us, teacher-lady."

"The D-day landings were in June 1944, almost at the end of the Second World War. It was the Allies – which means us and the Americans and the Canadians, Australians, New Zealanders, Free French and anyone else who was on our side (could have been your great-grand-dads) – doing our own invasion to get onto the Normandy beaches. Brilliant, flat, sandy beaches where you could drive tanks and lorries and land loads of troops. But there weren't any harbours. Not big enough for what they needed. So they got on and made one. Towed all the bits across and assembled them – in the Atlantic swell and under attack and much, much bigger. Though that's looking big enough from where I am," she added.

"He…thinks…big." It was like someone was twisting Dominic's arm right up behind his back to force him to say that.

"*Is* he one of your relations?"

Dominic's thin lips were pressed firmly together. He gave no sign that he'd heard her.

Then, from the former power station across the water came another of those wailing emergency sirens. Lights were flashing on the building site and the tall cranes, which had seemed to be in constant motion, stopped. *Miranda* darted away and Xanthe watched her swirl into the small creek that lead round the edge of the site. It reminded her of the way the Commander had leapt into his Polaris on their previous encounter.

"His safety record is completely appalling!" Dominic spat out the words. "No more argument. I'm towing you back to *Godwyn*. Now."

That was okay. They were all hungry.

CHAPTER THIRTEEN

Birdsong

Thursday May 30, LW 0634 HW 1256 LW 1856 HW 0111

"Hi, Siri." she stuck her head round the door of the young girl's cabin just as soon as she'd finished half a large baked potato with cream cheese and chives. "How are you feeling? You okay, K-J?"

Neither girl answered. They were lying on their single bunks as if they hadn't moved for hours. Siri was above, Kelly-Jane below, but Xanthe could see how easily the younger girl could have slipped away if the older was asleep.

"Jonjo suggested we go swimming. The boys are up for it but how about you?"

"Nah," said Kelly-Jane, "I ain't going. D'you wanna go, Siz? Wrong time fer me. I get cramps."

She screwed herself round to look up at Siri and Siri looked back at her. Then her blue eyes wandered to the porthole in the side of the cabin, quite high above her bed. It was small, maybe less than a foot across, round and with the standard issue cream-painted metal rivets surrounding salt-clouded toughened glass. The sounds of a summer afternoon were wafting in. There were walkers setting out and returning along the marsh wall.

"You saw me yesterday. When I was running off into the afternoon." Xanthe said to Siri. "Then you had to get out as well."

"You shoulda told me." Kelly-Jane was hurt. "I were worried sick."

"We could go the other way today. If you don't want to swim we could take a long walk. Take it together."

Kelly-Jane's hand went to the base of her stomach and rubbed it. Maybe that wasn't all her normal fat. Maybe she was feeling bloated and sore.

"S'up to Siz, innit."

"You think the saltings are spooky." Xanthe was talking to the younger girl. "But on a day like today they can be beautiful. They have flowers that you'll never see anywhere else and birds all settled into their summer homes. We could stay on the wall and walk to the top of the creek that runs up Broad Marsh – where we went sailing that day."

Kelly-Jane was being carefully don't-care but Siri's blank expression had begun to shift.

"Take a look out though that porthole, won't you?" Xanthe didn't mind pleading if that was what it took

It turned out they had to have Martha with them. But that was okay and Martha brought a backpack with sun cream and water and apples and biscuits.

Then Siri did something that Xanthe found totally disturbing. She produced two grubby Mothercare wrist-links and wordlessly insisted that she be attached to Xanthe and to Kelly-Jane, one on either side. It would mean they'd have to walk chained together, single file, for most of the time along the wall.

"That's because of her mum," said Kelly-Jane.

She didn't say any more and Martha didn't comment. But it started Xanthe thinking. Her mother, who was a magistrate and who sometimes knew things that other people didn't know, had sent her here in alliance with Rev Wendy, who also, in her over-anxious, ploddy and ideological way, knew things about… things. So maybe there could be some reason why Xanthe should try not to whinge about having to walk along a wall in the sunshine, linked up to an obviously traumatised child who felt safer that way.

There weren't that many people to notice them. The group of birdwatchers who were spending this half-term week on *Godwyn* had long ago twitched off to their hides. People who had boats on the saltings were settled in their muddy hollows, doing jobs or snoozing or playing their radios and drinking beer. People who had boats on the river would have to stay out there. There wouldn't be water in the creeks again until nine or ten o'clock tonight.

Martha made a few remarks but mainly they walked and looked around them in quiet. There were white birds feeding and nesting in a haze of sea lavender and the breeze was warm and stroked the sides of their faces and under their chins as they walked. They were walking away from the cranes of the ex-power station and it was too far away to hear whatever was happening with the construction of the replica harbour.

Xanthe was thinking of Eli – Eli and Iris, two people who had never been happy or in love with each other. She was remembering the way Eli had looked back at Rebow Cottage when he'd left it that last time.

She had assumed that it was the last time. He'd been standing and staring with his hands in his pockets. He'd certainly not been carrying anything. Then he'd taken one hand from his pocket and held it against his face.

Iris had done the same but Iris had known she had an audience. Eli had thought he was alone.

Iris's ebony walking stick had vanished from the house that night. She'd had it in the sitting room when they had been quarrelling and the next time Xanthe had seen it was in the soft mud at the highest tip of this Broad Marsh Creek, at the final bend of the channel before the old landing stage. And now she had it in the sail lofts.

She ought to take it to the police – she was sure about that. Wasn't she?

Except she'd look such a lightweight if it belonged to some other oldie. She should check it out first. Maybe ask Martha?

Martha was family; she might not want to answer. Everyone was family around here. Jonjo wasn't, but he wouldn't know.

Kelly-Jane got slower and quieter. Siri was silent.

Martha was looking around them all the time. Perhaps she was hoping to spot a ruff or a greenshank or a young marsh harrier. Xanthe knew the words, no more than that. There was a moment when they spotted the turrets of a Victorian Gothic mansion shrouded by dark trees and Martha opened up with some fragments of local history.

"That's Auntie Iris's childhood home," she told Xanthe. "Her father died on his way back from Dunkirk and her mother sold it not long after. It's a private clinic now. The company who own it wanted to buy the marshes too. We fought them off but then they bought the St Peter Peninsula and that old power station. And that worries me and Gareth because..."

They'd reached the top of the creek. Xanthe could feel Siri tugging at the wrist-link. "Yeah, this is where we sailed," she said without looking. "Where you and K-J were going solo for the first time. You have to come out again tomorrow. We could take ourselves a picnic. Do a full day."

No answer except a much longer, more impatient pull.

"That's not what you were saying? We could try a code..."

The younger girl stopped walking which meant that Xanthe had to stop too. And look behind her to see what was wrong.

"OMG, K-J, you are completely done in! Hey, Martha, we need to make this our sit-down spot."

They had Project sweatshirts tied round their waists, so they spread them out to cover the rough grass. Martha distributed the water bottles from her backpack. There were small birds singing their hearts out in the shrub and swallows wheeling in the cloudless sky. It was idyllic.

Kelly-Jane pulled her knees up towards her chest and used her untethered hand to massage her lower stomach. She was grey with pain.

"You need to free up her other hand, Siri. It's her wrong time of the month. And you are just too brave for your own good, K-J."

"You poor love," said Martha. "I used to get completely crippled up when I was your age. My m..." You could see she had been about to say something about her mother but had decided not to. "Are you okay taking paracetamol? It's all I've got with me."

"Not that bothered," grumbled Kelly-Jane, but she took the pills and drank some water and rolled over onto her side, facing away. Then Siri gently slipped her second hand out of the wrist link and began to massage the base of her friend's back.

Martha pulled out her phone. "I'm going to get Dominic to fetch us in the minibus when the boys have finished swimming.

There's a farm track leads down past the old house."

"Naw! Don't do that. My trouble's personal."

"No need to worry. For one thing Dominic's not that curious. He probably won't even ask why we want collecting and if he does I'll tell him I've got blisters or I'm running late for Auntie Iris or any number of things – all of which will be at least 50 percent true."

"You'll tell him later. You can't never trust adults to respect your privacy."

Xanthe could almost feel that low griping cramp and the struggle to squeeze back tears. So, it seemed, could Martha. She came right round and crouched below Kelly-Jane on the rough slope of the marsh wall.

"K-J, I know that your situation is really tough – and you know that if I ever have to make a choice between your privacy and your safety it'll be safety every time. It has to be. There are too many others at risk."

Kelly-Jane hid her face in her arms. All Xanthe could see was the back of her head and her slightly greasy hair. It had been hennaed once.

"But this thing isn't about safety and I don't have to tell. And I won't. I was young a long time ago and I discovered that not telling things sometimes made them easier to bear. Though not always," she added, after a moment.

"I can always guess with my sister," said Xanthe, who thought Martha was still talking about period pain. "She's so sweet-natured it's untrue, then suddenly she'll bite your head off and you'll think 'what was that about?' and then you realise. She often gets migraines with it and she has to stay home."

"Mmmm," said Kelly-Jane. She sounded more relaxed now,

even a bit sleepy. Siri carried on rubbing her friend's back as if she knew exactly where it ached. Then she yawned too.

"Take a nap, why don't you?" suggested Martha. "The minibus won't be here for at least half an hour. Xanthe and I will count damsel flies."

"I've got my research notebook."

"That's cool. Okay girls, we'll wake you when the transport's here."

Kelly-Jane was asleep already. Siri gave a small contented smile and moved as close as she could to her friend. Xanthe knew that she and Martha were being trusted to stand guard – against what? Still no-one was telling her.

She began to doodle in her notebook, thinking about the D-day components she had seen that morning. But then her sketching changed and she drew the creek ahead of her and the place where Excalibur had been found and the landing stage and the big house behind. She could see how neatly it connected to the field and the path across, leading directly to Rebow Cottage and the gate with the splintered sampler.

There was a cuckoo calling from somewhere in the trees near Broad Marsh House. Cuck-oo, cuck-oo. She remembered playing those two notes over and over when she and Mags had been learning the recorder.

"I hate that sound," said Martha suddenly. "Makes me think of all the eggs and all the baby birds that are going to be smashed so that one chick gets its best survival chance."

"I'm sorry. It's only ever said summertime to me."

"It wouldn't if you were a reed-warbler."

She fell silent again. Xanthe stared at the twists and turns of the empty creek and she thought about tide times.

Martha's phone chirruped as a text arrived. "Dom's on his way. Time we began waking these girls. It's been good to see them so completely out of it."

Siri's creamy skin was flushed pink. Her eyelids were moving slightly and she was murmuring in her sleep.

"She's dreaming," said Xanthe. "REM sleep. I can't wake her now."

"Let her be happy while she can," agreed Martha.

She began talking quietly to Kelly-Jane, trying to ease her back to consciousness. Xanthe sat back, watched Siri, and wondered.

Then the younger girl's eyes blinked open, not quite focused yet. She must have felt the warm sun and her friend beside her. Heard the birdsong maybe? Stayed another moment in her dream?

"Mummy…?"

"I'm sorry, sweetheart," Martha's voice was choked. "Your mum's not here. There's just us, your friends," she added, "Keeping you safe."

"Yeah, but her mum could be here, couldn't she?" said Kelly-Jane. "Watching over her, like, in spirit."

"Of course she could," said Martha fervently.

"And I do believe she is. We love you, Siri's mum. We're here for you. We're gonna help you keep her safe."

For once Xanthe was certain that she'd found the right words. It didn't seem to matter that she hadn't any idea what she was talking about.

CHAPTER FOURTEEN

Favours

Friday May 31, LW 0711 HW 1330 LW 1930 HW 0146

Who is taking fotos fgs? #bbarbie has u walking in slave chain gang and larfaminnit has capsize pix going viral. U need 2 stop them asap!

A text from Maggi? That was breaking the agreement. They were only supposed to chat at weekends but her Nokia brick had blipped this morning as soon as she stepped out from Rebow Cottage.

Let them larf. I don't care. Honest.

It was true, she had no urge to look at Twitter or Facebook or YouTube or any other place where people might be showing off their unkindnesses.

Don't agree. They r bullies. Shd be stopped. Anna is writing prog to run thru ISP addresses and find source. She says hi.

Say hi back but tell her don't waste time.

She likes it. Glad u ok xxx

They were like voices from another planet. Her lovely sister Maggi and their incredibly clever maths-geek friend, Anna. It was half term. Maybe they were sitting together on a bus to go shopping or more likely they'd met up at one or other's house to discuss GCSE revision.

Xanthe wondered whether she should text Anna to tell her not to bother trying to trace the photo source. Now that she had begun to guess what her kids might be going through, she couldn't believe that she'd ever lost a moment's sleep over Madrigal Shryke and her mind-games.

Except she knew that when Anna had decided to do something, no one could stop her anyway. And Mags was right; Anna did genuinely love complex mathematical challenges. She wrote computer code like other people wrote playlists.

Xanthe sent a couple of smiley faces back, switched her phone off and headed for *Godwyn*. The barometer was steady, weather set fair and she was planning to take her crew upriver for a picnic sail. After that she had only one more night to sleep in Rebow Cottage and she'd be moving onto the lightship full-time.

There were Companions still cooking breakfast and a comfortable clatter of plates and hum of conversation from the mess room. Food. Good.

But someone stopped her as she was collecting her tray and told her she was wanted in the office.

"Can't I even grab a coffee?"

"They said immediately. I'll bring you some."

"Then could I possibly have toast as well?"

Dominic and Jonjo were either side of the computer screen in the small round office. It felt as if they were in the middle of a quarrel.

"What do you hev to say about these, Xanthe?"

Jonjo's South African accent seemed more apparent as he struggled to contain his fury.

"About what? I've not seen anything. I don't have internet unless I'm here."

"Access on *Godwyn* is monitored and firewalled," Dominic

cut in. "I'm telling you. Xanthe hasn't used it at all this week. I watch out for her."

Jonjo was angry with her, Dominic defending. Huh?

"But you hev a camera and you also hev a phone."

"Yeah. But they don't link. My mum lent me her Macbook to upload any photos. I'm only allowed to use it for research."

"And thet's where?"

"In my bedroom."

"You used it last?" His jaw was set. He looked more like Action Man than ever. Almost quite scary, if she'd done whatever it was that had wound him up. Which she hadn't.

"Yesterday night. But not for photos. I was writing up some notes. And I can't access the internet when I'm there as there isn't any wi-fi."

"You could hev a dongle."

"But I don't have a dongle. You're making no sense."

Jonjo didn't answer. He was already on his mobile phone asking – no, telling – Martha to fetch Xanthe's camera and the Macbook from her room and bring them down to *Godwyn* as soon as she'd finished giving Iris her breakfast.

"And any other electronic equipment thet you can find," he added.

"What IS this?" Xanthe asked Dominic.

"There's been a major breach of security. It's connected with your social media activity. Or your friends'."

"My social media activity???"

She crossed to his desk and sat down in front of the screen. He was logged into Facebook. The larfaminnit.com photos were mainly of her and Nelson falling in the river, though the capsize drills she'd gone through with Kieran and David were up there as well. Okay, they were quite funny – capsizes usually were, if you were watching and not involved – but each one of them already had literally thousands of hits and they'd only been posted yesterday. There were YouTube video links as well.

"And I suppose you've been on Twitter and typed #bbarbie," she asked. "And you're both psychotic enough to assume that I'd have shared those pictures?"

She was almost too shocked to be angry. "Did you not understand that I'm here to get away from that stuff? Can you not grasp how sick it makes me feel?"

Though it didn't, really, not like it used to do. She was shocked by the scale of the Facebook activity, aware of the casual stupidity of everyone who'd clicked and shared and added a comment, but it didn't hurt her any more.

She wondered whether the kids had seen them. Nelson might laugh. She wasn't so sure about Kieran and David.

The Twitter string was worse. It usually was. #bbarbie had a photo taken from behind of her with Siri and Kelly-Jane linked by their wristbands with Martha appearing to drive them along the marsh wall. It was a silly photo but the racist abuse was unbelievable.

Jonjo was shoving his mobile at her.

"Hi Xanthe," Martha sounded shaken. "Jonjo's been on at me to take things from your room. I've told him no. Not unless I have your permission. What is all this?"

"I wish I knew. Someone's been posting photos on Twitter and Facebook and he's totally overreacting. He can't believe, apparently, that I haven't been deliberately showing myself up."

"Are any of the students in these photos?"

"Yes. Though it's not about them."

"Ah, but it will be from Jonjo's point-of-view."

Thank heaven for Martha's good sense. Xanthe was getting it now.

"You can bring him anything he wants in that case. If it's about the kids."

She ended the call before she gave Jonjo his phone.

"Okay," she told him. "Listen up. You remember you were grumbling about Dominic's iron curtain. Well, maybe one of the things he failed to communicate is the reason I'm working here. I'm here because I messed up badly on a pre-selection training week. I punched my main rival so I got chucked off and banned."

Yes, Jonjo was listening. His face was impassive, his grey eyes locked onto hers.

"At that time it felt like the end of my world. And since then I've been on the wrong end of a cyber-bullying campaign – as you're seeing here. It got so bad that I couldn't eat. I couldn't face college any more. I think I was having some sort of mini-breakdown. Then my mum and our vicar had an idea which was to make me forget about my problems by doing something useful for people who were worse off than me."

He managed a nod.

"So, that's why I'm here, but what is it with the kids? What are they hiding from? I saw you shut K-J up when she tried to speak out and Dominic treated me like I was an idiot. You all assumed I'd think that they're any old bunch of kids signing up for some outdoor education. Yet it's completely obvious that they're not. They're upset and terrified and they're cut off from their families and you're not letting me understand how to protect or help them."

"How did you find out?"

"I'm not stupid. Even Nelson only makes those jokes as his defence mechanism. But it was mainly from what Siri said."

"Siri's suffering from mutism."

"Maybe it's not total? She woke up yesterday and we were just women there and she felt safe for a moment. She said 'Mummy'."

A wave of sadness washed across his face. He was ready to level with her.

"Her mother got shot in a gangland feud. It was territorial: racketeers and drug suppliers fighting for control of an area. There was no question of her being involved. She was a single mother in the wrong place at the wrong time. Siri was with her, small child, attached to her mother's wrist as she was carrying their shopping home."

Xanthe went cold.

"…and the others?"

"All part of a witness protection scheme. We need to bring those killers to justice. This is one small area of a vast drugs ring. It's taken us years building the case and persuading people thet they're safe to testify. We know we heven't reached the big fish so, now the trial's finally started, the parents hev to be in London under twenty-four-hour guard. One or two of them hev to accept thet they'll be going down as well. Dominic's charity offered the kids a break and their parents agreed on the understanding thet we could maintain total secrecy. To spread these pictures across social media could not be worse."

She could see that. "I'll leave if you think it'll draw them off. I don't want to."

"I think it's the kids who need to leave. I've already got our people looking for another safe house."

"You're a policeman, not a youth worker." She was totally not surprised. "So why can't you get the photos taken down?"

He showed her his ID.

"I'm Special Branch and yes we're onto it. But we know we're too late. Look at all those hits. If these are not your friends you must hev made some serious enemies."

Thousands of them, all hating her and laughing. For a moment that old sick feeling twisted in her empty stomach. Then she thought of the kids and forced it down.

"Have you found the photographer?"

"No. I had hoped if we could identify the source thet we might squash it and stay put. I can see they're starting to settle. And if little Siri felt secure enough to speak – even a single word – thet's fantastic news. But I have to keep them safe. Thet's my first priority."

"Martha said something like that. Is she Special Branch as well?"

"Martha's an Essex Special Constable. It means she's a part-time volunteer. We took her out and gave her special training. This operation was planned months ago. If we move I'll try to hev her seconded to come with us but I know she won't want to."

He was silent now, thinking. The coffee came. They drank it. Then Martha arrived with Xanthe's toast and her Macbook and her camera and her dictaphone.

"So," Xanthe asked Jonjo. "Which of my things do you want to check out first?"

"Eh? Nothing at all. I owe you an apology."

Yes. He did.

"You could clear up one thing – if thet's ok," he added politely. "I noticed thet you weren't totally surprised? You knew something had happened before you looked at the computer – or did I read thet wrong as well?"

"My sister texted me to tell me I'd been tagged on social media. She thought I'd be upset and she also said that our friend Anna, who's a geek, was working to find where all this is coming from. But you've probably got some massive system that can do all that."

She gave him her phone.

"Anna and Maggi don't know anything about the kids. Read their texts."

He shook his head and then he laughed.

"Jesus wept! Maybe you girls are gonna put me out of a job. You got a comment, Dom?"

The Chief Companion's face was pale and serious. It was as if he was looking at something that was far away and could never be made right.

"*Godwyn* should be a place of safety," he said. "That's the heart of her mission. I think Xanthe should leave. Not for herself but because of the issues she brings with her."

"You think I'm a Jonah?"

She was hurt. She knew she'd suggested it. She saw he could be right. But she was hurt.

"I think you're a star!" Martha was scarlet with anger. "Snap out of it, Dom. Who got Siri back for us? Who's been putting up with insults from dotty Aunt Iris and, most important of all, who's managed to win those children's confidence and begin to change their outlooks? Not you, me or Jonjo. Sorr-ee."

Dominic stared at her. Then it seemed as if her blazing passion transferred across and warmed him. His colour was more normal and he obviously relaxed. She calmed down and paled.

Xanthe looked out of the window away from them. "There's almost water in the creek. We should be rigging the dinghies. Or am I sacked?"

"No you're not sacked," said Jonjo. "And thet's an operational decision for which I'm taking responsibility. But we still hev a problem thet someone took those photos. The first set was taken when the boys were on the river. I don't think they should sail today."

"Or maybe they shouldn't sail from here?" said Xanthe.

This weather was too good to miss. Why should the kids have to hide away from all the trolls who hated her as well as from whatever mega-villains were threatening them?

"You must have some sort of towing vehicle so why don't we split up? Kids and minders in the minibus – as if you're off for a picnic. Me and someone and a dinghy going separately. Then we'll meet at a beach and I'll take them out one at a time practising launches and landings. They'd love it."

"We can watch to see if we get followed," added Martha. "Or which of us gets followed. I am disgusted by the thought that someone was spying on those girls yesterday."

"Where would we go?" asked Jonjo. "I can't ever discount a snatch attempt. We need single track and very private."

Xanthe had been studying the chart. "On the other side of Meresig there's a channel called Coldlight Creek. It's mainly muddy but it has a lovely bit of sand and swimming at the entrance. I've anchored there with my family. I remember a lane through a farm."

"I'll alert the boys in blue," said Jonjo. "Get the access checked. Make sure there's back-up if we need it."

"I know Coldlight Creek," said Martha. "We lived across the river at Brittlesey when we were kids and my brother lands his oysters there. There's a locked gate onto the track but Gareth'll have the key. He'll have his dory, too."

"Dory?"

"Flat-bottomed boat that he do use for hauling. He'd lend it for safety."

For a moment Martha sounded like Gareth, as well as looking like him. Jonjo clenched and unclenched his fists. It wasn't aggressive, more as if he needed help to think.

"What does your brother know?"

"Nothin' but what he's worked out for himself. He's a Farran. He's got eyes in his head. But we're close – close-mouthed that is."

"I'll stay behind if Gareth's there," said Dominic. "Our visitors will be packing to go and I don't feel easy leaving *Godwyn*. I could check on Iris if you're late back."

"Commander Gold was at Rebow Cottage when I got dropped off yesterday," said Xanthe. "He'd bought her a new widescreen colour TV so she can watch his event this weekend. She wasn't totally grateful, though. She thinks she should be invited as his honoured guest. You're all related, aren't you? All Golds."

"We don't get on," was all that Dominic could say.

Martha leaned forward. Touched him.

"Tell them, Dominic. Spirit of trust and openness. Give it a go."

The Companion-in-Chief looked at his feet. Then he sighed.

"There's no need to nag. Commander Gold is…a relative. He's also the reason why I want to stay within sight of *Godwyn* when there's enough water for her to float. He wants the lightship for his event and I've said no. It's completely ridiculous."

"But you're afraid he might help himself – just as he tried with *Fritha*. It's why you've reinforced the mooring points with all that concrete and why you can't sleep at night when you know the tide is up." Martha finished for him. "I'll give you six out of ten for that attempt at an answer."

"Is there anything more thet I should know?" Jonjo was alert.

"If *Godwyn*'s safe, we're all safe. I care more about security than anyone. I really think we've talked for long enough."

Xanthe swallowed the last of her cold coffee and munched her toast as she hurried to collect her crew. She did notice that he hadn't answered Jonjo's question. And he'd sounded exactly like Iris.

Gareth did better than unlock the gate and get them down the private track and offer Jonjo his dory as their safety boat. He told them that his oyster-dredger was on a mooring further up the creek and he could bring her close in and anchor her if anyone'd like to come on board and take a look.

"Hey," said Nelson, "What swims in the sea, carries a machine gun and makes you an offer you can't refuse?"

"Not so funny," said Jonjo.

Xanthe didn't see that he needed to be so tense: there were a few other families on the steep sandy beach but not all that many and they blended in fine. They looked like a club.

"The Codfather," Martha answered Nelson. "I used to think that my dad had invented that joke."

"Along with that one about fish being clever because they swam in schools," Gareth added. "Then he'd look across at us and say, 'come on you two, time to get yer homework done, you don't want to end up like your old dad.' He'd run away, you see, when he were young. Didn't get on at home so he got a job on the paddle steamers. Gave up school when he were twelve."

"Iris told me about him," Xanthe remembered. "His name was Joe and he helped with the Dunkirk evacuation by making tea and sandwiches."

"Seven trips," said Martha. "And he was only fourteen."

"Would you do me a Dunkirk interview? Help me write down your dad's story? I'm sort of avoiding that subject with Iris now."

Then she remembered what Martha had said; she should have avoided it with them as well.

"Our dad drowned off of the *Igraine*." Gareth's voice darkened. "Eli went ter jail for it."

He shoved his hands in his jacket pockets, turned away from them and looked across the river to Colne Point and out to sea.

"Hey, bro…" Martha was warning him off.

"What's yellow and dangerous?" Nelson answered himself before anyone else had a chance. "Shark-infested custard!"

Gareth laughed, relaxed, turned back to them.

"Remember the other one Dad used to bring out when he'd had a drink or two?" he asked Martha.

"About the richest fish on the river?"

"That un's the *Gold*-fish, he used to say."

The children hadn't met a working fisherman before. They hadn't had much chance, living in East London. Xanthe, who had lived by water for most of her life, discovered that she knew nothing at all about the growing and the harvesting of oysters – which the Farrans had been doing as long as they'd been living near Flinthammock. Which was probably for ever.

"Romans ate these oysters here on Meresig. Flat oysters they would have been then, Natives. And not in the summer. Best sort of all, though they don't do so well now."

"Why not?" asked Xanthe.

"Could be pollution, change in water temperature, damage on the ground. Thing to remember about shellfish is that they're sensitive. They're opening and closing all the time: feeding and growing – or so you hope. The water's flowing through them but a'course you can't see that. So it ain't until afterwards, when you find they ain't growing or they're dying, that you begin to wonder what went wrong."

"Don't you, like, monitor the water?"

"We're talking about a river here, gal. A river that's open to the sea."

They were squashed together on board Gareth's little ship, anchored inside Coldlight Creek and finishing their sandwiches. Xanthe shut up after that and let Kieran and David ask endless questions about the machinery and the processes involved.

Nelson was unusually quiet, probably working out a new range of shellfish jokes. By the time Gareth said he needed to run them back ashore, he'd got one – which he answered as usual before they'd had time to think.

"How do fishermen go into business? They start on a small scale."

Gareth laughed aloud at that. He gave Nelson a serious answer though. "But have you seen how us humans guzzle – let alone what crabs and seabirds do, if you give 'em half a chance? Small scale's no good if you need to earn a living from yer oysters. It used to be seasonal but now people want 'em all year round. We don't sell 'em natives out of season, obviously. Just rocks – rock oysters, I mean, not stones. Ain't found a recipe for stones yet."

"My N-nan and G-grandad used to eat c-cockles and whelks. But we don't go there any more. N-not since we had to move." David sounded wistful.

"We had a holiday in Marbella once – before Dad lost his business. They eat loads of seafood." That was Kieran. He looked across at Kelly-Jane who nodded but didn't speak.

Xanthe'd learned to dread the silences when the children remembered their families and the lives they'd had to leave.

Gareth must have noticed too. "Any of you's interested I could take you for a walk around my oyster racks. They're in the other river, further up beyond Mell Creek. And I will just mention that I could be looking for an apprentice or two in the longer term. If I still have a business after that new hotel opens."

"No thanks," said Kelly-Jane.

"You're such a *girl*," said Kieran. "Can I come please, Mr Farran."

"It's Gareth. Call me Mr Farran and I'm looking over my shoulder for my late departed Uncle Eli, though the only thing I miss him for is he used to help me giving the sacks a shake at low water."

"C-could we shake s-sacks?" asked David.

"Don't mind you havin' a go. It's tough on the back and tough on the hands an' you'll need thick gloves and boots and waterproofs."

"W-we've got gear, haven't we, Xanthe?" They'd none of them got the habit of calling her Cap'n and she'd forgotten to be bothered. Different creeks, different flavours.

"We so have."

It was the first time David had positively wanted anything. And Kieran looked keen too.

"Is it somewhere we could go now?" she asked Martha and Jonjo. "Dominic said he'd cover if we were late."

"Don't mind if I come along," said Kelly-Jane. "Don't fancy shaking sacks though. Not if they're all smelly and slimy."

Jonjo and Martha were thinking aloud.

"No one's followed us today."

"How private is it?"

"It's about like this. We could stop at the Happy Haddock first off."

Xanthe and Martha looked at the girls. Siri's eyes said yes.

"Don't mind if I do," said Kelly-Jane.

The oyster racks were exactly that, racks: long metal structures about a metre high, embedded in the sandy mud at the river's edge and uncovered for an hour or two either side of low water.

Everyone sat on the dry sand near the top of the lonely beach, eating their chips and waiting. Then the racks broke the smooth surface, one after another and seemed to rise up as the water ebbed away. They were blackened by grime and draped with dark weed. On top of each rack lay hundreds of flat mesh sacks. They weren't large but each one contained dozens of oysters.

"Them's too small to be out on the river bed. Crabs'd get 'em. So we have 'em up here out of reach. Gives 'em time to grow. Each sack gets a regular shaking to move the little 'uns about, then after six months they's big enough to go out in the river. Leave 'em another nine months or so, then dredge 'em up – or hand-pick, depending on the tide."

"Everything's depending on the tide round here."

"That's just about how it is. Now my uncle Eli used to come down here. He was a lonesome old gizzard so he used to leave me a marker ter show where he'd reached on each of these rows. First job I'm needing you to do – those who's got their sailing boots on or who don't mind a paddle – is take a good look along and see if you can find any old piece of canvas sail tie. That'll tell us where he's been. He called them his favours. Came off a boat he once owned."

"The *Igraine?*"

"His one true love – as he always said."

"So these canvas sail ties," asked Kieran, who was up and ready to wade into the above-knee-deep water, "I don't really get what they look like."

"Nothin' much not once they've been in and out the river for a month or two."

All the kids were ready to search for Eli's markers. Nelson managed a quick one-liner about the oysters crossing the road to get to the other tide – "tide, not side, geddit?" They got it.

There were six long rows of oyster racks: one for each child and one for Xanthe. Jonjo kept lookout on the river wall, Martha stayed close to Siri and Gareth moved from person to person, pointing things out and explaining.

"It wasn't red, is it, the markers?" asked Kieran. "There's something completely tangled in here that was red once."

"Not red," said Gareth. "But you'd be surprised the things that do get caught up here. Bits of rope and old towels and fishing line and single shoes."

"I'm undoing it anyway," said Kieran. He was a steady, persistent type. "It's really long. I can't get it out properly."

Kelly-Jane left her rack and came to help her brother. "You know what it's like?" she said.

"No." They were all gathering round to watch Kieran extricate the mystery object.

"It's a bit like them flag-things you see on boat masts in the creek. Except it's way bigger."

"OMG!" Martha covered her mouth with her hand. "You know what this is, don't you, bro?"

Gareth was staring too as Kieran and Kelly-Jane pulled the object free. It was about two metres long and would have been a vivid red before it had got tangled round the oyster rack. Kelly-Jane grabbed it from Kieran and showered everyone with drips as she shook it.

"I found it," he whinged. "It's mine. Give it back."

"Stop it," said Gareth. "Stop that now, please."

There was something in his voice.

"It's a pennant," said Xanthe. "From a smack or a barge.

It'd fly from a bamboo pole at the top of the mainmast. I never realised they were that long."

"They ain't. This 'un's special."

"You recognise it?"

She guessed what he was going to say.

"It's hers alright. It's her best. Kept in reserve for a match or a birthday or summat. He must have had it all these years an' brought it down here. He must have meant it."

"For his…death day?" Xanthe began to feel horrified.

"Okay. Stop, everyone. We need to do this properly."

Martha pulled out a radio that they didn't know she had. She was calling Jonjo. She'd remembered that she was a policewoman.

"It's evidence," she explained, using her phone to take a photo of the oyster rack.

Jonjo came at the run.

"We need to bag this," she said. "Elijah Farran's inquest is on Tuesday. This could affect the verdict."

She told Jonjo what they'd found.

"Thenks," he said, sounding foreign. "I'm not so sure I'd hev seen the significance."

"Most people wouldn't."

"He left it here," said Gareth. "That meant it were for me. Eli were a crusty old so-an-so. I reckon he thought I oughta have it because of Dad." His voice was growly with emotion.

"Yes," Martha sounded emotional as well but she was staying focused. "That's right, and so you should, but the coroner has to see it first. It can't have got here by accident. It's a message. I'd say it's as clear as if he'd left a suicide note."

She forced herself to brighten up. "So, well done Kieran for spotting it. And K-J for helping get it out."

The kids were looking fed up. They didn't understand what was going on and what they did understand, they didn't like.

"We'll give this rack a special treat," said Xanthe. "Show us what to do, Gareth."

"That's simple enough. Like shaking a duvet. Yer grab each sack by its corners and yer give it a wriggle. So's the oysters shift around and there's not the same ones getting all the best space."

"We could work in twos. C'mon Nelson."

He heaved a big sigh, moved up to the nearest sack and did as she'd suggested. Then he stopped still. His hands hung down by his side. He appeared to be deep in thought.

"What's the best way to catch a fish, teacher-lady?"

She was totally amazed by him. How did he keep it going?

"Mr Midshipman, I wish I knew."

"Have someone throw it at you," he told her, breaking out once again into his glorious grin.

CHAPTER FIFTEEN

Blackout

Friday May 31, LW 0711 HW 1330 LW 1930 HW 0146

"It were easy enough if you owned a good boat. The real danger came when you were landing the goods – onto the beach or up the creeks."

"What sort of stuff was it?" The kids had left in the minibus with Martha and Jonjo. She and Gareth were in the Land Rover, towing the dinghy back. She wasn't that bothered about old-time smugglers; she was keeping him talking as a distraction. It had obviously upset him, finding the *Igraine*'s pennant tangled in his oyster racks, and he'd been really angry with Martha except he couldn't say much because of the kids.

"Brandy and cigars. Bottles of gin. Not drugs, not like today."

"Alcohol's a drug. So's nicotine."

"Government weren't trying to keep them things out of the country for health reasons. Those were things that people wanted, so government put tax on 'em to earn revenue."

"So the smugglers were like tax dodgers. And that's not right either."

"Taxes in them days weren't exactly supporting a national health service or education."

Xanthe had stopped thinking that smugglers were okay when she'd discovered about the way they smuggled people. Or used people to smuggle drugs. But Gareth was talking from way back. Maybe it was different.

"What does it matter what I think? You were telling me what happened. You said the Golds started smuggling to pay for *Igraine*.

"And Farrans didn't like it.

"Was that because they thought it was wrong?"

"More likely they were jealous. They weren't doing so well on the fishing – wherever they went Golds had got there first. *Igraine* were that much handier than Farrans' old boats. She had all new gear as well."

"What happened?"

"Farrans turned 'em in. *Igraine* were seized and no end of contraband was found on board. It meant transportation for the Golds and *Igraine* was forfeit. Those boys was lucky they weren't hanged."

Yuck. Xanthe was glad she lived now, not then. "They must have known about the risk."

"But they all swore blind that they wasn't guilty. Never mind what they might of done other times, this time they said it were a plant. And when Farrans came out as *Igraine*'s new owners the Golds didn't reckon they needed to look far to guess who'd stitched them up."

"Do you think they had, the Farrans I mean?"

"Nothing proved. The younger Golds – the ones what hadn't been convicted – carried on as best they could."

"They didn't try to get revenge?

"They weren't exactly gonna leave it, were they."

"Did they fight?"

"Out of the Plough and Sail on a Saturday, a-course they did. The rumour was a bit more subtle."

"What rumour?"

"That them Golds left cuckoos in the Farran nests."

"Cuckoos?"

Xanthe thought of what Martha had said and about the reed-warblers and maybe also that bird that had flown out of the wood. She'd meant to look it up.

"Children what didn't belong. Farrans was dark and Golds was fair and every so often there'd be some fair-haired baby turning up in a dark-haired Farran nest."

"The mothers would have known."

"No doubt they did but Farran men weren't exactly notable for tolerance so they'd probably have chose to keep it quiet. Anyway it were probably no more'n rumour. It's a small village, Flinthammock, and us families have been interbreeding for years."

"You know what," said Xanthe. "I don't want to hear this. I don't want to go round staring at people and wondering if their dads were who they said they were."

"No more do I. So you get what I was saying? There's some questions best not asked. Though I'd have thought as I could have trusted me own sister…" He glowered over the steering wheel as they bumped along the narrow lanes.

"And Iris?" – she'd try anything to keep him off that pennant – "I thought she was the little rich girl from the big house. But didn't you say that she was a Gold, before she got married?"

"That's right. Her dad were second or third generation from some of them Golds that got transported. His lot struck it properly rich."

"And he came back here?"

"He were a clever man, Augustus Gold. He liked fast boats and inventing things and he bought Oveseye. Then he made a man's mistake and he married what they call a trophy wife."

"Who left her child as soon as she heard her husband had been killed. Why would she have done that? Poor Iris, maybe I oughtn't to be surprised she has such weird ideas."

"Except she were left with my Aunt Ann Farran and she were a good woman. There's sommat gone curdled in Iris. She shouldn't never have married Eli."

"She's weird about that too – she says the *Igraine*'s a death-ship, keeps on about her 'coming for him'."

Gareth laughed. "*Igraine*'d have been pushed to do that!"

She was glad he'd cheered up. "Why?"

"Cos goodie cousin Dominic and I took 'er out and scuttled 'er on the Gunfleet sands," he said triumphantly. "That were after Eli had drowned my father, Joe. We put an end to 'er. We should ha' put an end to all that feudin' an all."

Then it couldn't have been the *Igraine* in the mirage. It must have been some other random smack. Iris had got the whole thing wrong. All her talk about dark powers! It was a relief.

They'd reached *Godwyn* now so they slid the Pico off its road trailer and wheeled it over to the other dinghies. Then they carried the sails and all the detachable bits into the storage shed and Gareth got back into the Land Rover.

Rebow Cottage time. *More* Iris. This wasn't *her* family.

"Hey, Gareth, would it be a big deal for you if I didn't come back to Rebow Cottage yet? I'm feeling there could well be an evening breeze."

"You go for it, lass."

"And it mightn't be so easy to go sailing by myself when I'm living with the kids on *Godwyn*."

He waved her away. "You'd best get off then if you're going. I gotta bit of thinking to do. I won't lock the back door in case you're after Aunt Iris's curfew. I shoulda thought to show you Eli's trick for gettin' in – he had his crafty side!"

"Cool. Thanks Gareth."

Xanthe crossed over the wall and dropped down onto the marsh so she wouldn't be seen from *Godwyn*. The shelduck resented her and the greylag geese with their half-grown goslings scrambled anxiously away from the edge of the scrape where they'd settled for the night. She'd been meaning to ask Gareth what it was he'd expected her to have known about *Fritha*.

Clouds of pollen blew into the air as she pushed her way through the long grass, keeping out of sight. There was thistledown on the evening breeze and unexpected insects darting across her path.

She didn't run. She knew she was already tired. She began wondering who had taken those photos. She switched on her mobile to see whether Maggi or Anna had any ideas but she couldn't get reception.

It had to be Madrigal, didn't it? But how had she discovered that Xanthe was in Essex?

As she climbed back over the river wall and began stepping along the line of muddy slabs and bags that formed the Fisherman's Hard, she could see it was going to be a struggle getting out onto the river. The young flood was gathering pace and the breeze was funnelling in. She wished she had oars, or an outboard, or someone to give *Fritha* a tow. But, as she had none of those things – and there was utterly no one in sight – she decided to tow herself. So she slipped, splashed and occasionally swam the first, shallowest stretch, pulling the Firefly behind her.

Why was she doing this? Getting cold and muddy and even more tired. She could be back in Rebow Cottage running herself a bath or stretching out in that smooth white bed.

Stick with it and she'd soon be out, close-hauled and heading seawards, free as a bird. Were birds free? Or was it only humans who thought so? Birds probably felt totally stressed out. They had to eat all the time, didn't they? And guard their chicks.

The water was a darkening blue and that further shore looked bleached in the evening light. The cranes on the construction site stood skeletal against the sky. Their floodlights were already on. She glanced across at the D-Day components with the tugs lying alongside. It wouldn't get properly dark for a couple of hours. She'd be back in the Flete by then. Xanthe emptied her mind and headed for the horizon.

Fritha's jib was backed, her mainsail shivering. She had turned into the wind and stopped herself. Xanthe had slumped forward, dropping the main sheet and pushing the tiller away as she fell asleep. The Firefly was hove to.

The night was all around them. It seemed extraordinarily dark.

She pressed the side button on her sports watch. Eleven o'clock. She felt as if she'd never experienced such blackness. So dense she could almost touch it. Breathing it in to her lungs like fog. Had that brief moment of illumination from the watch damaged her night vision? She closed her eyes to help them readjust.

Fritha's gentle motion told her they were at sea. There was still a friendly breeze and a couple of hours' flood. It wasn't a disaster. She had her compass. Gareth hadn't locked her out from Rebow Cottage. She simply needed to spot some sort of mark. Get herself a bearing.

Xanthe opened her eyes again, let go of the tiller and leaned quickly over the stern. She filled her cupped hands with seawater and splashed it cold against her face. The dinghy's sails flapped. A cloud slipped onwards revealing the smallest sliver of a waxing moon. That could be crucial. She needed the sky to stay clear.

There was no sparkle in the water. That gleam of moon was going to have to be enough to help her compare black against black and distinguish sea from sky and land. If the wind direction hadn't shifted while she'd been asleep, it would be still blowing on-shore and the flood tide would be tending to take her up the coast. The last thing she remembered was the green flashing light of the Bench Head buoy that marked the official entrance to the river.

Where was it now?

Fritha had lost her equilibrium; she was restless: she wanted to sail. Xanthe brought her round so that the wind was on her port side. She kept her close-hauled, standing away from the land. She couldn't risk being pushed ashore until she knew what shore it was.

The Firefly seemed quicker and lighter. There was a gleam in her sails. The mainsheet in Xanthe's hand felt new. Not new as in modern braids, new as in right for *Fritha*. And it was leading from the centre of the dinghy not her stern. Had Gareth made some rigging change she hadn't noticed?

She was going to work on the assumption that she was

somewhere off the seaward edge of the St Peter Peninsula. There was possibly some last lightness in the western sky and that small silhouette could be the outline of the ancient chapel. Nothing glowing from the peace camp, but maybe she wouldn't be seeing that?

You shouldn't do assumptions and possibilities in navigation. You needed fixed points.

So where was the Bench Head Buoy or the Colne Bar or the Inner Bench Head – all those fixed, illuminated, navigation marks that she'd memorised from her chart? And where, for that matter, were the lights of Meresig or even the floodlights of the construction site? Or the neon from the towns that stretched northeast along the coast. Big towns like Clacton that should paint the night sky orange?

Fritha was slipping clean and fast though the water. She was sailing like a new dinghy, tuned to perfection. Xanthe felt as empowered as if she was sailing *Spray*. She pulled her compass from inside her jacket and allowed herself to bring the dinghy round so the wind was astern of her port quarter. Just north of west. This course should be taking her back towards the Nass.

The water sizzled soft beneath the dinghy's smooth hull. All else was silence.

Nothing from St Peter's and nothing from Meresig. No construction noise, no distant music, no car engines. And still no lights. Meresig was a holiday island. It had campsites and caravans. Pubs would only just be closing. It was half term!

She tried to take a peep under the Firefly's mainsail, setting full out to starboard. This new arrangement of the sheets was good. There was a swivel jam cleat she hadn't noticed before. It made the dinghy much easier for a single sailor. She clamped both sets of sheets and shuffled cautiously for'ard. She knew she mustn't risk an accidental gybe yet she felt peculiarly desperate to identify some source of light. Where were the floodlights for the power station?

The tiny moon vanished again behind the clouds. Total blackout.

Xanthe kept the dinghy balanced and struggled to think what she should do. She should not go rushing on, full sail, into darkness. At the very least she should take the mainsail down and run with jib alone until she was certain where she was.

The main came down without a rustle as if it was fresh, white Egyptian cotton. When she'd put it up, it had been terylene, slightly yellow and crackling with age. If *Fritha* was young again perhaps Xanthe had lost her bearings in time as well as place?

There was a creak of warps and spars, men's low voices, the possible glimmer of a bow wave? A larger, heavier boat was closing rapidly from astern.

Xanthe shone her torch on the bright triangle of *Fritha*'s clean white jib. She gybed the dinghy and shouted.

The black shape passed only metres away as if she was invisible. She was a gaffer with a long bowsprit and all sails set. She was confident and fast and she wasn't showing any lights.

Xanthe upped her own mainsail and followed in her wake. The *Igraine* was leading her home, she was sure of it. No matter what Gareth had said.

The moon came out, the All Clear sounded and the lights of the building site blazed across the water. Xanthe hauled her wind and headed for the Nass. There was the familiar twinkle of western Meresig and the line of channel buoys helping her back into the Flinthammock Flete.

Only *Fritha* seemed old and somehow despondent.

"This was left here for yer." Gareth was holding an ivory envelope with a complex emblem of intertwined swords. He looked tired. It was one in the morning.

"Sorry," she said. "I didn't expect you to wait up."

"Reckoned you'd have had trouble getting outa the Flete on that tide."

"Yeah, I did. But it wasn't that which made me late. I think I might have gone to sleep or something."

"Yer back now."

"Yeah," she said again. Part of her longed to tell Gareth about the darkness and the silence and the change to *Fritha*. Most of her was aching to go to bed. She took the envelope.

"Seaxes – that's for Saxons," he added when he noticed her staring at the logo. "It'll be an invitation from Dominic's old man."

"Dominic's…?"

"Father. Property developer from across the river. If it's yours, he wants it. Land, boats, the drippings from your nose. Mostly we don't mention the relationship."

"His *father*?" she repeated. "But now you're going to tell me that they don't get on."

"They don't."

"Why am I not surprised about that?" She thought of the earnest, monkish Dominic with his Rules and his Project and his terrible anxieties, then compared him with the self-satisfied wannabe Viking.

"And Commander Gold's been here?"

"Here when I arrived. Iris had been complaining that she couldn't work the TV that he gave her. Dominic was long gone. He says she needs a full-time carer. Got one arriving as soon as you leave, he says."

"They're related – Dominic's dad and Iris?"

"Though not exactly as you might expect."

Her brain couldn't deal with this answer: her body was begging to go to bed.

"Do you have you to get up early?" she asked Gareth.

"Ain't planning on going ter bed just yet. I need to get my quota so I either dredge now with the tide or I'll have to hand pick in the morning. Rock oysters. Not natives. Reckon I'll go over t'other side for 'em. Shouldn't take too long."

"Then I'm double sorry I stayed out so late."

"It wasn't a problem. I needed ter think."

She didn't ask what he needed to think about.

"Thanks again for *Fritha*."

"Get on arright?"

"Yeah." It was too late to talk about the darkness. Or the change in the feel of the dinghy. Or that new way of running her mainsheet. Or anything at all. She was way too tired and Gareth had oysters to pick.

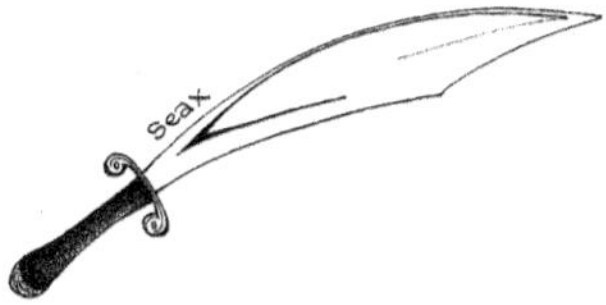

CHAPTER SIXTEEN

A Challenge

Saturday June 1, LW 0745 HW 1402 LW 2002 HW 0222

She left opening the envelope until next morning. Anything from the Commander of the Saxon Shore was likely to be bad news – unless he'd relented and was offering her access for her project research. Since the night that he'd tried to steal *Fritha,* she'd have struggled even to accept that from him.

This was a formal invitation:

The Commander of the Saxon Shore
And the Directors of Saxon Holdings
Challenge
Miss Xanthe Ribiero
To appear in a Charity Sailing Match
On Monday June 3rd, Dunkirk Day
In the presence of the Hundreth
RSVP

"I don't want to do it," she told Martha, once she'd explained.

"Of course you don't. It's a publicity stunt."

"Like everything he does," added Dominic.

He looked exhausted. He must have been up even later than she had, guarding his beloved *Godwyn* against a possible hijack by the man Xanthe now knew was his father.

She'd seen those powerful tugs and cranes. She didn't think Dominic's worry was so stupid. The narrow creek was his best defence, but on a high tide – and if they didn't much mind what damage they caused…She even felt sorry for him.

"What is this…Hundreth?" asked Jonjo.

"It's like a society for people with money," Martha answered. "Or power. Especially the people who control planning around here. Saxon spends thousands schmoozing them to wave their construction projects through. We stopped them when they tried to take over the saltings – the birders were great – but once they bought the power station it was different. There was only us and the peaceniks beside the chapel. I personally treasure them but all they want is to be left alone to chant into the sunrise and that. They don't exactly do lobbying and politics."

Xanthe had gone up into the *Godwyn* office to ask advice. She hadn't needed all this local information. Jonjo seemed a bit switched off as well. He probably didn't exactly do peaceniks.

Martha had her hands cupped around her mug of tea. Dominic was staring out of the window, strained and vigilant.

"Arthur Gold put forward this scheme of an immense war-games adventure park. The Hundreth could see serious money pouring into the area and Saxon PR keeps telling them that it's the patriotic thing to do. They offer annual steadfastness awards and big lunches with lots to drink and feel-good entertainment – like this sailing match idea. He used to fund *Godwyn*," Martha added. "Until Dom couldn't take his money any more."

"I'm ashamed I ever touched a penny. I thought he was trying to make amends."

"Amends?" Xanthe queried.

"It doesn't matter. It's…in the past. We don't get on."

That old phrase.

"So no-one's gonna mind if I say no? I've realised why Saxon's been ringing such bells with me. They sponsor a racer called Madrigal Shryke. She was the reason I got thrown off the training camp."

She owed them more honesty than that. "That's not true – *I* was the reason I got thrown off. If Madrigal's sponsors are promoting a sailing match there has to be a possibility that she could be involved. I know I'm being a wuss but…I don't much want to meet her. There was even nearly an injunction."

"I'd say!" Xanthe could hear that Martha had got the picture. "Sir Hubert Shryke is Chairman of the Saxon board. He's Arthur Gold's senior partner *and* a member of the Hundreth. He's completely certain to be there."

"Is thet where those photos are coming from?" Jonjo asked, sounding interested again.

Larfaminnit.com had hosted a new album that morning – a video sequence of Xanthe pulling *Fritha* down the Flete. The editing was brilliant. It was totally hilarious. YouTube viewers were loving it. Jonjo had asked his bosses to get it taken down but they couldn't see any reason why they should do so as none of the protected children were involved.

"The Flete was completely deserted last night – unless they'd fitted up the shelduck to take photos. My friend Anna has identified the sharers of the first batch but she can't put a name to the photographer. So now she's working on discovering the camera type. It's not a phone or anything; it's something high-tech. Long-distance surveillance, she thinks."

She'd found another text from Maggi when she finally remembered to switch on her mobile. Anna'd tracked the initial posting to one of Madrigal's thousands of friends-of-friends. The Twitter images had been posted via a temporary secretary in a PR firm. Big money had then been spent boosting the posts on both platforms on behalf of a client who claimed commercial anonymity. Madrigal hadn't liked or shared any of the photos – she was about the only person who hadn't.

"It's completely unconnected with the children." Jonjo sounded relieved. "They're just victims of your fall-out with this girl."

"Yeah, think so. I need to take them sailing now if you're comfortable that they're not getting snatched or anything. I want to take them all the way to the sea while the weather's still so calm. But I ought to post that RSVP. They can't be expecting me to come or they'd have given more notice."

"Martha," said Jonjo. "Are you okay for duty today? I could use a recce across the river and delivering Xanthe's message could be exactly the front I need. I'd take the second RIB."

"Carry the war into the Enemy's camp," said Dominic, looking energised and fierce. "Tell him that we won't be pushed about to suit his greed and self-aggrandisement. Proclaim our Defiance!"

Xanthe wondered whether she mightn't do better to buy a stamp. "I don't want to be in their sailing match but I don't totally want to be rude. I'm going to go back to racing."

Jonjo nodded and Dominic went silent again.

"There was another thing," Xanthe added. "I've been using Gareth's Firefly dinghy and she could do with some TLC. Would it be okay if I brought her up the creek and asked the kids to help me haul her out and work on her? It would only be if they wanted to."

"You'd be working on the dinghy in front of the lightship?" said Dominic. "Yes, it's a weak point. We could all get out there together. Be seen to be busy."

She held back from mentioning that it was *Fritha* and her crew she was thinking about. Not *Godwyn*'s defences.

Dominic carried on anyway. "I can certainly permit that. Bring her up as early as you like. We'll leave the Project dinghies in the Flete. The tide's getting later each day and, starting next week, I'd like you to focus on the youngsters getting their stage one certificates. They're missing out on education – this could give them something to show."

"So you're happy for them to work with me on *Fritha* later today? If they agree."

"I'll help Martha supervise while Jonjo takes the RIB across with your reply. My aunt's carer is settling in and I don't have any more outside visitors to worry about just now."

Which surely means that *Godwyn*'s more vulnerable, Xanthe thought, but she kept that thought to herself.

It hadn't taken long to clear out of her Rebow Cottage bedroom and say goodbye to Mrs Farran.

"You'll be coming again, won't you?" asked the old lady. "I could carry on helping with your homework. I don't think you've done very much. Your mother won't be pleased."

Xanthe was never going to risk another interview with Iris Farran but she couldn't help admitting that the old lady had a point. She hadn't done much work on her essay. She hadn't actually done any…

"Thanks," she said. "I expect I'll see you at the inquest on Tuesday."

"Inquest?"

"For your husband. The one who died."

Maggi would have told her that was unkind. But Xanthe couldn't make herself feel all that sorry for Mrs Farran. Also she had to decide before Tuesday what she should do about that walking stick – and maybe also the sampler? She should definitely talk to Jonjo when he came back from his recce.

Kieran and David loved the idea of working on *Fritha* once sailing was over for the day. They each chose an area of the Firefly's varnished hull and settled painstakingly, methodically, to taking off the surface layer as evenly as Xanthe managed to explain to them. Nelson worked in wild bursts. Kelly-Jane was uncertain and Siri took no notice at all. She'd sailed beautifully once again. She seemed to have completely natural balance and an instinctive ability to read wind-shifts that Xanthe recognised and admired.

"Try these," said Martha, returning from the sports equipment store with a couple of old-fashioned kites.

The kids were getting tanned, Xanthe noticed. It was a good thing that Kelly-Jane had been mothering them with high-factor sun-cream as no-one, not even Siri, had got burned. They'd been here for a week and, outwardly, they were looking better.

"You're a brilliant team, did you know that? Carry on like this and we'll be able to get a coat of varnish on while there's still plenty of heat in the sun. Then we'll walk across to the chandlery and I'm going buy us all ice creams. Except *Fritha*. She's getting proper new sheets and halyards. She's a racing dinghy, not a museum piece."

"Are you rich?" asked Kieran.

"She must be if she's done all those competitions, dumb-ass."

"Did you win loadsa prizes, teacher-lady?"

Xanthe looked at Martha for help.

"When we told the students you were coming, we said a bit about what you'd achieved," she explained. "We thought they'd like to know who was going to be teaching them."

Xanthe swallowed and did her best. "You don't exactly get cash, you get points and, if you're hoping to get a place in team GBR, you want the selectors to notice how you did. You might also be looking out for sponsors. When I wrecked my first boat, I got my sister to video me in the local regatta and I used that to persuade the dock company to buy me a new one."

Spray II...would be gone by now.

"You're saying that you already have to have a boat and be winning things before anyone will help you get a better one." Kelly-Jane commented. "That's okay for me cos I wouldn't want to. But Siz might."

"I w-would l-like you to t-tell us about all the r-races you've w-won."

That was David.

"Yeah, well, best get back to work now."

Xanthe made out she was really involved in getting *Fritha*'s forefoot silky smooth and this somehow made her unable to talk. Mainly she was sick with shame. She'd had so much and she'd chucked it all away.

They were sitting on *Godwyn*'s aft deck that evening playing cards when they heard the rifle shots – two clear, sharp, cracks from across the river. The birds heard them too. They flew up from the marsh, honking and wheeling, parents and youngsters in panicky skeins. Then subsided again into wary silence.

Maybe they should have been used to distant noises? In the short week she'd been living in Flinthammock Xanthe had come to expect sirens and flashing lights from the construction site at least once or twice a day. She'd asked Dominic what he'd meant by his comment about his father's safety record.

"He pushes his workers as if they were robots – or slaves. You'd think he was hosting the Olympics, not building a hotel."

"That's what it is – a hotel?"

"On the megalomaniac scale. No thought of appropriateness to the area."

"Or the pollution involved," said Martha. "Gareth's expecting he'll lose all his young oysters. He'll be back to where he was when Dad died.

"We should have scuttled my father, not the smack."

"No violence, Dom."

Then they had remembered that Xanthe was there.

"Don't mind us," said Martha. "Family stuff. Probably sounds worse than it is."

Xanthe wasn't sure that was possible.

A text from Maggi plopped into the quiet evening after the birds had settled back onto the marsh. She felt her crew watching as she read it. Had to twist away from them when she realised what it said.

Cannot believe u are doing this. Wimp or what? Parents gutted. Your chance to vindicate says dad. Mum and college p all accepted invite. Tutor too. Griselda ok. Spray promised. What is wrong with u?

There was a follow up:

Have u seen fb?

How could she have known that they'd have asked her family and her tutor and her college principal? And Griselda, for crissake! And *Spray!*

She got up, not very steady, and pushed back her chair.

"I need to go find Dominic," she said to Martha.

The kids were looking sick. There must have been so many sudden calls, so many bad atmospheres, so many conversations from which they were excluded.

Okay, maybe she could do this differently.

"You can read these texts," she said, passing her mobile to Kelly-Jane. "And share them. They're from my sister and she's called Maggi. You'll find she's not very happy with me. I have to speak to Dominic and check Facebook but I'm gonna to need a team meeting when I get back. I'm relying on you to manage it. And, okay, David, you'll get the story of my racing career but you might not necessarily like it."

Martha looked shocked and ready to protest. Xanthe wasn't stopping to listen to her. It felt as if she'd been manoeuvred into upsetting everyone in the world that she respected – her parents, her teachers, Griselda. Her crew were the last people who might have respected her. So at least she owed them honesty. And if she had to take decisions, she was going to consult them. She might have talked to Gareth if he'd been there but he wasn't. Nor was Jonjo.

Facebook was awash with photos of her and Nelson joshing about; her and the other kids flying kites, eating ices. Anyone would think that Xanthe was having so much fun that she couldn't be bothered to take the time to join the Dunkirk commemoration.

Which they did, of course:

Sacrifice forgotten? Was this generation worth fighting for? Our ancestors crossed the channel: this girl won't cross a river!

There was a new, sponsored, St Peter's Saxon Shore page with thousands of likes already. It showed the whale, the beetle and the spud pier being towed into position to make a mini Mulberry harbour. Then it repeated the invitation to all East Coast Little Ships to visit the Saxon Holdings Memorial Facility. Every boat that visited would be welcomed and entertained, all free of charge and a substantial donation made to the Royal National Lifeboat Institution or a Veteran's Charity of the owner's choice.

The first vessel had arrived last night. Xanthe's experience – some of it anyway – had been for real.

Former East Coast fishing smack Igraine from Flinthammock on the River Blackwater in Essex, answered her country's call on May 27th 1940. She sailed to Ramsgate to assist the evacuation but was not, in the end, required to continue on to France.

The Igraine returned to her home river but had the extraordinary bad luck to hit a mine off the end of Flinthammock pier. Her owner, local fisherman Abraham Farran, drowned but his son, the late Elijah Farran, subsequently spent many years rebuilding the smack.

In the later years of the twentieth century, the Igraine became a familiar sight as she continued to use traditional techniques to fish home waters long after the majority of her sister ships had gone out of business.

Circumstances finally forced Mr Eli Farran to abandon her and for many years she was presumed lost. Saxon Holdings are proud to have recovered the Igraine and to have invested a substantial sum restoring her.

After the forthcoming commemoration ceremony the smack will be moored off the Saxon Shore Hotel as a permanent tribute to the unsung heroes of the East Coast.

She was a lovely-looking smack, Xanthe could see that. And Iris had been right: it had been the *Igraine* that she had photographed on that extraordinary morning of mirage. She must have been well out to sea, crossing Ramsgate to join the other Little Ships and then the early morning light rays had bent round the layers of hot and cold air to make her image visible maybe twenty miles away.

She couldn't now make any sense at all of what Gareth and Dominic had claimed. They said they'd 'scuttled' her but here she was, back in her home river, doomed to be stuck at St Peter's forever. Maybe she'd become a bar for hotel guests to enjoy their evening drinkies.

In the scale of Xanthe's problems that didn't feel such a big one.

Madrigal Shryke had liked and shared the St Peter's Saxon Shore page and so had most of her thousands of friends. She had added a comment to say how humble she felt that she'd been asked to play some small part in the Commemoration as one of Britain's young sailors To Follow. Then there was a long, predictable, conversation with friends asking her how she felt hearing that Xanthe, her former sailing rival, had also been invited.

I'm cool. I'm strong enough.

Later she'd posted a status update describing her disappointment that Xanthe had refused the invitation to the Charity Sailing Match:

Maybe it's hard for people like her, whose families weren't involved, to understand why it's so important for us English people to remember.

Likes and shares for that one were spreading like a petrol slick over water.

"What do you think?" Xanthe asked Martha and the kids. "You've read the texts from my sister. I got an invitation to be part of a charity sailing match to commemorate Dunkirk and World War Two and I turned it down."

Anyone who said she was a coward – yes, they were right. She could see it now.

"Martha's already told you that I used to be a racer. I didn't know how lucky I was. I got a sponsor and a really good boat and I made it to the junior pre-Olympic training camp. Then I lost my temper and I punched my main rival. She's the one who's going to be at the Dunkirk sailing match."

She didn't give them a chance to ask anything.

"It was a totally dumb thing to do. I knew she was needling me. She'd been doing it all week."

The mental stuff had been just as much a test as the sailing – and she'd failed it, dismally.

"So I'm banned for six months and all the Test regattas will have happened by then and the long-list selection. I had to tell my sponsors what I'd done and offer to give my boat back. That was almost the worst thing. I loved my boat."

She remembered how Madrigal had dissed *Spray* and the casual way she'd let her get damaged. She must have guessed how Xanthe had felt.

"There was a load of bad publicity on social media and I wasn't handling it. My mum sent me here to keep out of the way. Then, when I got asked to appear in this sailing match and I guessed Madrigal might be there, I wimped out. I'd been told to keep away from her and I didn't want to start it all up again. I didn't realise they'd asked my family and everyone."

She had to be completely honest. "I also didn't know that my sponsors would be letting me use *Spray*. I'd do pretty much anything to get my dinghy back."

"Are you s-sorry you p-punched her?" asked David.

There were loads of things she regretted – but still not that. Not exactly. She'd never forget the shocked look on Madrigal's pretty pink face when she fell backwards into the water. And when she'd replayed that scene in her head she was almost certain there'd been one or two of the people standing round who had wanted to laugh. Or who had covered their mouths to try and look shocked when they weren't. People who might even have been…pleased?

"She sort of needed punching. Though not punching, obviously, because that put me straight in the wrong. I should have been able to punch her without actually punching her, if you see what I mean. I am genuinely ashamed about that bit, about losing my temper."

Their faces told her nothing so she carried to the end. "And now that I've met you I realise that you know more about violence and intimidation than I've ever imagined. Which makes me feel even more stupid for making such a fuss about my issues that are only to do with sport."

She knew the saying that sport was like war but minus the shooting. But theirs had been a gangland war. With shooting. Siri's mother, who wasn't even involved, had been killed. With Siri strapped to her wrist. There couldn't be much that was worse than that.

"Your sister sounds as if this sailing race is pretty important to her," commented Kieran.

"Yeah, and the rest of my family. Seems like I'm the one who's changed."

There was that silence whenever she used that f-word.

"That isn't so much the issue – they'll get it when I explain. But I am bothered that I might have made things worse for you – because of the pictures on Facebook and stuff."

"I think Jonjo will have sorted that now," said Martha. "There won't be any more photographs."

But Xanthe hadn't completely finished answering David. "And the other main thing that I'm sorry about is if I might have made it worse for anyone else who's being bullied by Madrigal."

"Because when p-people see all the b-bad things that have happened to you, they'll be m-more scared of upsetting her."

"Yes."

There was a defeated sigh around the group.

"When you go into witness protection they tell you you're going to be okay," said Kelly-Jane. "You think you'll have new names and your parents will have different jobs and you'll live somewhere new and that it might be better. Cos maybe you didn't like your old school all that much and maybe there was stuff in the playground that was…wrong. So, even if you do mind leaving your friends and your house and never being able to tell anyone the truth, you think it'll be worth it for your family not to be scared any more."

She spoke as if all this had been bottling up inside her and now it was bursting out.

"But you still are scared," said Kieran. "And your parents are. And then maybe you work out that your dad's going to be put in prison anyway. Whatever he says."

"And he'll be a g-grass," added David.

"So if anyone finds out who he really is – and what he might have said – he'll get beaten up."

"Or k-killed."

"Then you could wish they hadn't done it in the first place – offered to help the police."

"Yeah but, no but—they totally had to. Waddever!" Nelson was passionate.

"Because of Siri's mum," said Kelly-Jane.

"And the big bosses going too far."

Their voices came in a rush. All of these kids had something to say about being bullied and scared. And resistant and brave.

Siri had withdrawn deep within herself. She'd not moved nor spoken since they'd heard the rifle shots. There was nothing anyone could do that would bring her mother back. She would always be collateral damage in someone else's dirty war.

"I don't know why Jonjo hasn't got back," said Martha. "But there's nothing I can do except report it."

She looked at her watch yet again and stared across the marsh towards the other side of the river.

"You have to give a different answer now, don't you?" she asked Xanthe. "You have to go to this match and face her."

"If it stops them thinking I'm personally a coward or that people with my colour skin don't care about history then I suppose I do. But it won't."

"Don't bother then," said Kelly-Jane.

"Except that it's about remembering the dead," said Nelson.

His big brown eyes were fixed on Siri. "They lived in the

same road, her mum and mine. Could have been any of us walking past that day."

"But this don't feel like that. It's more like bullying the living," said Kieran.

"And getting publicity and making money," his sister agreed.

"I hate M-madrigal," said David. "Even though I've never m-met her."

"My sister says it's wrong to hate," said Xanthe. "But – I might not necessarily agree."

She took back her phone and sent Maggi a text.

U & parents don't know half. St Peter's project stinks. Remember WW1 conchies? I might be one. Will decide am. Mad stinks 2 xx X

She was so grateful to David: so grateful to them all.

CHAPTER SEVENTEEN

Mined

Sunday June 2, LW 0822 HW 1436 LW 2036 HW 0256

There was an explosion in the night. Maybe there were several. One after the other, under water – or under mud, more like. They happened soon after it had started to ebb. They weren't big and no one on *Godwyn* exactly heard anything. All anyone could have felt was possibly the vibration; a muffled shock that made the lightship flinch.

Xanthe was up first, then Kieran and David. They'd agreed an early start to wipe the dew off *Fritha*. The barometer was rock steady and if the day stayed as hot and as fine as forecast Xanthe reckoned they could get two full coats of varnish on the Firefly and still have her dry enough to turn over before dark.

They'd started down the short companionway to the working area beside the creek before they realised that it wasn't there. The protective bank that Dominic had built round *Godwyn* had been almost completely blown away. It wouldn't be dew they would be wiping off *Fritha* – if they dared reach her now – it would be mud and pebbles and grass. The hull had been rolled round and over and was dangling above a newly-formed precipice with a sheer drop into the almost-empty creek.

"I think there's been a mine," said Xanthe. Her mouth had gone dry. "Like a buried bomb. It could be seriously dangerous. We mustn't shout or stamp."

She had to get the boys away. Then she needed to tell Dominic and get the others out.

"Here's my phone," she said to Kieran and David. "I know you're not keen on police but we have to have them now."

They nodded. It was obvious enough.

"Go right to the end of the path – run once you're on the gravel – and ring 999 from beside the sail lofts. Tell them we think that there could have been sabotage, then don't go anywhere until they come. And if anyone else arrives, like other boat owners, you have to warn them that they should wait with you for the police."

Could she be overreacting? Was it just subsidence or something?

Kieran and David ran.

Xanthe woke Martha first and asked her to wake Dominic. Then she roused the other kids.

"I might be wrong – and I hope I am – but we need to evacuate. Grab some clothes and pick up your shoes but don't put them on. Tread as gently as you can and meet me by the gangway. Try not to be scared. I don't think you're in danger."

She saw Kelly-Jane giving her the bullshit look.

"Seriously, I think it's *Godwyn* that's in trouble here, not you."

Once the embankment had been destroyed there would be little to stop those tugs coming across the river on the next night's high tide and towing the lightship away.

Fritha's equipment was on board *Godwyn*. Xanthe gave each of the crew something to carry: rudder and tiller, centreplate, sails.

"We tell people not to take possessions." Martha had caught up with them.

"And you're completely right. Can you give K-J a hand with the mast, please, Martha? And maybe a sail bag as well? Think of it as salvage. We haven't any time to argue. Kieran and David are waiting by the sail lofts on their own."

"On their own?"

Martha gave one agonised glance at *Godwyn*'s upper deck before she hurried away with Siri, Kelly-Jane, Nelson and all of *Fritha*'s gear.

"Don't worry," Xanthe called after her. "I'll go hassle Dominic."

The Companion-in-Chief was so totally predictable. He'd made his own phone calls to the emergency services and now he was standing on the outside deck, directly below the tower that housed the foghorn and the lamp. He wasn't even looking at the damage. He was gripping the metal rail and was staring across the river to St Peter's. She felt she could see every bone in his head.

"*Godwyn* stays on station." He spoke without looking at her.

"Yeah, sure, 100 percent. But you need to get ashore and tell that to the police. She's ok right now. Your father can't get his tugs up to take her because there isn't any water."

The backs of his hands were white and all his knuckles were standing up like mountain peaks. There was a vein pounding up the side of his neck. That must be his heartbeat.

"I do get it, Dominic. I've met your father. I realise he's got loads of influence so if he can prove that *Godwyn*'s a danger he might insist on towing her away for public safety."

"He could not!"

"That's OK then. But, if she was mine, I'd be calling up a lawyer – and I know one if you don't. And at the very least I'd be getting along to the end of that path to join Martha and the kids and to convince everyone that you've got the situation totally under control."

He didn't look like a man in control. He'd started to sweat.

"You can do this, Dominic. This is England. It's the twenty-first century. You've got the law on your side. Have some water or something."

The Companion-in-Chief swallowed. She could see his epiglottis convulse. Maybe he physically couldn't get the words out. She took her own advice; fetched a glass of water and handed it to him. He took a deep breath and downed it in one.

"My father part-owns *Godwyn,*" he spoke hoarsely. "He made me pledge her when I founded the charity. But when Jonjo went over to St Peter's yesterday he shot out the cameras."

"Cameras?"

"He'd installed cameras for surveillance. On the top of the scaffolding. They should have been covering the site but they were pointing across here, 24/7. Your friend Anna proved it."

"Anna?"

"She made contact with Jonjo directly. Decided you weren't really listening. She'd worked out the trajectories and the relative density of each image. Plus the type of camera used. They were part of the building contractors' safety spec. Safety spec – that's a joke."

He was bitter.

"He's been watching me all the time, everything I've tried to do."

"So Jonjo...took them out? With a rifle. That's what we heard?"

"I persuaded him to do it. He only wanted to evacuate the

children. I was too angry. Even more when I saw my father flaunting the *Igraine.*"

"You were right." She surprised herself there. "Are we thinking that the Commander's got Jonjo?"

A silent nod.

"You're guessing or you're sure."

"I'm sure."

"Like he's a prisoner?"

"Hostage." Dominic sort of panted out the word.

"Okay, so Jonjo's a hostage – and your dad wants to trade him for *Godwyn?*"

Dominic shook his head. "Not yet. I've still got something else I can use against him – it's my nuclear option. At the moment he just wants you."

"Huh? So what was all this about?" She gestured downwards at the mess of blown-away earth.

"Pressure. Threat. Retaliation. The pattern of behaviour I've lived with all my life. He must have bribed someone to bury these devices when I was constructing the berth for *Godwyn.* They'll have been here since I founded the charity, waiting for me to annoy him more than usual. And now he's detonated them."

Godssakes! Dominic must be well into his 40s. Could be 50, even!

"My father's furious with me but mainly he's trying to keep the other half of Saxon Holdings sweet. He realised who you were when he found you checking out some pillbox or something. His partner has a daughter who wants your head – so it suits my father to give it to her."

"I know that. But what about the kids?"

He looked at her. It was as if he'd forgotten what was totally the most important thing. And it wasn't her feud with Madrigal and it wasn't his precious lightship either.

"I see…No, the children look like regulars to him. He despises all my guests. He thinks Jonjo's some sort of security guard employed by me. He doesn't know he's Special Branch."

"Which means Jonjo's got to sit there and look stupid. Carry on pretending he's your hired muscle. He's not going to do or say anything that links him to those kids."

Dominic was staring as if he couldn't work that out. It was a good thing Xanthe had been checking back down the path.

"The police have arrived at the sail lofts. And I can see a Bomb Squad truck. You need to get along and take control or they might decide to blow up *Godwyn* just to make sure."

That shifted him. He was off the observation deck and striding down the gangplank with a step that could have rattled every rivet in the hull. Xanthe almost felt guilty for scaring him. No one was going to blow up the lightship while his big boss father wanted her so badly. She must be learning mind-games.

The worst danger Xanthe could see was *Godwyn* being officially cordoned off and none of them allowed back for hours – or even days. So she found herself a less conspicuous route out. She climbed over the bulwarks on the Roffey Creek side and let herself gently onto the surviving ledge of mud from which she was determined to liberate *Fritha*. There was still a trickle of water. She could wallow and wade and haul her round to one of the jetties. She wasn't sure exactly why she needed access to the dinghy – she was just definite that she did.

"We gotta put our deaf ears to that telescope again," said Nelson.

"Just c-carry on," agreed David.

"Otherwise we're being wimps as well."

As well as…who? Xanthe didn't think Kieran intended to make her feel bad but he might have succeeded – if she hadn't already made up her mind.

"Yeah," she said. "We carry on exactly as we planned. We put in a morning's work on *Fritha,* while we're waiting for the tide, and then we sail right the way around Oveseye and come back to finish her this evening.

Martha disagreed. She wanted to fetch the minibus and take Xanthe and the children right out of the area. However as Jonjo wasn't around, Dominic could only think about *Godwyn* and she couldn't make contact with Gareth; her position was weak.

"Think about it," Kelly-Jane told her. "You've got professional disposal experts working on the lightship plus sniffer dogs and their handlers checking the whole area. There are two teams of uniformed police questioning all the other boat owners on the saltings. How much more security do you want?"

"We only need a trailer to move *Fritha* to the sail lofts," said Xanthe. "And I think K-J's right about security."

"Please," said Siri. There was a wisp of word as well as the appeal from her eyes and a butterfly touch on Martha's arm. Irresistible.

"Okay, okay."

"But the totally first thing we need to sort is work out how we're going to answer Him Over There."

Martha looked at Xanthe in surprise.

"Surely that's your decision?"

"I've decided all right. The only thing I haven't quite got my head round is *how* to send my answer. Not what I'm going to say."

"So is it yes or no?"

Xanthe couldn't believe she'd ever had a moment's hesitation. Yes, she admired the conscientious objectors of World War One and anyone who truly stood up for non-violent beliefs – like the peaceniks by the chapel, maybe – but something had clicked inside her head when she'd seen the mess that the Commander had tried to make of *Godwyn*.

This was his own son's cherished boat. *And* it was a charity and – control-freak though Dominic might be (and obsessive and insensitive and irritating) – all he was trying to do was to run the lightship as a peaceful retreat for bird-watchers and offer a safe shelter to children in need.

Okay, maybe he had persuaded Jonjo to shoot out the cameras but they shouldn't have been snooping in the first place.

"I'm going to the race, for sure. And it's not to do with anything except for standing up and not being scared – and definitely not being pushed around."

They were in the sail lofts eating sausage sandwiches for their breakfast.

"So how should I tell them?" she asked her crew. "It seemed to me they splashed my refusal over Facebook almost before they could have got it. I'm certain they never expected me to come. But we can't ask Jonjo because he's still not back. Dominic thinks they might be holding him."

"Like a hostage," said Kieran. It was a statement not a question. These children understood too fast.

"Will you ring Arthur Gold?" asked Martha. "Do you need a number?"

"He gave me a card with his contacts but I made out that I couldn't be bothered to pick it up."

"I'll send your message from my phone," said Martha. "Or Dominic can."

"Could you…" said Xanthe. They'd think this was stupid.

"Could you maybe send it in Morse?"

Not many people her age were good at Morse. She was. So if the Commander needed to go check it up, then she'd have one small moment of advantage.

Martha was looking worried. "Only if you do the encoding. I got sent on a two-day amateur radio course but I didn't carry on practising. I'd have to look up virtually every letter. But yes, I could type it in, if that's what you want."

"I'll speak it. We could speak it all together if we practise. Send the recording. Show him that we're solid."

They did it like a band with speaking and stamping and clashing rowlocks and twanging metal shrouds:

Need . Godwyn . Safety . Officer . Then . Okay . For . Your . Match . XR

Dash-dot, dot, dot, dash-dot-dot (pause)
dash-dash-dot, dash-dash-dash, dash-dot-dot, dot-dash-dash, dash-dot-dash-dash, dash-dot (pause)
dot-dot-dot, dot-dash, dot-dot-dash-dot, dot, dash, dash-dot-dash-dash (pause)
dash-dash-dash, dot-dot-dash-dot, dot-dot-dash-dot, dot-dot, dash-dot-dash-dot, dot, dot-dash-dot (pause)

dash, dot-dot-dot-dot, dot, dash-dot (pause)
dash-dash-dash, dash-dot-dash (pause)
dot-dot-dash-dot, dash-dash-dash, dot-dash-dot (pause)
dash-dot-dash-dash, dash-dash-dash, dot-dot-dash, dot-dash-dot (pause)
dash-dash, dot-dash, dash, dash-dot-dash-dot, dot-dot-dot-dot (pause)
dash-dot-dot-dash, dot-dash-dot (ENDS)

"I don't see how anyone learns that stuff," grumbled Kelly-Jane.

"What do spy chiefs call sausages-in-batter? Morse toad in the hole."

"I hope it g-gives him b-brain-ache."

But Martha's phone rang back immediately. She put it on speaker and the Commander's rich voice boomed out into the morning. "Capitulation not before time, Miss Ribiero. Be here before noon on Monday and we'll organise a race to the beaches. I'm considering the position of the so-called safety officer – or should I say saboteur?"

And when Martha instantly tried to call back and demand an explanation and more news of Jonjo, there was no reply and no messaging facility.

"I didn't, like, get that – the saboteur bit?"

When Kelly-Jane didn't understand something, she didn't like it. And she definitely wasn't going to like this when she did understand.

"I'm sorry, K-J, they had cameras pointing over here to spy on us. That's how they got the Facebook photos and everything. But it was still about me, not you. Jonjo shot the cameras out last night. Unfortunately he got caught."

"It sounded like that man was threatening him."

"Yeah, well, I mean, it could be that I have to win the race to get him back but this could all go public – which means they can't hurt him or anything. And I'm telling you that there's nothing I want more in the world than to out-sail Madrigal Shryke, this one time that I'm officially allowed. My *Spray* is completely equal to her dinghy any day. Also Jonjo's a professional. He's tough and he's cool. I just know he'll be okay."

Fritha was clean and dry and varnished and gleaming rich gold and amber. Xanthe and the kids were gathering buoyancy aids and scattered pieces of sailing gear and Kelly-Jane had finished packing a picnic lunch, not helped by Nelson.

"Why won't we get hungry on the beach? Because of the sand which is there – sandwiches, geddit? And what's the best thing to put into a pie? Your teeth."

Iris Farran arrived when they were ready to head off across the saltings. Xanthe's heart sank. Iris was in a wheelchair, being pushed by a carer in a crisp lilac overall. She had a pink fleecy rug tucked carefully around her and was wearing a white sun hat, a flowery blouse and an immaculately clean, cream cardigan with small pearl buttons.

She came straight for Xanthe. Didn't bother saying hello to Martha. Ignored all the children. "He shouldn't have invited you. I know it's a mistake. You're not to go."

She had the invitation envelope on her lap. The one with *Commander of the Saxon Shore* and all the fancy seaxes. Xanthe must have dropped it when she was packing to leave.

Xanthe saw that the old lady's eyes were wet. She remembered how she'd heard the Commander telling her she could watch it all on her new flatscreen TV. Xanthe could see that Iris was hurt.

"I'm not a guest, Mrs Farran. I've only been asked for the sailing. It's some sort of entertainment."

"They could have asked an English girl."

"They have. They've asked two of us at least."

Martha stepped forward quickly and put her hand on Iris's sleeve. "Xanthe's been in training for the British team, Auntie. Uncle Arthur's asked her and one of the other girls to show people how talented they are. I think it's very modern of him."

No, it wasn't modern. It was more like a mediaeval jousting match; she and Madrigal going head to head with the Commander chucking down the gauntlet.

"They didn't have her sort at Dunkirk."

"And fishermen wouldn't have females on their boats and women in the WRNS couldn't go to sea. Lots of things have changed since then, Auntie, and I think they've changed for the better," said Martha. "Xanthe is as British as we are."

"But she's a..."

"Just don't say that word!" Xanthe exploded. "If being white British means living all your life in one muddy little village, getting mean and moany because you're too scared to try anything new, then I'm happy to renounce it. My father is from Ghana; my mother's from Sierra Leone. They both work here and I'm proud of them. My sister and I were born in this country and we are official British citizens but we've also lived in France and in Canada. So, when I'm an adult, I'm going to take a global view."

There were red spots in Martha's cheeks and her dark

eyes burned. She might have had to take a couple of deep breaths but her voice stayed calm and controlled. It was a nice voice. A bit Essex but without her brother Gareth's strong accent.

"I'm sorry, Xanthe, if that's how you see us, here in Flinthammock. We don't all necessarily have a completely free choice about where we're able to live."

Xanthe felt sick. How could she have spoken like that in front of these pushed-around kids, made homeless in their own country? How many times had Maggi tried to shut her up?

"I'm…sorry," she began, "I didn't mean…"

But Martha wasn't going to stop. "I'll speak for myself and then we'll move on. I live here – in this 'muddy little village' – because this is where I belong. There was a moment – after my dad died – when my mother and my brother and I thought seriously about leaving Essex and starting somewhere new, but we chose not to. And it wasn't because we were scared. At that time it felt that we needed more courage to stay. But it was the right thing to do and I'm proud that we did it."

"I'm truly sorry and I didn't mean it about you and your brother. I think you're brave and kind and I'm glad that I've met you. And my sister would totally kill me if she'd heard what I just said to your aunt."

"Then we'll have to leave it that we're different," said Martha. "And I think your sister might agree that you've had some provocation."

The atmosphere was better. Martha was smiling at her. The kids were moving about again. It had been like a sudden summer storm, breaking out of nowhere.

"I don't understand what you're saying," said Iris to Martha. "Where were *her* parents in the war, I'd like to know?"

"Not born, I should think." Martha's smile widened. She was looking at Xanthe, offering to fight this battle for her.

"Her grandparents then?" The old lady wouldn't be stopped.

"Do you actually want to know?" Xanthe asked her.

"Only if you feel like telling us," said Martha.

"Yeah, sure, I'd be delighted. My mother's father was living in Freetown, which was a big British navy base, and he was liaising with the British officers to keep their ships provided with fresh food and everything. It was a necessary job and he made a lot of friends who then looked after my mother when she came to study here. My father's father was in the army – the Gold Coast regiment – and they went to fight in Burma. He was in the jungle for seven years and when he eventually came home he was mentally damaged. I think that's why my dad worked so hard to be a doctor."

"Oh," said Martha. "That's really something. What do you think, kids?"

They nodded, most of them, but they were obviously fed up, standing around listening while their sailing time ebbed away.

"What about you, Auntie? Did you understand what Xanthe was saying? Did you hear her answer to your question?"

Iris was looking down at the invitation envelope. She hadn't understood anything. She was still hurt and miserable and suspicious.

"You must to be careful of her," she warned her niece solemnly. "She has dark powers. Have you seen that she has raised the *Igraine*?"

"Dark powers! Yeah – that sounds like me. And do you know

what else I've raised? I've raised your ebony walking stick!"

She asked David to fetch it from the sail loft and, remembering that Martha was a policewoman as well as a Farran and a local, she described exactly when they'd found it – and where.

"And how did you know that the stick was hers?" asked Martha.

"Because I'd seen it in Rebow Cottage. When she and Mr Farran were watching TV on the evening before he died. When I think that someone hit someone with it. I'm just not sure who."

Tears were trickling from Iris Farran's eyes and Siri had moved up close and was holding her hand. The carer looked approving.

"Don't cry, Nana."

Now, at last, the rainbow effect. Iris looked at Siri and smiled – and Siri smiled back at Iris.

"She ain't your Granny," said Kieran angrily but Kelly-Jane shook her head at him. Her eyes were bright with amazement.

The carer, who didn't know that there had been a miracle, wondered whether the girls would come to tea one day.

"Would you like that, Auntie?" asked Martha. "Would you go home now and make them your special scones?"

"But not me!" said Xanthe quickly.

"No," said Martha, kindly, "Definitely NOT you."

CHAPTER EIGHTEEN

Vigil

Sunday June 2, LW 0822 HW 1436 LW 2036 HW 0256

"You can say what you like," Martha told him, "The children are not sleeping on *Godwyn* tonight. I know you're going to be there and I know there'll be a security presence and I know that the lawyer Xanthe told you about has got all approaches ringed around with injunctions like electronic tripwires, but in the absence of Jonjo – which is *your* fault – I'm responsible for their safety and I've contacted county HQ and they're agreeing with me. End of."

The Bomb Squad and the sniffer dogs had gone; the police had taken names, addresses, wads of statements and they'd left too. In the time it had taken for Xanthe, Martha and the kids to have a totally brilliant sail all the way round Oveseye, with some significant exploring near Flinthammock Pier, *Godwyn* had been meticulously searched from stem to stern and the entire area around her had been checked and pronounced 100 percent safe. There was no official objection to them going back and carrying on as normal but Martha wouldn't have it.

"So where are you going to sleep?"

Dominic was doing his best to keep his voice casual. Xanthe'd been sent to the Happy Haddock – she was getting like a regular there – and they were all in the sail lofts eating hungrily out of polystyrene containers with small wooden chip forks. There would be no washing up today.

"Undisclosed." Then Martha relented, "Shall we tell him, crew?"

"It's a t-tower," said David.

Xanthe loved the way he said it with a shiver of excitement in his voice.

"It's in the m-middle of a f-field and it looks right down the r-river."

"And when it was wartime the Navy built it so they could keep a look-out against invaders," added Kieran. "Then p-zow they'd press the button and the whole river would go up. They'd laid mines."

No-one was noticing Siri. Not even Kelly-Jane.

"It's mainly used for storage now," Kieran carried on. "But there's a room on the top floor where we're all going to sleep together like we were in a tent or something. But when we want to wash – or whatever – we're going across to a farmhouse."

Martha smiled. "You've guessed it, Dom. It's the old watchtower beside Mum's. We could all have slept in the farmhouse but we're thinking this'll be more fun. Plus the view's amazing. We can look right down to St Peter's and they'll never know."

"Spy on them like they spied on us." Kelly-Jane got angry whenever she thought of the photos.

"What's the difference between a dog and a flea? A dog can have fleas but a flea can't have dogs."

"What about you, Xanthe?" Dominic sounded resigned.

"I'm staying on *Godwyn* tonight – if that's okay?"

"You don't have to. There'll be some volunteers to help me keep watch and the tower might be useful for your project."

"It would, except I'm hoping for a good night's sleep before tomorrow. And I've more I want to do on *Fritha*. I wish I could speak to Gareth but he's not answering his phone."

"Hey, who's for a round of cards? Just to let the food go down." Martha's voice was uncharacteristically loud.

It wasn't long before she and the kids were gone, all buzzy and excited, and Xanthe found herself walking back to *Godwyn* with Dominic.

"Do you think Gareth could be in danger?"

"More likely to be in the Plough and Sail."

"Since yesterday evening? I don't *think* so!" She hated the way Dominic talked down his cousin. "I'm sure he had something on his mind. Something to do with that pennant."

"Pennant?"

She hadn't realised no one had told him.

"When we were down at the oyster beds, all of us, Kieran found a long red flag, tangled into one of the racks. It couldn't have been there that long – a tide or two, maybe. Gareth reckoned it had been left there by Eli and was meant for him. He said it was from the *Igraine* and Martha thought so too. She and Jonjo bagged it up as evidence but Gareth got quite emotional. He and Martha would have had a row if we hadn't been there."

"Farrans!"

"What is it with all of you and that boat? Iris has been accusing me of practising some sort of black magic ever since I happened to take some mirage photographs that happened to show *Igraine* crossing the estuary. That was the morning you dragged me back…"

She was glad he looked embarrassed.

"Was it because she'd caused trouble for your family?"

"It was a set-up." He sounded as angry, as if the accusations of smuggling had been yesterday.

"But now the *Igraine*'s moored alongside the Mulberry pier. She'll probably get her own page on Facebook."

"He won't ever stop," Dominic muttered. He sounded more bitter than angry now and Xanthe guessed he was talking about his father.

"So what did the investigators discover about last night's explosion? Was it an explosion?"

"It was a couple of pieces of old ordnance. They could have been there for years."

"I suppose things like that do turn up sometimes. I mean, this was a World War Two defence area and that was almost like being a battle zone."

"Except that I had the whole of this mud berth checked before I brought *Godwyn* here." He spoke bitterly. "And all the extra material that I used to build that quay was professionally screened."

"Is that, like, normal?"

He looked at her and didn't answer. Was Dominic normal? Were any of them?

"I wish I could talk to Gareth." She hadn't necessarily meant to say that aloud.

"I know you're trying to help, Xanthe, and I'm sincerely grateful for all you did this morning but I truly don't care about the present whereabouts of Gareth Farran. *Godwyn* is my priority. She's like a trust."

"And you're feeling seriously threatened by your father. Okay, I get it. So what would you like me to do?"

His answer shouldn't have come as a surprise. But it did.

"Beat that girl he's setting against you. Get Jonjo back if you can – but beat her anyway. For your own sake. Sail her into the ground."

"Okay. Thanks. I'll give it my best. I was really offering to take a watch for you."

"There's no need. I've asked a few of the Companions. Do your exercises. Get some sleep. Do whatever you need to be ready for tomorrow."

"Any other advice?"

"Don't trust my father. Not ever. He's a liar, a bully and a snob. He's worse than any Farran. And what he has he holds."

"You don't think he'll give back Jonjo?"

"He wouldn't give you the phlegm from his cough – except as a distraction while he siphons off your heart's blood."

But he'd given Iris a flatscreen TV and he'd previously given Dominic money for *Godwyn*. And now he was giving all those Dunkirk Little Ships donations just for being there. Did that mean he would be taking something really important in return?

She must have been staring. Dominic went a bit red.

"That's been my experience of him, anyway."

"Thanks. And I mean it. Thanks for the warning. We left the project dinghies in the Flete. If I should need to borrow one is that okay?"

He nodded. "And go out sailing on my own?" She knew she was rubbing it in.

Another nod and he walked rather awkwardly away.

Xanthe put herself through a half hour's intense muscle-toning routine then she took her sleeping bag and some water. Plus a torch, a notebook, chart, tide table, compass and a block of Kendal mint cake. She was going to get a few hours bivvy down near the CND pillbox and she was going to look across the river and she was going to think.

She walked along the inland side of the river wall although she didn't think that anyone would be watching her. She wanted to be private, to go off radar.

At least that was what she had thought she wanted.

She felt in her pocket. Yes she'd got her phone. Ought she to text Mags?

No, she ought to call her. It was the weekend now. They'd made an arrangement.

"Hi, sis."

"In your own time, sis! I was gonna start dragging your creek."

"Are Mum and Dad bothered? That I haven't rung sooner?"

"Trying not to be. They keep telling each other that you're grown up and perfectly able to cope on your own."

"To be fair, that was the deal."

"Except the way they say it, it's like news. And they sort of take turns as if it's the other one who needs convincing. It didn't exactly help when they were watching 'Down on the Marshes' on TV East and saw something about your lightship getting blown up."

"Since when did they watch that stuff? And anyway why weren't you at the Club? It's Sunday. You could have been racing."

"Duh. It's called revision – which Anna and I take more seriously than you ever did. And they've been watching TV East ever since you left. There's some guy across the river seems to have the local PR machine totally whirring his way. Anna said he was the one who installed the surveillance cameras. His group sponsors Madrigal."

"Yeah well. I need to get on now. Good luck tomorrow. In your exams, I mean."

"You on Planet Zog? It's maths tomorrow."

"Best make sure you're sitting next to Anna then. Ouch! Did I say something? Sorry, can't hear that. You're breaking up. I must be going out of signal. Say goodnight to Mum and Dad and tell them that I'm doing that challenge. Sorry, can't hear you. By-eee."

She found the same space that Siri had used, and she settled down in her sleeping bag to think about all that had happened over the previous week and what might be yet to come.

It was getting dark and it wasn't especially warm. There were lights on the other side of the river and distant sound too. Not clanging and sirens but snatches of music. Fairy lights along the newly assembled pier; deck lights and light spilling out from cabins and portholes. Xanthe guessed there would be hospitality, food and drink, maybe a band.

If this was the nose drips, whose was the heart's blood?

Her sleeping bag was in a tough outer sack. She was glad of that as she snuggled down at the base of the river wall and breathed in the slightly salty, vaguely fishy, potentially rotting smell of the tideline at the saltings edge. She looked upwards and wondered how long it would be before she would spot the first of the stars.

Then she found herself trying to remember that Sherlock Holmes and Doctor Watson joke to tell Nelson. This wasn't what she should be doing. She'd come here to think. She needed to ask herself what the Commander was after and specifically what traps Madrigal would be springing on her tomorrow. Yet all her brain was offering was the struggle to polish a punch line.

The stars are out, Holmes, and the moon is rising in the northern quarter. I see Orion's Sword, Ursa Major and Sirius the Dog Star. What do you deduce from that?

Watson, my old friend, it strongly suggests that someone has stolen our tent.

Xanthe giggled weakly and shifted into a more comfortable position. She wished she'd brought something to go under her head. Her buoyancy aid…ah, that was good.

Behind her, as darkness closed over the saltings and the marsh and the flood tide came welling up the creek, Dominic turned *Godwyn*'s light onto full strength and it shone out like a beacon across the black waters.

She found herself thinking sleepily about the chapel of St Cedd-on-the-Wall. She'd been near there a couple of days ago when she'd been sailing with the kids to the mouth of the river. So small and plain against such an enormous sky.

There hadn't been time for the kids to land. She might have noticed an inner channel that would reduce the need to go far out to sea but there was a complex system of anti-erosion defences that she wanted to check out at low tide first. She'd heard the Companions talking about the guided walks they took along the far side of the river so that people could experience that extraordinary sense of space and travelling out of time. She wondered whether that was what had happened to her in that black night with *Fritha* when the *Igraine* had come ramping home?

The Saxon Shore Development was a huge scheme. Where had all that money come from?

Little Miss Oy-ris – our own personal crock of Gold. Remember that, Eli, me boy."

But Eli didn't have enough money to buy himself a pint of beer. And Iris needed to take lodgers.

And who's the richest fish in the river? That un's the GOLD fish.

Y'r fancy man.

No, your brother.

She'd never understand the intertwining of the Farrans and the Golds. It was like a Monkey's Fist knot: complex and tight and almost all of it invisible from the outside. Xanthe sighed. Maybe she'd should walk back to *Godwyn* and spend the rest of the night in her cabin.

It was after midnight. She could hear a boat coming up the channel inside the Spit: it wasn't heavy enough to be a tug, nor purry like *Miranda,* but it did sound familiar. A fairly standard outboard on some fairly standard workboat? Xanthe stood up and gathered her things.

There was a small figure hurrying along the wall, heading in the direction of Flinthammock. It almost collided with Xanthe and let out a tiny, inarticulate cry.

"Siri! Whatever are you…? Does Martha…?"

Xanthe hoped Martha didn't know that the youngest and most vulnerable of her crew was out alone in the night. If she did, she would be frantic. Something must have gone badly wrong for Siri at the tower.

Xanthe took the child's hand. She made herself stand completely still.

"It's okay now Siri. I'm Xanthe. I'm here too. You're safe with me."

Were they safe? Xanthe was texting Martha as they stepped quietly along the marsh wall. Then they heard the workboat engine stop. There was splashing. Someone was coming ashore at Fisherman's Hard. The light from *Godwyn* came swinging round and caught him in its beam.

"Jonjo?"

"Xanthe! Siri! Whatever…?"

"Never mind about us for a moment, we're on our way back to *Godwyn*. You've got away! That's so fantastic! But whose boat did you use?"

He shrugged and sounded surprised. "I didn't exactly ask permission. I took it because it had an engine thet I thought I could work."

"It couldn't be Gareth's workboat, could it?"

"Gareth's? Why…?"

"Because he's been out of contact for two days and the last thing he told me was that he was going across that side of the river to pick oysters. It was after the evening when we found the pennant."

"Hell, I don't know. I was just glad to get away."

Martha called back at that moment. She hadn't known Siri was gone. "That child walks through walls. Kelly-Jane would have been devastated."

"I've got good news too, we've just met up with Jonjo."

She could hear the relief in Martha's voice. "Oh thank heavens!

Could you pass me across for a moment? I need to tell him why I've moved the kids up here."

Xanthe passed Jonjo the mobile. She was still holding Siri's hand. They could hear Martha's kindly, anxious voice bringing Jonjo up to date with the explosion at the lightship.

"You're in charge," Xanthe said to Jonjo when the call was over. "You're the pro and it's such a big responsibility. Martha's been completely terrified of getting it wrong. I couldn't say anything to start her worrying about her brother now."

"We don't know anything anyway. Look Xanthe, where is this watchtower? I need to get there. I'll take Siri back with me."

Siri, pulling away and shaking her head. Letting go of Xanthe. Poised to run.

"What is it, sweetie? What's upsetting you so much?"

Xanthe put her arms round the child. Tried to pour a feeling of safety into her.

"Dead. Fish."

Huh?

"Sounds gross. Poor little Siz."

Xanthe still didn't get it.

"Their. Home."

"What is this watchtower?" Jonjo asked.

"I don't think it's anything now. Maybe storage? It was built in the war as a lookout point. They could detonate a minefield if there was an invasion."

"Then I think I can guess what's troubling young Siri. It's the collateral damage again. If you detonate a mine at sea, you'll be killing all the nearby fish as well. More innocent passers-by caught up in someone else's war."

"Oh yuck."

Maybe Siri would be better just staying locked away from the pain of life.

"Were you going back to *Godwyn* to keep safe?"

Siri nodded.

"That's good – that's what *Godwyn*'s for. And me too. Except I ought to check that the boat isn't Gareth's."

But it was.

"Where exactly did you find it?" she asked Jonjo again.

"Tied under thet pier thing. I can't go back. My job is with these children."

"For sure – but you must see that you've probably left Gareth in danger."

"Only if he's doing something illegal."

That was a bit rich coming from someone who'd been shooting out other people's cameras but Xanthe let it pass.

"I've no idea what he's doing," she said – which wasn't totally true. "Look Jonjo, there's been a lot happening over here. Obviously Siri needs you to take her to *Godwyn* first off and Dominic can fill you in on everything else. I've got permission to borrow one of the Picos. So I'll take that with me, return Gareth's workboat and be back later."

"Thet'll be seriously late. Okay. I can't see any alternative. You'll need to take a lie-in tomorrow."

Lie-in? Tomorrow! He didn't know what was happening tomorrow – and she wasn't telling him. It was today, now, anyway.

"Sure."

Siri gripped her hand. Shook her head.

"Siri, please, can't you trust him?"

No words. A tighter grip.

"Has Jonjo done anything wrong? Has he ever done anything to make you afraid of him? Don't look at him, sweetheart, look at me."

Siri looked at Xanthe, a long impenetrable look. Xanthe didn't dare move or hardly breathe. She remembered Min, the Chinese boy, his abuse by the fat policeman. She prayed to something somewhere that she was doing right.

Slowly Siri's eyes filled up with tears. She took a long shuddering breath.

"No," she said, definitely.

"Okay, my love. You're afraid because he's a man. But I believe that he's a good man and it's his job to keep you safe."

What if she was wrong?

Siri was looking at Jonjo who was also standing completely still. Then she transferred her hand to his. It was a tiny gesture but it was also huge.

"Thanks, Siz. I'm texting Dominic to say that you're both on your way. Look at *Godwyn*'s light. It's beaming out for you. You'll be back in your cabin before I'm halfway down the Flete."

"Immobiliser cable?" she called after Jonjo as the two of them set off.

"It's in the boat. And I found it on the downriver side. Third section along. Hidden beside some old wooden one."

The Dunkirk Little Ships were there. They'd almost all be old and wood.

"A boat with a mast?"

"Thet's correct. And one of those things thet stick out from the front."

Monday June 3, LW 0900 HW 1508 LW 2108 HW 0330

There were clouds crossing the moon and a wind was beginning to get up. The music had stopped. The edges of the pier were still illuminated, but only a sprinkling of anchor lights indicated the sleeping Little Ships. Gareth's workboat was a dull olive green and she and her clothes were dark. She'd cut the engine and drifted onto the pier. If anyone had happened to look at her directly she would have been seen, but it was two in the morning now.

Gareth was exactly where she'd expected. He was hidden on board *Igraine*, waiting for the tide to turn so he could cast off her warps and let her drift free on the ebb.

"I spotted her here, must have been Friday. Would have taken her last night except there was too much going on. They'd caught that South African chap, Dominic's policeman, and Artie Gold was coming and going all night with the dratted *Miranda* of his. So I pushed off early and picked my quota, then I made sure I got some kip before I were back here again."

"You should have told Martha. She's been really worried."

"Couldn't exactly leave my phone on, could I?"

"You could have sent her a text. She's had total responsibility for the kids without Jonjo there and there was an explosion on *Godwyn* and she hasn't even been able to admit that she's been worrying about you."

He looked a bit ashamed. "Knew they was up to something last night. Didn't know it were an explosion. Kids okay, are they?"

Xanthe nodded and sent Martha a quick text herself.

"I was angered when she started playing policewoman over

that pennant. They could have taken a photo. I weren't going to run away with it."

"But now you're going to run away with the smack?"

They were whispering in the darkness.

"Too right I am. Thought I'd buried this piece of trouble nigh on thirty years ago. Cousin Dom and I swore a solemn oath we'd never tell anyone where we'd sunk her. He must have cracked."

The noise of the boat's hull against the fenders and the tugging of her warps had changed.

"Tide's turned," said Xanthe. "And we've only a couple of hours before it's light. Were you planning to put a headsail up here or wait until she's drifted off? Where are we going, anyway?"

"I didn't ought ter let you be saying 'we'. You've enough of yer own problems."

"Not yet I haven't. And I need a boat to get away from here. Without your workboat I'm stuck. I'd been going to tow one of the Picos across but they're so white. I might perhaps have misled Jonjo about that."

"So we'll both be eatin' humble pie for breakfast – if we get any. Let's slip them warps and then we'll see what you think about headsails. I've always worked with engines myself but she ain't got one. Ain't much of a sailor."

"You own *Fritha*!"

"She's a different story. Reckon we'd best get going."

The tide was making an eddy on the downriver side, pinning *Igraine* tight against the pier. Xanthe eased the staysail up without so much as a rustle and held it aback until the bows swung silently away. Then they were out in the main stream and Xanthe was working out by feel where the main and peak halyards were. It wasn't until they were half a mile down river, sailing smooth and fast, that either of them spoke again.

"Where *are* we heading?" Xanthe asked.

"There's a little cut round the back of Meresig, right far up that Coldlight Creek. Goes up into the marshes to a farm. There's an old barge quay. But it do get shallow."

"What does she draw?"

"I'd reckom about four foot six"

"That's almost a metre and a half. We'll never do it in the time. How legal is this, Gareth? Whose boat is she really, Farrans or Golds? And how was Dominic involved?"

"It were thirty year ago and I were that distraught. I were fifteen and my dad had died and Eli were in prison, so I took it out on the boat. Cousin Dom helped me sink her. I didn't exactly question his rights. He and his dad..."

"Didn't get on," Xanthe finished for him. "I know, I know. I think it's hideous. He's been standing guard over *Godwyn* expecting a snatch attempt by his own father. So don't get me wrong, I'm on for taking anything that'll upset the Commander. But with this wind and tide we could be out to sea and down the coast. That was why I was asking whether we were legal. Because I was beginning to wonder what my parents would think if we arrived home with *Igraine* for breakfast at the club?"

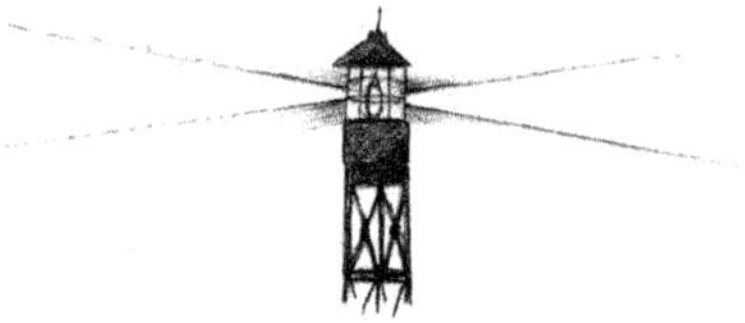

CHAPTER NINETEEN

Black Flag

Monday June 3, LW 0900 HW 1508 LW 2108 HW 0330

There was a glimmer on the eastern horizon soon after they'd passed the entrance to the River Colne and by the time they were half way down the Essex coast it was daylight. Xanthe had spoken to Dominic at about four in the morning when she knew that the tide would have turned and the threat to *Godwyn* had passed for another night.

"Listen up, Dominic. You told me that you had, like, a nuclear option. You said that there's something you could say to your father that would totally keep his hands off *Godwyn*. I want you to use that, now, for Gareth and *Igraine*."

"Where are you Xanthe? Jonjo told me you were using one of the Picos to take the workboat back. You've been far too long"

Dominic sounded tired and cross. Gareth took the phone.

"Xanthe's been helping me remove the smack, Cousin Dominic. We're out of the river now and I'm a-looking due east, where that old sun is a-coming up, red and bloody, behind the Gunfleet Sands."

"The Gunfleet!"

"Where our uncle Eli drowned hisself not a week ago."

Xanthe sat stock still, hardly bothering to put her hand on *Igraine*'s tiller. They were towing the workboat aft, the breeze was on her quarter and the smack was so well balanced she was virtually sailing herself. No-one had told her where Eli died. OMG! All the way out here!

"Them sands don't look quite as they did back then – that night you'll remember…"

"I understand your reference, Gareth Farran. I don't forget the Gunfleet Sands. Neither do I break my word. We promised each other we would keep silent for ever."

"That we did. So why did you tell your old man?"

"I have told no-one where we scuttled the *Igraine*. Certainly not my father. If I knew the date of Judgement Day, I wouldn't tell him."

"Then how did he get his greedy hands on her?"

"I have no idea." There was exhaustion in Dominic's voice. "Unless the surveyors found her when they were building that wind farm."

"An' if they did, why would they tell the Commander? She was never his property. *Igraine* belonged to Farrans. Look at the work Eli put into her."

"Farran sweat, Gold money. Did you ever ask yourself Cousin Gareth, why I helped you sink her?"

"We were kids. You were on half term from your posh school. You probably thought it were a lark."

"If only that were true. It was A-levels and I was desperate to apply to university to study theology. My father wouldn't even discuss it. It felt as if he was going to dictate my life forever. Then I discovered that he'd been lending Uncle Eli money. Not out of kindness – I knew my father better than that – it was to make Eli do something in return. He'd made Eli pledge the *Igraine* against his debt."

Even Xanthe knew that this pretty fishing smack had been the most important thing in Eli Farran's life.

"Eli went to prison after your father died," Dominic continued. "It was probably my father who put him there. He was obviously broke and he owed your mother compensation, which he would never have been able to pay. The *Igraine* had been pledged so that when you came up with your crazy idea, I saw my first chance ever to stop my father getting something that he wanted."

"Dunno why I ever thought to ask you."

"I was glad that you did – though she's a Gold boat properly."

"No she ain't."

Xanthe took back the phone.

"Don't start that again – Farrans and Golds! It's so totally immature. The point is, Dominic, that your father is planning to use *Igraine* as the showpiece for today's event. But we've got her and as soon as anyone wakes up at St Peter's they'll see that she's gone. However, because Jonjo has also escaped, your father will assume that it's him who's taken her and that he's working for you. I want you to call him and sound like you're the mastermind. Then you tell him that if he tries to get her back before all the legalities of her ownership and *Godwyn*'s are sorted out, you're going to go public on whatever it is that only you and he know. He's high profile. It'll hurt."

There was silence. Then Dominic disconnected.

But no-one came after them as the red dawn lightened and the billowing low clouds cleared. They shared Xanthe's mint cake and took turns to sail and catch up on sleep.

"How *did* Eli die?" Xanthe asked Gareth at one of their handovers.

"They didn't tell you?"

"I asked but they offered me counselling instead."

"Took his little flat dinghy out ter the sands. Anchored as though he were fishing, waited until dark, then he overturned her. He tried to make it look like an accident except everything were properly fastened and she don't overturn easy. He couldn't swim. Probably filled his boots and went straight down. Wind farm patrol boat found the dinghy first thing. Body weren't far off. Fetched up against one of them turbines."

She thought about it for a while.

"You'd think he chose to die out there because he was trying to get back to *Igraine*. Which would be why he left you her pennant. He obviously didn't know that she'd already been salvaged – but how would he have known that she'd been sunk there in the first place?"

Gareth looked a bit awkward.

"Well, don't tell Cousin Dominic but…I let on ter him. Once I'd grown up a bit and I'd stopped feeling so angry. Poor old beggar, he loved this boat. I knew he couldn't do anything about it – he hadn't got the money to have her raised or anything – and I reckoned he needed somewhere to look out and grieve."

Watching the grave? She remembered Donny's Great Aunt Ellen saying something like that.

"What about you? Your father drowned. Did you have anywhere to think about him – anywhere special, I mean?"

She thought he wasn't going to tell her, but he did.

"Should you ever happen to be passin' quite close in to Colne

Point, near where the chart marks an old wreck, you might see a scrap of black flag on the end of a stick. You'd likely think it were marking an old lobster pot. But it ain't. That's where my dad died. Only Martha and my mum know that. An' Uncle Eli of course."

They didn't talk to each other, these Farrans: they left signs. As the smack sailed them along the coast, Xanthe told Gareth about the broken teapot and the trampled sampler at Rebow Cottage and she described finding Iris's walking stick by the landing stage in Broad Marsh Creek.

"It was almost like he was leaving a trail – which started at Rebow Cottage and ended up at your oyster racks – and then the Gunfleet Sand. I even heard something smash in the night. But I still don't know how he'd got in. I'd done what Iris wanted, I'd locked and chained the door."

Gareth laughed. "Elijah Farran were a crafty old beggar – and that cat were his accomplice."

"Joe?"

"Named for my dad an' friends with everyone. Except he don't like Artie Gold –I've seen him spit. Anyways he an' Eli worked out a little routine when Eli got locked out by the missus. He'd bring Joe a bit of something tasty – cod's roe or whatever – and come up the back path to that cat flap. Then when Joe hopped out to get his treat, Eli would nip a pole in quick to stop the flap from swinging back. He had an old bamboo flagpole ready to reach through and wriggle off them chains and bolts. *And* put 'em on again after. I don't reckon she ever suspected a thing."

It was a good story: it made Eli seem more human. As if he was someone who might have once been a boy.

"Why do you think he did it? Breaking those things and throwing her stick in the creek?"

"Expressin' his feelin's? Auntie Iris used to say as he were a bully, but I allus reckoned she had him well under her dainty little thumb. He wouldn't have been no good with words but I reckon there'd been something that night that had pushed him over."

"That could have been me. He told her she'd brought a darkie into his parents' house."

It had shocked and upset and angered her then. Now, explaining to Gareth, didn't bother her at all. Except, if had been so bad that it'd driven Eli to kill himself…she wasn't sure how she felt about that.

"Don't reckon it were that. Not that finally tipped him. I saw him that night you first came. He came down through Broad Marsh on the tide, then round the back of Meresig into Coldlight. He were upset right enough but he were only going to spend a bit more time in his boot-room and out around the creeks until you'd gone. We had a bit of a chat like. That's why I were so took aback when I heard he were dead. There must ha' been som'at else. Danged if I know."

Gareth went below, then, for a couple of hours sleep, which gave Xanthe more time to think as the waves heaved and surged and the ebb tide hurried them past the sunshine coast. By the time they were rounding the Naze and Gareth was on watch again she had realised where she'd been going wrong.

"I think Iris hit Eli with that stick after they'd had that quarrel. I even heard her. But I was just totally sexist – and angry – I assumed it was the other way round. I thought he'd hit her when she called him a sot."

"In 'er dreams! Poor old boy hardly never had enough money to drink more'n a half pint unless I treated him for shaking out my oyster sacks. But you might be right about the hitting. I did the identification and there were a mark across his face but I didn't think nothing of it. It would have been a terrible blow to his pride. She might as well 'a finished him there and then."

"Will you say so at the inquest?"

"Probably not."

"*Because there's things that's best not mentioned if you want to live together for the next two hundred years*. I don't actually believe that. I'm quoting."

"And I'm agreeing. *That-a-ways you can still say a civil good morning to folk or accept if they want to buy you a pint in the pub.* Eli'd had a pint or two that night – more'n he could usually afford."

"Mrs Farran might have thrown him some money. I think he was threatening Commander Gold. He said he knew something..."

"Did he now?"

"Yeah – but he didn't say what, and obviously *there's some questions best not asked.*"

"It don't suit you, being sarcastic like that."

She wasn't below for an hour before she was needed on deck again. They were approaching Harwich Harbour and the tide had turned.

"I know I said we could go to the club – but I'm not so sure. I've been thinking about the race this afternoon and my stomach's tying itself into double granny knots. I don't think I can face any of those people – even my parents – until after I've gone head to head with Madrigal. And, ideally, beaten her."

"D'you want to jump?" Gareth asked. "You could use the workboat an' take off. I'm grateful that you shipped along but I reckon I've got the hang of the sailin' now. Nice little boat."

"Iris called her a death-ship, which does seem harsh. It's been the people that have caused all the trouble, not her."

"I won't be asking Cousin Dom to scuttle her again, if that's what yer thinkin'."

"Right now, all I'm thinking is where we should leave her here she'll be safe. I'm thinking of somewhere that's less public than my parents' club. My friend Donny's got a mooring off Gallister Creek. It's up the River Stour and he lives there on a Chinese junk with his mum. They went to Holland for half term but they'll be back now. It's GCSEs. We could leave the smack alongside *Strong Winds,* then I could take a taxi back to Flinthammock in time for the race. I've got some money."

"Y're avoiding y'r own family."

"Only until this evening."

CHAPTER TWENTY

Black Star

Monday June 3, LW 0900 HW 1508 LW 2108 HW 0330

The stretch of water between Shinglehead Spit and the Saxon Shore was crowded with boats. There were neat, white, modern yachts and woody old timers – big, black Thames barges down from Fishling with their rich tan sails, and rakish smacks from Meresig with flying jibs and topsails set. Although half-term was over there were scatters of dinghies in every direction. They must be from local sailing schools, Xanthe supposed.

Igraine had been left in the Stour, safe alongside *Strong Winds* and Gareth had set off back up the coast in the workboat.

"I'm going to need her, anyways. I've still got me livin' to earn."

Dominic had been the only person around when Xanthe had reached *Godwyn* and she had yelled at him. She was late and tired and strung out. She would have yelled at anybody.

She wanted him to help her get *Fritha* back into the water – as soon as there was any water – and he couldn't see why she needed her.

"I thought you said that your Laser would be there – *Spray*, isn't it?"

"I need to get across, don't I?"

"All the Picos are down by Fisherman's Hard. They're accessible. Or I could lend you the RIB? I don't understand your obsession with that Firefly."

She didn't either – which was one of the reasons she was cross. She had all that time with Gareth and she'd never asked him what it was that made *Fritha* special.

"*You're* an obsessive, Dominic. You do stupid, unreasonable things because you think they're right. No-one has a clue what makes you tick and you don't seem to care. Look at the way you treat Martha."

"Martha? Martha's my cousin. She's almost like my sister…"

"Yeah, yeah. And you're probably the main reason she's stuck around Flinthammock all her life. In case you need your nose wiped or your shoelaces tied and you can't manage to do it yourself because your head's got jammed in the turret of this lightship. What happened to your mother, I'd like to know?"

He went sheet white. Grabbed a piece of *Godwyn* to steady himself.

"Oh hell, Dominic, I'm sorry."

When would she ever learn to stop assuming that everyone would have had two functioning parents? She'd scarcely met any uncomplicated families around here. His mum must be dead or have abandoned him or something.

"I shouldn't have said that. Please believe me. I'm so, *so* sorry. It's none of my business. Total disconnect between tongue and brain."

He breathed deeply. "Not a disconnect," he managed, "more like a super-conductor."

"I *am* sorry."

She wasn't going to make excuses: say she was tense, or tired, or anything.

"Remember this morning?" Dominic was struggling to

explain. "The nuclear option? That's what you called it."

"Yeah, I remember. So it's to do with your mum and it's totally painful. You don't need to say another word. Of course I'll use one of the Picos. I don't understand why I'm stressing about *Fritha.* Your father said I didn't know what I'd been given and he's right. There'll be plenty of time for me to find out later. I have to remind myself that there is life after racing. Shake hands, Dominic."

He did everything she wanted. There wasn't enough water to launch in the creek but they brought the Firefly out of the shed on a trolley and took her to the boatyard slope near the marina sill. Then they put her on a long line that they attached to the frame of the RIB.

As soon as the RIB could float, and there was even a puddle of water over the sill for *Fritha,* they set off with Dominic towing and Xanthe hard at work. She was reeving on the new sheets she'd bought from the chandlery and fitting a set of almost new – but very old – sails that Martha's mum had left for her while she'd been away. They were cotton, she supposed, and still nearly pure white, with that sail number 486.

There was something about them that was whispering to her, but she couldn't understand what they said.

"She fetched them from the watchtower," was all that Dominic knew and Xanthe was too busy to phone Martha or ask any more.

She felt completely lonely and at the same time absolutely visible. Everything she did was a distraction from the task ahead. She needed to focus on Madrigal.

Soon.

Now.

It was quarter to twelve when Dominic landed her alongside the Mulberry Pier. There was almost no wind and the few wavelets bulged as lazily as setting jelly. The fleet of Little Ships, moored six deep, had run up a rich variety of flags which were hanging lifeless in the still air. The seaxes and the flags of St George that festooned the half-built hotel dangled limply downwards and only the Saxon Holdings banners fixed stiff as wallpaper along the jibs of the massive cranes were able to spell out their message clearly.

There was wind on its way, she was sure of that. The question was when? If she hadn't been insulting Dominic she'd have had time to check windfinder on the internet. She knew that she was better than Madrigal in a real blow. She was physically stronger for one thing – that 'classic West African figure' meant that she was at least a stone heavier. Madrigal was a lake racer. She was sharp and superbly balanced, ready to make *Imperium* move to the least quiver in the atmospheric molecules.

Would she be good on the tides? Her connection to Saxon Holdings meant she could have been down here, training. And if you knew your currents you could get very close to your fellow competitors in light winds and you could drift alongside hissing like a water-snake, destroying their concentration with nicely planted insults.

"We are sorry, ladies and gentlemen, members of the Hundreth, that it is approaching high noon and the young African racer Xanthe Ribiero (name mispronounced) to whom we had hoped to offer the opportunity to begin to expunge her recent disgrace, has not seen fit to arrive. We extend our condolences to His Excellency the Deputy High Commissioner of Ghana who might have hoped that his country could begin to make some showing in this quintessentially English sport."

Her arm shot up to wave; she opened her mouth to yell but there was a crackle and a whistle and a new, young voice cut across the Commander's plummy tones.

"It's only five to twelve and if Xanthe hasn't made it yet there'll be a good reason which she can explain for herself. Until then, if you look out on the river now, you'll see her sister, Maggi Ribiero. Her dinghy's called *Kingfisher*. I'm Anna Livesey and I'll just say that Maggi is also a great sailor in her own right. Any country would be glad to have her in their team but her view is that sailing is a skill and a pleasure and it's something to share and to celebrate, not something to turn into a sort of war and use any means to bring down your opponents. Like some people I could name."

Anna had hacked the PA system. Maggi was out there in *Kingfisher.*

But they were meant to be taking their GCSEs!

Xanthe ran up the metal walkway though the sea of big hats, designer dresses and navy blazers with brass buttons. Everywhere there were seax ties and lapel badges and seax silk scarves tied casually to the straps of expensive handbags.

She couldn't see her parents. Griselda was there but she was standing with Madrigal's personal trainer. Only her history tutor, Mrs Oakenheart, a big, blonde, clever woman, smiled and waved. But where was *Spray*? She needed to get out there and take on Madrigal, take the pressure off Maggi.

Maggi…here…racing! Had their parents gone crazy? They'd never been allowed to miss so much as thirty seconds of schooling to be on the water. Let alone a GCSE exam!

Had she maybe got the wrong date? No, Donny had gone off early this morning before they'd arrived at Gallister Creek. It was beyond her.

"We are an Island Race…" The Commander had got control of the system again. She did her best to tune him out.

Then she saw one of her sponsors, Mr Hutchison Bennett.

"We've done as you asked us," he said, without even saying hi or asking how she was. "I can't say the board is happy with the new image – there's no commercial advantage for us in that area – but we're still backing you, Xanthe, and we'll give you this one chance. I can't understand why you've left it so late. Hurry along now, your dinghy's ready, I'll help you down to the water."

There was her dinghy. But it wasn't her dinghy any more.

Spray had been re-sprayed. The cool, Vela-grey hull, so pale you'd call it white, was now black. The dinghy was already rigged and Xanthe could see that the sail scarcely flapping in the calm air had lost the GBR letters that she'd been so proud to earn. In place of the official country code there was a black, five-pointed star.

"It's a compromise." Mr H-B was still talking. "We felt you were being unreasonable in demanding a completely new sail made in the Pan-African red gold and green colours. Nevertheless we were prepared to accept that your withdrawal from the GBR squad and your forthcoming application to sail for an unrecognised country did put you in a difficult position. We couldn't make contact to talk it over so we went ahead as we thought best."

"But…" said Xanthe. "I haven't ever…"

"You wrote to us, offering to give the boat back after that unfortunate incident in Weymouth. We hadn't any intention of withdrawing our sponsorship – we'd heard something of the other side of the story and we were quite ready to sit out the ban with you. We didn't much like the social media coverage but we'd decided to ignore that as well. Then you messaged us about your decision to search for your roots and you listed the changes that you wanted us to make."

"I did what?"

She stood completely still and stared at him.

"We couldn't get in touch with you directly and your mother told us that you needed some time on your own. We respected that and we would have waited. Then we heard from today's organisers that you were eager to make some sort of public statement. They've invited the Deputy High Commissioner."

"OMG. I am so sorry." How many more times would she need to say that? "I never thought you would allow me to keep *Spray*. But the rest of it…isn't right at all!"

"You don't mean *Spray*, do you? You mean *Black Star*. You were completely definite that you needed your dinghy to have a new name for this new beginning."

"NO!!"

Mr Hutchison Bennett was a pale-complexioned man with receding brown hair and permanent worry lines. Although his chief executive job with the Port of Felixstowe sent him around the world to the most exotic places, he looked as if he'd scarcely ventured outside his Suffolk office. His grey eyes blinked behind his spectacles.

"Is there something wrong, Xanthe? Have we misunderstood each other?"

"In spades! But it's none of it your fault. You've been totally amazing! It's all mine for simply assuming that you'd dump me. And then for going off-air and leaving other people to write the scripts. Oh, *Spray*!"

"Not *Black Star* then?"

"No! Never! I was never going to go racing anywhere else. GBR is the best in the world. Why would I not want to be among the best?"

Mr Hutchison Bennett looked pleased for a moment. Then his worry lines were back. "You'll withdraw from today's event in that case? I'll square it with the board. You're too late anyway."

There was a burst of patriotic music then the Commander's voice came booming back. "…so we will leave the police to do their duty in searching for the stolen smack and we will not hasten to judgement over the involvement of this embittered young girl and her deluded friends. Once again, Your Excellency, ladies and gentlemen, veterans, distinguished guests, members of the Hundreth, I bid you welcome to the Saxon Shore!"

There was some applause. The way people clap when they can't be bothered to put down their glass.

"We are gathered to commemorate a great national event and we are also at the outset of a major new project which will regenerate this forgotten corner of our country. You can already see the progress we have made developing these redundant blocks into a unique mix of luxury hotel living and serviced executive apartments that will gaze onto a floating armada of historic vessels."

Blah! Blah! They wouldn't be gazing at *Igraine* or *Fritha* and not *Godwyn* either, as long as Dominic held his nerve.

"These empty fields will provide the venue for battle

re-enactments and exercise to drill the youth of today into a compliant force ready for any occasion that they may once again be needed to repulse the invader. We will not tolerate the un-English, the slackers or the vagrants, and today I am able to inform you that we have permission to re-dedicate the ancient chapel of St Cedd to the warrior gods of old mythology."

She could see him cloned across a range of big screens, his white hair flung back, his face looking out as if onto a new dawn. She longed for Anna to pull the electronic plug on him.

"So, for your appreciation today we have invited the best of our home-grown sailors to race round my own island of Oveseye. They will be led by that brightest English talent, our own Madrigal Shryke. Her former rival has shirked this challenge. There will be no *Black Star.*"

Xanthe looked at Mr Hutchison Bennett and he shrugged.

"I suppose you'd better…?"

Then she looked at *Black Star,* her own beloved *Spray,* re-branded without her knowledge or consent.

"Young members of our island race, racing around an island. The finish line is before you and the first race will be judged on normal handicapping rules. But today we commemorate a defining moment in our national consciousness – when our Little Ships played their decisive part in bringing our own folk home from a foreign shore. For today, the newly sponsored Saxon Dynamo Grail has been placed in the chapel of St Cedd. There is a second race. Speed alone will count."

There was another burst of static as if Anna was trying to get through. It stopped abruptly.

"Meanwhile lunch will be served to our distinguished guests

and the youngsters must set off as swiftly as their ancestors. The Blue Peter is flying. They have four minutes."

Four minutes? And *Spray* still on the trailer.

"Sir Hubert sent his daughter's rigger over. You only have to run her down to the water."

Madrigal's team had set up her dinghy's equipment? Oh great!

"I'm sorry. I'm not going to."

But even Mr Hutchison Bennett seemed to have been infected by the Commander's speech.

"I think you must."

"No," she shouted back, leaping back down the sloping gangways. "Sorry. We'll talk about everything later. I've got an alternative statement that I'd like to make."

Fritha – whose name meant peace. She'd use *Fritha* – never mind that she was many times slower than the modern dinghies. She couldn't remember the Firefly handicap rating. Corrected time might help her position in the race round Oveseye but there was no chance of her beating *Imperium* on speed.

Somehow none of it mattered. *Fritha* was the boat for today. She must have known it all along subconsciously.

The wind was coming. Sudden random gusts were sending catspaws across the water. She saw a lady catch her hat and laugh. A dinghy from one of the sailing schools gybed and was over. The smacks were taking in their topsails.

Spray loved heavy weather and so did Xanthe: she'd never sailed *Fritha* in anything other than the most favourable breeze. She'd have to trust her. All she needed to do was to get out there and join the race.

Dominic had left and the Firefly was trapped on the wrong side of the pier. Someone arriving even later than Xanthe had moored a small motor cruiser on the outside. However could they do that! Should she take *Spray* after all? Ignore the unwanted makeover, trust that her gear had not been set up to fail? She was undoing the motor boat's stern line even as she rejected the idea.

"What d'you think you're doing? Leave that warp alone. Sir Hubert told me I could moor here."

"I can't help that. I need to get out please. This is my dinghy. I'm in the race."

The man looked at her. She saw his recognition. "You're that…girl."

"I'm Xanthe Ribiero and I need to make the start."

"You're violent and you're in trouble."

"Utter rot." A familiar voice, used to being heard. "Heaven knows what you thought you were doing when you moored that tub on the outside of a wooden dinghy. Now you can make yourself useful. You can pluck her off and pull her out into the stream. She needs to get to the start."

It was Griselda. "Hullo Xanthe. What a *fantastic* find! Get on with it, man. Don't just stand there gawping."

And when he still hesitated she took action. She was across the Firefly and into the motor boat and telling the owner to get his engine on while she attended to the lines.

"Okay, Xanthe, get your mainsail up. F 486 – utter *magic*! I never thought I'd see that again. The Blue Peter's down. You've got less than a minute."

Even before Griselda finished speaking, Xanthe heard

that distinctive wailing sound. The All-Clear. The race had begun.

"Hmph," said Griselda, "That was a fraction over-sharp, I'd say. Never mind. Do your best. You needn't be afraid to reef. That was Elvström's trick in '48."

Elvström? '48?

As she hardened in her sheets she heard Griselda shout. "Where's *Spray*?"

"Still on her trailer." Xanthe shouted back. "She's *Black Star* now and I don't trust her rigging."

But her words were snatched by the rising wind. The club racers and all the sailing school dinghies were streaming upriver. And that could be Maggi in *Kingfisher,* way out on the starboard side of the line.

Fritha was slipping through the water as if she'd been oiled, not varnished. This was the dinghy she'd dreamed.

The wind was wildly fluky. Violent puffs from varying directions interspersed with moments of complete, disconcerting calm. Xanthe sat forward, blessing her new smooth-running sheets, loving the dinghy's responsiveness and poised like a hawk to take full advantage from every shift.

The fleet was beginning to stretch out on the long upwind leg. She could definitely see Maggi there with the leaders.

"Okay sis, you've bunked off school. I'm shocked, so I'd better be keeping you company."

Everything was coming together. Xanthe was a racer; this was what she did. She felt she was breathing pure happiness as she and *Fritha* began moving up the order.

Her new tacking system was good. If she eased the mainsheet slightly, cleated it, then used the jib, she could almost accelerate as she came round. She passed dinghy after dinghy as their skippers made mistakes in the complex conditions. The leaders weren't getting away from her. One or two might even be coming back slightly.

Not *Imperium* though. *Imperium* was way ahead. She was sporting an enormous red seax on her sail and treating the race as if it was a procession. Madrigal must have made a super-perfect start. The only person not to be surprised by the over-early signal?

The wind dropped away again, almost to nothing. Xanthe stayed still, using her weight and her helm as little as possible. Only her head and her eyes moved as she searched for those elusive puffs. Everyone else was doing the same: sitting still, keeping watchful, trusting the tide to carry them upriver towards Oveseye and the first mark.

A familiar purry engine almost made her jolt. It was *Miranda* and her owner. *Miranda* with passengers: Siri and Kelly-Jane, Martha – and Iris Farran!

The Commander came cruising close beside her. Much too close. He had a colourful Seax streamer and a race official's pennant flying from the varnished flagpole on *Miranda*'s short aft-deck.

Mrs Farran smiled and waved. She was tucked around with coats and rugs and was wearing a thick silk headscarf on her white curls. She looked tiny but triumphant. Martha almost waved as well – except Xanthe could see that Siri was shaking her head and Kelly-Jane was deliberately folding her arms and looking away. Siri understood about dinghy balance. Kelly-Jane understood about Siri.

Xanthe knew that her pupils wouldn't be expecting her to wave back. She was shocked that they were there.

The Commander positioned his motor launch at exactly the right distance for her wake, slight as it was, to fan out in front of *Fritha*, imperceptibly slowing the Firefly.

"Interference!" shouted Xanthe.

The judge's boat would be anchored somewhere near the mark beyond the island. Much too far away to notice what was happening and, at this moment, she couldn't see any other race official. Except the Viking. One by one the dinghies she'd already overtaken began catching her up again.

She tacked. It was strategy not a defeat. She drifted at an oblique angle until she had a clear view of the end of the island and knew that the judge would have a clear view of her as well.

Miranda was forced to alter course but now it was Xanthe who was ahead of the spreading ripples and was using their momentum to help herself along. How peculiarly satisfying! She gave the girls a nod and a grin that she felt certain they'd interpret correctly.

Possibly the Commander understood it too. He opened his throttle and swerved away.

"Neat!" said a familiar voice from astern. There, drifting up river with her dinghy in perfect equilibrium was Griselda. She was sailing *Black Star*.

"I thought I could do my bit to keep your sponsors sweet," she added. "As well as our distinguished visitors, of course. Your sister's sailing nicely. Plenty of talent on these East Coast rivers, I've always said. Ah, well, on I go. I expect I'll see you later when the wind gets up again."

Black Star was overhauling *Fritha* inch by inch. Xanthe could see Griselda's lean weather-beaten face, creased with concentration and delight. Then her coach appeared to make the slightest error of judgement. It left an opening for Xanthe to alter course and foul her wind from behind.

Xanthe didn't hesitate. She slipped across. Got in the way. Watched *Black Star*'s purposeful progress falter and slow.

"Very good," Griselda called back. "I was afraid you might have learned some scruples while you've been on leave."

She corrected her own course and began to draw away again.

Where was the wind? Xanthe sighed in frustration. *Fritha* couldn't begin to compete with *Black Star* and the other top Lasers in these conditions.

She looked ahead to the leading group, watched them approaching the island. *Imperium* reached the mark. Madrigal's progress was silky smooth. She was demonstrating a textbook rolling gybe. She'd need all her momentum to counter the tide, thought Xanthe.

Then the sail deflated. *Imperium* stalled. Madrigal glanced at her wrist and pushed her tiller hard away from her. She was swinging the Laser into an eddy, an unsuspected patch where the current set crosswise round Oveseye, following the course of a submerged creek. Within seconds *Imperium* was slipping out from the shadow of the island and was heading confidently down river in the gossamer breeze. It had been a beautiful, knowledgeable manoeuvre.

"Very neat in*deed,*" commented Griselda.

She spoke rather loudly and Xanthe guessed that she had been meant to hear: that Griselda was telling her that she wasn't partisan; that she was still supporting Madrigal as well as herself; that they were still her two key competitors for the one top spot

Xanthe stared intently, lining up the mark against a clump of trees on the further shore, trying to establish the coordinates Madrigal must have used to step onto that invisible tidal conveyer. She noticed Maggi in *Kingfisher* and one or two others of the leading dinghies trying something similar but without the same success. Madrigal's placing had been impeccable. Her glance at her wrist was possibly the giveaway.

The sky had paled and high white wisps of cloud were moving swiftly in the upper atmosphere. Down on the far southwestern bank a vicious purple bruise was spreading up and over the vanishing shore. The instructors accompanying the sailing school groups hurried to gather together their students, take in their sails and attach them securely to the safety boats. The more experienced club racers tensed in anticipation.

For one last time the water surface seemed to congeal. It glassed and slopped. All the dinghies slowed until they were nothing more than feathers on the tide. Those who had already gybed but who hadn't succeeded in following where Madrigal had led began to drift helplessly backwards.

It was as if the weather was holding its breath. The dinghy sailors, watching, held theirs too.

Then Xanthe spotted a small, multi-coloured raft: four kayaks bobbing together downstream of the mark. She recognised the occupants – David, Kieran, Nelson and Jonjo. She could see that they had their paddles crossed horizontally in front of them, linking them together. She realised that they were looking at her, not at the distant darkness or the spreading cloud. They had no idea of the danger and were waiting to cheer her on her way.

CHAPTER TWENTY-ONE

The Chapel on the Wall

Monday June 3, LW 0900 HW 1508 LW 2108 HW 0330

The hard, dark line of the wind swept the greying river. Lightning flashed above Fishling and the sky around them howled. *Fritha* leapt into life as if she'd been galvanised. Her sails were straining, her lee gunwale was almost submerged as she rocketed ahead.

Xanthe had both feet hooked beneath the toe straps and was hiked out horizontal. She had loosened the sheets as far as she dared but she couldn't hold the Firefly upright. She didn't have the weight to maintain her course. Until the squall passed all she could do was abandon the mark, bear away and run.

She was rounding the island now and rampaging down the river. She saw everything sideways, her head just a few feet from the surface of the water as she strained to keep *Fritha* from capsize. There was Madrigal; there was Maggi; there were the racers from Meresig and Brittlesey – taut, white triangles against the iron-dark sky. All of them still battling for supremacy as well as for survival. What a race it had become!

But it was a race she would have to abandon. She had to get back to the kids. How could she find the strength to bring the Firefly round into the wind? How could she drop out?

An orange RIB tore across her path, leaping and slamming between plumes of spray. The driver was Dominic. He was standing forward, gripping the wheel, peering ahead into the storm. His pale hair was soaked, his face bleached with anxiety as his tall, bony frame absorbed the impact of each smash. He hadn't gone back to *Godwyn*.

The dinghy beside her capsized: another appeared to have blown out its sail. Xanthe lifted herself a few degrees above the horizontal and looked round. Everything that had been blue, mellow and reflective was now slate-grey, foam-flecked, indigo. All the official safety boats were busy. She hoped the Commander had got *Miranda* and her passengers safely under cover.

A Laser surged towards her. It was *Black Star*. She had rounded the mark and was heading down river with her mast jutting forward at a crazy angle. Griselda was letting the dinghy run. It was all she could do. Then, even as Xanthe watched, the whole rig blew out of its step and collapsed. *Black Star* lurched, swivelled, stopped. Griselda thumped her fist on the gunwale before she began loosening the mainsheet in order to push mast, sail, boom and vang off the hull before she swamped.

There was nothing Xanthe could do to help. She stared upwards at her own bellying mainsail. F486. The blocked black lettering on the strong white cotton.

Suddenly she had it. She'd seen this exact sail in storm conditions before. It was in a drawing in one of the many classic racing books on the shelves of the Sailing Academy library. But the sail had been reefed.

You needn't be afraid to reef. That was Elvström's trick in '48.

Griselda hadn't listened to her warning about *Black Star*; Xanthe hadn't listened to Griselda.

Elvström. The Danish sailor who'd won more Olympic gold

medals than anyone (until Ben Ainslie came along) had won his first gold in a Firefly. F 486.

This was the dinghy. She was sailing an Olympic champion's boat! Gareth had assumed she would have realised. The Commander of the Saxon Shore had been outraged.

What else could she remember? This was good history. It was 1948. London – Torbay, actually. Elvström had been a teenager – hadn't he? Very young, anyway and, crucially, lighter than his opponents. Too light for the Firefly – this actual dinghy! – in heavy winds. So he'd reefed her hard and had survived to win.

This would be her only chance. She couldn't wait for the squall to pass; she steered *Fritha* close under the lee of the island, tore the jib down and put two rolls in the mainsail. Then she thought of the kids and their kayaks and put in two more rolls. Rescuers had to think differently from racers. They needed to be quick, but they also needed to arrive.

She pointed the Firefly into the wind and headed back upriver. Out of the corner of one eye she saw Griselda coping with the wreckage of *Black Star*. She was over the stern of the dinghy, gripping the transom and kicking furiously, swimming the Laser ashore.

The wind shrieked and a flurry of hail pummelled her cheek. It made her want to shut her eyes but she had to keep them open. How could Jonjo not have checked the weather? The hailstones came pinging off the mainsail as if it were a trampoline. Then they turned to rain. Great fat drops bombing onto the water.

Suddenly she was there, where the kayak raft had broken apart in the wind and waves. She let her mainsheet fly and *Fritha* stopped. She saw Dominic heaving Kieran into the RIB and

Jonjo had his kayak clamped firmly against David's, holding them both rock-steady. Two out of three.

Where was Nelson? She twirled her dinghy, staring every-which-way until she saw him coming towards them. There was rain streaming off him. His paddle was flailing and his smile splitting his face in two. She hauled her sheet and sent *Fritha* darting towards him.

"What does the sea say when it sees the shore?" he shouted. He must have had that one ready for her.

"Nothing," she shouted back, feeling the rain running warm down her own face. Or maybe it wasn't all rain. Had she ever felt such relief?

"It just waves!! Go show'em, Cap'n Xanthe!"

The kids flourished their paddles. Jonjo gave a thumbs-up. Dominic gestured to her to head back downriver to rejoin the race but Kieran, level-headed Kieran, pointed his paddle to the mark.

He was right. She hadn't yet rounded it. She'd be disqualified. Though she was out of contention anyway.

With her reduced rig it was the work of a moment to tack back those extra few metres and pass the buoy on the correct side. The judge's boat was moored there with a number of dinghies clustered alongside for safety. Madrigal, Maddie and the rest were downriver, almost out of sight.

Xanthe hoisted her jib and unrolled *Fritha*'s mainsail twice. Then she was gone.

Hell, she was so happy she wished she'd unrolled it all. The wind had lost its initial bite and the downpour was flattening the water, but the Firefly was still a two-man dinghy and she was only one girl – albeit with the blessing of her sturdy figure. Once she had rounded Oveseye, it was a long broad reach to the Mell Creek marker. She had to hike out to keep the dinghy flat and, although part of her was beating herself up for her cowardice in keeping *Fritha*'s mainsail so small, she couldn't help noticing that she was upright and most people weren't. The fastest racers – the survivors – were far away. The rest had capsized, retired or been stopped by the organisers.

She glimpsed one solitary spectator as she passed the place where the pier had once been. Xanthe guessed she was female but she was wearing a long dark raincoat with a hood covering the top part of her face and the visibility was poor. She definitely wasn't anyone that Xanthe knew but she was waving uninhibitedly.

At that moment, Xanthe and the woman seemed to be the only two people in the world. Xanthe let *Fritha* come up for a moment and released one hand to wave back as she passed. It was possible that the woman cheered.

The rain and wind had eased slightly but the Firefly wasn't sailing so well. She felt sluggish. Xanthe realised that her dinghy had been filling up with water. This would never have happened in the small well of a Laser but *Fritha* was big and deep and… boat-shaped. Either she had no self-baling system or it had been overwhelmed by the downpour.

Xanthe had no choice. She turned the dinghy head-to-wind and baled vigorously as the sails flapped and the minutes passed.

"1940s design fault there. I wouldn't have caught you otherwise." It was Griselda. Somehow she'd re-stepped her mast, refastened her cleats and was back on the water. "Someone made a damn silly error when they rigged this dinghy. It wasn't you, was it?"

"No, it was NOT."

She emptied the last of the rainwater and swung away down river.

Griselda was sailing more cautiously now, checking *Black Star*'s equipment. "Don't wait for me," she said. "Push on, for heaven's sake."

It was pointless. Xanthe had already heard the All-Clear sounding repeatedly to greet the finishers as they completed this section of the challenge. She hoped Maggi was okay. Her sister had never enjoyed heavy-weather racing since she had broken her collarbone in an October gale.

There was no siren for her as she passed St Peter's and no comment from the loudspeaker. The other dinghies had gone on again, racing for the chapel and the invited spectators would be inside the marquees finishing their lunch and watching events on screen. Presumably all those smacks and barges were running some race out to sea somewhere. If they had cameras with them, beaming back footage, there'd be enough entertainment to content the Deputy High Commissioner and the Hundreth and all those other distinguished visitors. There'd be lavish food and plenty of wine and conviviality with the owners of the historic Little Ships.

Yet again, Xanthe wondered why.

She took out the last two rolls from her mainsail and lifted her centreboard to run freely towards the point. The sky was clearing. She could see Laser sails in the distance. Maybe eight or ten, clustered together. She supposed she'd meet them on their way home.

Miranda came flying down the river. She was something

extraordinary at full speed. More rocket than boat. She rounded the point and vanished from sight.

"You're dawdling," said Griselda. *Black Star* was sailing freely now.

"Ok then, watch me," replied Xanthe, adjusting her course. "Any route to the chapel, okay?"

The tide was almost at its height. She'd give Griselda a race. The Laser was quicker than the Firefly of course and her coach was a former champion, but Griselda wasn't sailing home waters.

"OMG!"

She thought she'd had enough shocks for one day but there was *Godwyn* being towed slowly down the channel by a Saxon tug on the far side of Shinglehead Spit. Her vivid scarlet was unmistakeable. Dominic had abandoned his post for a single afternoon to watch over the kids in a storm and his father had stolen his life's work.

And she'd almost certainly facilitated this by forcing Dominic to use his 'nuclear option' to protect Gareth and *Igraine*. There was nothing she could do to help and she had failed to achieve the single thing that Dominic had asked of her. Beat Madrigal.

Black Star was sailing like *Spray* again and Griselda was pulling away fast. She was taking the obvious route, following the marked channel well to the outside of Sales Point.

Xanthe adjusted her course. There was more than one way to win a race and, if Griselda didn't notice what she was doing, Xanthe could win this one on navigation.

They were the last to join the small fleet of racing dinghies pulled up on the shell bank before the Chapel of St Cedd. Xanthe would cherish the moment that she and *Fritha* had shot out from inside the rubble and the sea defences that were protecting the point from erosion and had heard Griselda shout, "Damn!" Everything else was failure.

Miranda had dropped anchor a couple of metres off, within easy wading distance from the long flat shore. The weather front had passed, the sun was shining, the air seemed washed and luminous. There was even a rainbow arching over the small plain chapel.

Not so plain today. The building had been festooned with red and gold and purple banners with gilt tassels and black symbols: not only the ubiquitous seaxes but horned helmets and fists clenched inside gauntlets. The banners had been disarranged by the wind and soaked by the rain. They looked wrong and unnecessary in the glowing landscape. The wannabe Viking was posed in front of the ancient building holding an ornate gold cup.

"Speed alone will count. You couldn't have put it more clearly," said one of the Brittlesey racers, an eighteen-year-old who Xanthe recognised as one of their top competitors. "I was here first. I claim the prize for the River Colne."

He was relaxed and confident.

"I was impeded. Harassed all the way by…*that*." Madrigal was white with fury, except for two red spots in the middle of her cheeks. She gestured towards Maggi.

"Wherever I went she was in my way, fouling my wind, forcing me to luff, pushing me across other competitors. She wasn't sailing to win; all she wanted to do was make me lose. She was sailing me down the fleet from the moment we left St Peter's. Every one of you must have seen what she was doing."

Maggi stayed quiet and smiled: the other sailors nodded and laughed.

"It's an accepted tactic in fleet racing," commented a cheerful lad from Meresig. "I bet you've used it yourself."

Madrigal ignored him. She was shaking with anger as she appealed to the Commander of the Saxon Shore.

"She took no notice when I called for water. I protested her several times. She could have taken penalty turns at least. She ought to be disqualified."

"But that still won't make you the winner," said the boy who was holding out his hand for the trophy. "Because I was here first."

"Did you want to make a formal presentation, sir?" he asked politely. "If not, my friends and I'll be heading back. The tide's on the turn now. It's been an excellent afternoon and I hope you'll invite us again."

Commander Gold muttered something and shook his hand. A cameraman took a single, unenthusiastic photo. The club racers began walking back to their dinghies.

"Hi, sis," said Maggi to Xanthe. "You took your time."

"Hi, yourself. Why aren't you in exams? It was maths today."

Maggi rolled her eyes. "Because Anna and I already took maths at Christmas. All the top set did. Have you no memory?"

"Obviously not! It's good to see you, sis. Gimme high fives!"

But they didn't bother slapping palms: they gave each other a huge sisterly hug.

Madrigal had not left with the other racers.

"Your sister is a deceitful little cheat. She should be ashamed."

"*Are* you ashamed, sis?"

"No, I don't believe I am. Perhaps I'll feel differently when I watch the video that my friend Anna's just uploading to YouTube and Facebook. She recorded the entire final section as she walked along the river wall. Though obviously it wasn't quite as good as using high powered surveillance cameras from the top of Daddeh's construction site like some people."

Madrigal rushed at her, nails ready to claw. Stopped abruptly when she noticed Griselda. Took a huge, shuddering breath and pasted a smile onto her ravaged face.

Xanthe almost admired her. She searched for something neutral to say.

"It was impressive how you found that current round the top of Oveseye. Have you got one of those new GPS watches?" she began, but she never got a chance to finish.

"Uncle Arthur! Where's the peace camp? WHAT HAVE YOU DONE?!!"

Martha appeared, breathless, from the secluded wood beyond the wall. She had Siri and Kelly-Jane with her but not Iris.

The Commander of the Saxon Shore put on that smug look that Xanthe really, *really* loathed.

"We've helped them move away, since you ask, little Martha Farran. They were never going to be happy here once we begin rebuilding the Othona boot camp. And when all the Little Ships and our distinguished visitors began arriving, my workmen had nothing else to do. We decided an assisted evacuation was in order."

He wouldn't give you the phlegm from his cough – except as a distraction while he siphons off your heart's blood.

So this was what it had all been about. Diverting public attention while a non-violent community was evicted and their homes flattened. And his own son's lightship removed. *Godwyn* was still in view being towed implacably towards the horizon. Where was she going?

"I'll never speak to you again."

He smiled. "No need, my dear, no need. You stay on your side of the river and I'll stay on mine. I've offered your aunt Iris an apartment in my new St Peter's Saxon Shore complex in exchange for that poky little cottage of hers. She'll be lodging with me on Oveseye until it's ready for her to move in."

"You're not planning to accommodate her with your WIFE then? In the asylum."

Martha had squared her shoulders now. Her brown eyes blazed.

The Viking stood very still. No one else dared move. Except that Xanthe noticed her mother and Anna arriving quietly from behind the chapel. She signalled to Anna that she should record what was happening, if she could.

"I've no idea what you mean."

He tried to turn away but there were enough of them to block him.

"You know exactly what I mean," she said, articulating every word. "You may have forgotten that I'm more than 'little Martha Farran', your dead half-brother's younger child, I'm also an Essex Special Constable. You may not realise how often our work in the community requires us to call at sad, secluded places like the private clinic at the top of Broad Marsh Creek."

The top of Broad Marsh Creek! The house behind the

landing stage where Eli had hurled away the walking stick on his last desperate night!

"I know that you placed your wife there many years ago, when she suffered permanent damage working as your drug mule. Nothing could be proved against you – or done to help her. I've been watching ever since but I promised Dominic that I wouldn't mention her existence for as long as she remained safe – AND AS LONG AS THIS SITE STAYED SACRED!"

This was Dominic's secret, his mother – a drug mule. Now Martha had pressed the red button.

"I don't think my son will thank you…" the Commander began.

"He'll be fine," said Martha. "We understand each other. We always have done."

The Commander wasn't listening. "The poor woman was already an addict when I met her," he carried on, pulling his walrus moustache as if he was sad. "I've been supporting her these forty years."

"Using Iris's childhood home." Martha wasn't wasting any sympathy on him. "I've always wished I knew how you ended up with all Augustus Gold's money and property while his only daughter was left in Rebow Cottage, married to your brother Eli and taking in lodgers."

"Oh!" said Xanthe. "I think I can tell you that."

Everyone turned to look at her.

"I've been studying local history while I've been living in Flinthammock. It's not the sort of history that's going to help me write my extended essay for Mrs Oakenheart – but it is a Dunkirk story. It was on the last night of Operation

Dynamo, that everything changed for Iris Augustine Gold."

"You were not there." The plummy voice was angry.

"I realise that. And I'm an outsider here, as I've been reminded often enough, but outsiders sometimes get a clearer view. I've interviewed Iris Farran and recorded her answers and I've thought about the moments where she wouldn't answer and where she got upset and insulting. I've come to believe that the reason she behaves like a disturbed and spoiled child is that she was so badly let down by everyone around her on the night her father died. And that was June 3rd 1940, the last night of the evacuation."

"YOU WERE NOT THERE!" Suddenly he was shouting.

"But you were. You were 'Artie' in those days and *Artie was in the middle with the light*. And *Artie saw...*"

"Artie didn't *see* anything at all, ignorant, barbarian girl. We were showing no light. You have no conception what we were enduring. Artie *heard*."

"Okay, set me straight. What did Artie hear? You were on a lightship in the middle of the English Channel. Possibly it was *Godwyn* herself, the lightship you have just stolen from your son. What did you hear? Exactly. And by the way, my friend's recording this."

He didn't seem to care. He stood beside the chapel he had desecrated, looking outwards. The rainbow was fading from the tranquil afternoon sky but they could tell he wasn't seeing it.

"I heard something bumping alongside in the dark. We were rattled by then. Stuck there in the middle of the carnage – defenceless and almost useless. There had been bodies – burned, drowned, mutilated bodies – but bodies don't make that kind of noise. Our first thought was E-boat – and what could we have done against armed raiders? It wasn't the enemy, however; it was a little Calais fishing boat escaping before the surrender. She'd been strafed by a Messerschmitt and it was a wonder she was floating. They were mainly French on board. Exhausted, wounded, end of their tether. But the man at the wheel wasn't French and he wasn't a fisherman either. He was the Major from the big house, Miss Iris's father, Augustus Gold – the man who paid my mother her wages. It was obvious he wouldn't be doing that for much longer. He'd one leg shot off at the knee and an arm gone. He'd tied himself to the wheel but he wasn't going to make it into Ramsgate. There wasn't anyone else fit to take over so he'd run alongside our lightship for help. Specifically he wanted…me."

He wasn't the Commander of the Saxon Shore any longer – or the Chief Executive of Saxon Holdings plc – he was teenage Artie Farran, the boy who'd grown up, unhappily, in a fisherman's family and had escaped from home by joining the lightship service as soon as he left school.

"The Major knew that he was dying and it wasn't long before he did. And before he went he told me something that changed my life."

Everyone stood completely quiet.

"He told me that Fisherman Farran wasn't my father." His voice grew harsh and strong. "The Major was my father. He didn't pretend it was a mistake – or a love affair. I was the cuckoo in the Rebow Cottage nest. He'd forced her. Planted me on the Farrans as a revenge from them turning us in all those years before."

Xanthe could have felt sorry for him – for this ex-teenager, learning the callous truth about his birth in such terrible circumstances. But she didn't.

"So you chose to behave like one. That's what cuckoo chicks do – they chuck out all the others from the nest so they get everything. You never went back to your real mother in Flinthammock. She had lost her husband as well, don't forget, when the *Igraine* hit the mine on her journey home. Both the fathers of her children in a single day. You didn't go to comfort Iris, the little girl who loved you and who you now knew was your secret half-sister. You went straight to the big house and confronted Mrs Gold. I don't know whether you bullied or charmed or blackmailed her – in the shock of her grief – but I'm quite certain you were the reason that she didn't take Iris when she left for Scotland. She took you."

"I was a boy. I was the oldest. She was glad of me."

"And even if she hadn't been, I don't imagine you would have given her any choice."

He smiled. Strong and triumphant. The Survivor.

"It weren't enough though," A new voice joined in unexpectedly. "She were a spender, that Mrs Gold. Your little crock at the rainbow's end weren't as full as you'd ha' liked and there were some of it that had, in law, to go to Iris. So you turned smuggler."

"God save us, it's the oyster-grubber. Who invited you?"

"This foreshore wasn't private property last time I heard. And I ain't been grubbing oysters; I've been lifting lobster-pots. I reckon there's plenty of folk who'll be interested in what I found."

"Sounds as if the salt has finally turned your brain." The white-haired Commander stood stocky and proud.

"Reckon my little bit of lifting might have landed me the Goldfish," Gareth answered. "You see, when old Eli left me *Igraine*'s red pennant, tangled around my racks, not so far from the low water mark, I realised that he'd had a bit of time to spare. He'd left Broad Marsh around high water – we know that as he left his wife's stick high up in the creek where you can only reach at the top of the flood. That left at least six hours before he were fixing the pennant at the bottom edge of the oyster racks. An' I guessed how he might have spent 'em."

"Swilling, I'd imagine."

"He'd had his last pint by then and he'd sat in the snug at the Plough and Sail an' he'd written his confession."

"Knowing that you'd come swilling there later?"

Gareth ignored him. "Then he'd returned home one last time with some little bits of business to attend to there and he'd made sure his paper were wrapped up watertight. And once he'd done all that he needed – to settle his accounts with his wife, like – then he got hisself into that little flat boat at the top of Broad Marsh, which was to be his ferry to his death and he took his package to the black flag. That's the flag above the lobster pot off the end of Colne Point that marks where my dad died. And, as I now know, it's one of them places where Eli used to haul up smuggled goods for you."

"I'd stop there if I were you, oyster-grubber."

"I'll let my uncle Eli speak in that case. Before I hand his letter to the police. Or even to my sister."

Gareth pulled a well-wrapped package from inside his oilskin trousers, took out a letter and began to read. Everyone else stood close by. They believed that they had the Viking surrounded.

This is the last will and confession of me, Elijah Farran, written Sunday May 26th in the Plough and Sail pub, Flinthammock. It may also be the last pint of Blackwater Brewery mild-and-bitter that I will ever savour unless my nephew Gareth Farran arrives before I leave and can be persuaded to stand me another. He's a good lad, is Gareth, and I hereby leave him all that I have to leave, which is the Truth.

My house is no longer mine and the woman I married (who has never truly been my wife) invites strangers there without informing me. I was once the keeper of the prettiest and most generous-natured sailing smack on the whole of the East Coast but she was taken from me and sunk. I took that to be our just deserts for the killing of my brother Joe but I have mourned her every day for nigh on thirty year.

I dreamed of the Igraine last night. I dreamed that she had been raised from her watery grave and was sailing back to me. I woke up in that stable, blubbing like a girl. Then, when I saw my half-brother, Arthur Farran Gold, declare on TV that he would be welcoming the Little Ships of Dunkirk with dirty money I knew this must be the end.

The money that my half-brother Arthur Farran Gold is offering today is money that has been earned from criminal acts over many years and I can no longer be a party.

This is what I have to say.

To whom it may concern. I hereby state that since the bad winter of '63, which destroyed the whole year's oyster harvest, I have been an accomplice in my half-brother's smuggling operations. When I began doing runs and lifting pots for Artie I believed that all that was involved was continental spirits and tobacco. I knew it were risky but it didn't feel wrong, not exactly.

I would like to say that when I stopped believing that it were spirits and tobacco I stopped doing the runs but that would be false and this document is my last truth. Artie had loaned me more money than I could afford to repay. When he said he would take the Igraine if I refused to continue, I should have let him but I could not bear it.

I confess that I also involved my brother Joe after he had lost his job. This led him directly to his death when I were lifting stuff. I would like my nephew to know that his dad were innocent until that moment. And also that it were an accident. Her boom came across with a wallop an it hefted him straight in. Then she ran, and it were a full cable afore I could turn her back to search in them black waters.

I have done many wrong things in my life and I am sorry for some of them. I find I need another final pint and I thank my nephew Gareth in advance for picking up the tab and for the many times he has overlooked that I can no longer stand my round.

Signed by Elijah Farran and witnessed by the Landlord of the Plough and Sail.

CHAPTER TWENTY-TWO

The End of the Rainbow

Monday June 3, LW 0900 HW 1508 LW 2108 HW 0330

"Arthur Farran Gold, you are under arrest for…"

But the old man didn't wait to hear what Martha was charging him with. He had Madrigal clamped against him and he had a well-maintained World War Two revolver that he knew how to use.

"Don't struggle," he told the terrified girl, backing away from the chapel down the long, flat foreshore, with his arm round her neck and his gun at her head. "Your father's as deep in this as I am. Come along with me nicely and you've a chance to survive. Although our sponsorship of your Olympic bid may have come to an end."

He was pulling her with him all the time he was talking. Her big blue eyes were horrified and her pretty face skull-like with shock.

She wasn't resisting. She was walking backwards on legs that were apart and as rigid as a doll's. Xanthe remembered someone telling her that people automatically lost continence when they realised they'd been taken hostage. Had Madrigal wet herself – or worse?

Already they were halfway to *Miranda*.

Gareth made a sudden direct dash forwards but a bullet caught him and he went down. Griselda was on her stomach and elbows swarming after Madrigal when a second bullet landed inches ahead of her, splashing black mud up into her face and temporarily blinding her.

"Don't!" Madrigal screamed, though it wasn't clear who she was trying to halt.

Xanthe was bent double and jinking as she ran. She wasn't going for the abductor; she was looping round and sideways and heading for Gareth. Martha couldn't move as she had Siri and Kelly-Jane on the ground and had positioned herself protectively in front of them. Maggi was there with her, also lying flat, murmuring reassurance to the younger girls.

June was phoning. Anna was videoing. When the Viking had tried a shot at her, she took cover beside the chapel and carried on. This was evidence and they would need it.

"He'll be out of range in a moment," Martha said. "I've called 999. They're alerting the coastguard as well as the police. I've asked them for a helicopter."

"I've called an ambulance," said June. "For the man who went down."

"He's my brother," Martha thanked her. "I have to concentrate on the criminal situation. My colleagues will get to Sir Hubert and Lady Shryke as urgently as possible. Whatever the accusations, that's their daughter out there."

"You okay?" Xanthe asked, as she flung herself down beside Gareth. Fool question, obviously.

"Might not make the Fishling mud race this year but you didn't oughta worry about that. You get after Artie Gold – and that poor young girl."

Right as usual. Vile as she was, Madrigal hadn't deserved this. Xanthe wished she knew the range of a revolver or how often someone would need to reload. More essential World War Two research, not done.

The Viking had reached the water's edge. She heard another crackle of shots and saw spray kicking up around the stern of Gareth's workboat.

She ran on. He was forcing Madrigal into the launch. Had his gun on her all the time. He was fit and relentless. Impossible to believe his age.

He was starting his engine but *Miranda* had touched ground in the shallows. She wasn't instantly able to rear up and roar away.

The Viking let the engine idle, threw a kedge out from her stern and hauled off. Why hadn't Madrigal grabbed that moment to try and escape?

Little Luke, Anna's step-brother, had explained something about the feeling of having a real gun pointed at you. Not the proxy in a video game but a gun that could fire actual bullets, which could rip into your soft flesh and sever arteries, shatter bone and make you bleed. Madrigal could be scared witless.

Miranda was away now, heading towards the horizon, her wake a long, foam-fringed curve as the Commander steered for *Godwyn*.

Xanthe knew she had to follow – even though she had a snowball's chance in hell of even keeping them in sight. Gareth's workboat was there, but it had been holed and there was fuel spilling across the water from the smashed outboard.

The last of the dinghies to arrive – and therefore the easiest to take – was *Black Star*. She'd like to have taken *Fritha*, of course she would, but the Firefly was much heavier and would need several willing hands to push her off the shell bank. Anyway,

Black Star was still *Spray*, the moment you looked beneath her colour and asked her to sail.

A lovely, playful, little breeze; the last of the rainbows fading into memory; the white sails of distant dinghies beating back to Meresig or reaching for the Colne – it was an idyllic scene.

Xanthe flung herself into the Laser as if she was launching a surfboard. It was a great start but the wind simply wasn't there to keep up the power. She had everything adjusted in seconds, was in her own familiar dinghy ready to sail at the peak of her skill. And she was about as effective as a bath duck bobbing on a pond.

What was the Viking's plan? Was he intending to rendezvous with the lightship or was that course merely coincidental? He had a hostage and he had a vessel that was surely faster than the fastest police launch. But with cooperation from countries all around the North Sea you couldn't really hope to escape unseen, not in daylight, and it wouldn't be dark for hours yet.

A puff and a surge, a half a degree directional change: Xanthe's response was instant and instinctive. Her own dinghy was an extension of her own self. She could think, plan, sail. None of it fast enough to be any use to Madrigal.

Tan sails in the distance – the gaffers were returning from their offshore race. And over to port, coming down the River Blackwater as fast as their restored engines would carry them, Xanthe saw the fleet of Dunkirk Little Ships. There were the white painted motor yachts, a couple of barges and that wonderful restored paddle steamer that could have been Joe Farran's when he was a small boy making sandwiches. The skippers must have had heard the news of Madrigal's abduction and had leapt on board their craft like knights of old dashing to the rescue of a damsel in distress.

She spotted a police launch emerging from the Colne and was that possibly the sound of a helicopter drumming in the distant air? *Miranda* would be surrounded. Arthur Gold would surrender. They'd surely save Madrigal.

For a moment she felt delight, then fear drenched her like an ice-bath. The Viking was ruthless. Now he would be desperate. The danger for his hostage would be extreme.

Did people understand – would they offer space for negotiation? They didn't know what he was capable of. Did Madrigal know? Her father was his business partner – maybe his criminal accomplice – but she wasn't responsible for her parents. Xanthe could maybe calm the situation? She just needed to get there.

Where was the wind when you needed it?

But the motorboat had turned. No need for *Spray* to speed up, *Miranda* was hurtling back. She would reach Xanthe well before any of the others reached her.

OMG – now she felt lonely; now she was scared. If she managed this well she had the chance to save Madrigal: if she messed up…she didn't want to think of it.

Stay calm. Think clearly. Find the words.

"Xanthe! Help me…*please*!"

Madrigal was calling out to her as soon as she was close enough. The Viking was driving slowly, almost casually, now. But he still had that gun and it was still pointed at his partner's daughter. No wonder Maddie was hyperventilating, no wonder her face was like a creamy saucer holding her two enormous baby-blue eyes, drowning in tears. She was stretching out her hands as if she was praying and Xanthe was ashamed of herself for noticing her false nails, each painted white with a tiny red St George cross.

"You can save me! He says he'll let me go. Please Xanthe, I'm not a great swimmer. And it's so far out..."

He was letting Madrigal go?

"Why?"

"I am leaving these ungrateful shores but an English rose should never be transplanted."

Pompous git.

"You're running away from your crimes."

Stop it, Xanthe, she told herself. Don't antagonise him. If he's letting Maddie go, you have to make it easy for him.

"Please, Xanthe, come alongside. Take me on board your dinghy. Help me. *Please!*"

She didn't trust Arthur Farran Gold. She didn't entirely trust Madrigal Shryke either. But what choice did she have? She could hear the helicopter, the police boat, the engines of the Little Ships,

"I'm not waiting any longer," he spoke harshly.

He looked ready to fire up *Miranda*'s amazing engine and be gone with a roar.

"Yeah...okay...of course."

She noticed her own breathing change as she manoeuvred *Spray* alongside the sleekly-varnished hull of the powerboat. She was totally concentrating so as not to show her fear. She slipped her dinghy's painter round a smart brass cleat but kept hold of the end so she could leave in a hurry.

"Help me, Xanthe."

Madrigal didn't seem to have control of her limbs – and yes, she did stink.

"I can't...quite...seem to..."

"I won't wait," growled the Viking. He left the steering position and moved towards the two girls. He still had that gun.

Xanthe let go of her painter's end and steadied herself against *Miranda*'s gunwale as she reached up to help Maddie.

Suddenly she had been grabbed and tipped into the cockpit and Madrigal was into *Black Star* and away.

The Viking was smirking and his gun was on her.

"Deportation time, Miss Ribiero. Sit quiet and we can make this easy."

He was moving back to the controls but not taking his eyes off her, those peculiarly level and direct blue eyes that hid his scheming soul. "The plebs will let us through with you on board."

"No-one was going to hurt Madrigal either."

She was so angry that fear didn't come into it any more. But the Viking hadn't noticed.

"Her parents and I go back many years," he answered, unctuously. "She persuaded me it was wrong to deprive them. I hold the bond of family sacred."

He didn't expect her to have any answer. He pushed down hard on the chromium throttle and placed his non-gun hand on the steering wheel as *Miranda* leapt ahead.

Xanthe leapt too. Backwards, to grab the varnished flagpole from its solid brass casing, then forwards, to crack it down onto his gun arm.

He shouted and *Miranda* gave a wild lurch, tipping Xanthe over the low cockpit coaming. She didn't feel the pain as his bullet winged her shoulder. The impact of hitting the water at such a speed was enough to knock her out.

There were vessels all around them now. Plenty of witnesses who saw the Commander of the Saxon Shore drive his powerboat direct and deliberate into the lightship's metal side and who watched him perish in a pyre of flame and thick, black, billowing smoke.

"Invoking Rule 69 doesn't begin to cover it," Griselda was shaking with her fury as she hauled Madrigal ashore. "You saved your*self* at the expense of your fellow sailor. Then, when you must have seen her go over the side, you made no attempt at all to turn back and assist – in total contravention of the laws of the sea – let alone your common humanity. You are banned forever from my squad. And if we discover that that the money your family gave for our new academy was dishonestly earned, I'm prepared to tear it down brick by brick before I allow a future generation to be fouled."

"I think that you can safely allow the law to take its course."

June Ribiero didn't look at Griselda or at Madrigal. She was gripping Maggi's hand and watching as the air ambulance finished lifting her older daughter from the sea. The first of the Little Ships had been standing by throughout and there were paramedics on the shore who were in radio contact with those in the air. She'd been reassured that Xanthe was still breathing and her pulse was strong. She'd recovered consciousness and they would now be giving pain relief and heading straight for the nearest operating theatre. Xanthe's father had said a hurried goodbye to his old friend, the Ghanaian Deputy High Commissioner, and was already on his way to meet them there.

June was in shock but was holding herself together. She didn't take her eyes from the helicopter but spoke as calmly as she could for the sake of the other children. She knew that what she had to say was important.

"I came here today with a heavy heart. The trial of the gangland hit-men was on the verge of collapse as some key witnesses no longer felt confident about the safety of their families. I believe that what we have seen and heard this afternoon has finally removed that central threat and justice will be done. These were the men behind the mobsters."

The helicopter was gone; there were police and rescuers around the lightship and the smoke still poured from the burning powerboat. Maggi was clinging to her mother as desperately as her mother was clinging to her. They needed to leave now. Martha was there in charge and Anna had all the evidence.

June managed to smile at everyone.

"And don't let's be too hasty at Weymouth," she said to Griselda. "You are training sailors from across the world and there may even be young hopefuls here who would benefit from every breath of encouragement that you are able to give."

Kelly-Jane put her arm around her friend and hugged her tight, but Siri didn't speak.

Monkey's Fist knot

Research Notes

The extended essay that Xanthe fails to write throughout this story is a central part of the International Baccalaureate Diploma which she's chosen to study instead of A-levels. As she's been so distracted by other matters during her time in Flinthammock I thought that perhaps I could help her with her bibliography.

Clearly Xanthe's tutor will already have given her a copy of Margery Allingham's *The Oaken Heart.* This is an autobiographical account of the first years of the Second World War experienced in the village of Tolleshunt D'Arcy, which lies a few miles inland from the River Blackwater. Allingham was writing throughout 1940, when invasion was expected and security was a central issue. She chose, therefore, to disguise the names of her own and nearby villages. Tolleshunt D'Arcy was renamed Auburn, Maldon was Fishling and Tollesbury became Flinthammock. I have borrowed some of these place names together with names from Allingham's first published work, *Blackerchief Dick,* a smuggler's tale set on Mersea Island. Two other River Blackwater classics, Rev. Sabine Baring Gould's *Mehalah* and Alfred Ludgater's *Mistress of Broad Marsh* have similarly been plundered. I've reverted to early spellings for Osea and Mersea Islands and have shuffled some of the names on the Bradwell side of the river – all to reinforce the obvious point that this story is fiction.

Xanthe, however, will need to stick to fact. She'll want to find copies of J.P. Foynes *The Battle of the East Coast 1939-1945* and Russell Plummer's *The Ships that Saved an Army: A Comprehensive Record of the 1,300 Little Ships of Dunkirk* . If she's still keen on using contemporary sources, *Looming Lights* by George Goldsmith Carter (published 1947) describes his experience on board a Channel lightship at this period and *We Fought Them in Gunboats* by Lieutenant-Commander Rober Peverall Hitchens (1944) is frighteningly atmospheric – though less directly relevant. Athough both these books are long out of print I'm hoping that Xanthe's parents' club, the Royal Orwell and Ancient, might have copies in their library.

I was fortunate to inherit these titles, and many others, from my father and my uncle, both of whom served in the RNVR. Dad (George Jones) had poor eyesight so was mainly employed in organisational roles, including a stint in Freetown, Sierra Leone. Uncle Jack was in direct combat and was badly wounded in the Dieppe Raid of 1942. He needed to lash himself to the wheel of his MTB (Motor Torpedo Boat) in order to get his boat and his men safely home to England.

While Xanthe is exploring her club library she's sure to find a copy of Michael Frost's beautifully-written *Boadicea CK213: the Story of an East Coast Fishing Smack*. It won't help her with her extended essay, as it ends at the outbreak of the Second World War, but it will tell her yet more about the sailing and fishing qualities of a smack very like the *Igraine*. (In the interests of accuracy I should point out that it was the smack *Iris Mary* who sailed from Tollesbury to Ramsgate, offering assistance with the Dunkirk evacuation, and it was the *Teasel* who was sunk by a mine off Tollesbury pier.)

A more recent title, which Xanthe will definitely enjoy, is Giles Milton's *Russian Roulette,* which describes Augustus Agar's extraordinarily daring use of a high-speed CMB (Coastal Motor Boat) in an attempt to rescue Paul Dukes (fellow MI6 agent to Arthur Ransome) by skimming across the surface of a minefield in the eastern Baltic. Agar was an outstandingly brave and talented Naval officer who has lent nothing more than his first name and his connection with Osea Island on the River Blackwater to the morally corrupt Augustus Gold of this story. Xanthe will find all her dislike of modern smuggling amply reinforced if she reads Tony Thompson's *Bloggs 19: the Story of the Essex Range Rover Triple Murders.* I hope she'll take the taste away with a re-reading of the most romantic and beautiful of all Dunkirk stories, Paul Gallico's *The Snow Goose.* I feel sure her parents keep a copy in their cabin.

Readers who are sticklers for fictional accuracy (and quite right too) will have noticed that there has been an inexplicable gap in Xanthe's school career. She was already doing her GCSEs in 2007 when the events of *Ghosting Home* took place, yet this story with its black Barbie dolls and Macbooks and increasing use of social media sits much more comfortably around 2010, the seventieth anniversary of the Dunkirk evacuation. This was the year when I was doing my own research for a new edition of *The Oaken Heart* and was interviewing several *non*-fictional 80- and 90-year-olds in the Tolleshunt Darcy/ Tollesbury area – none of whom bore any resemblance to the Farrans or the Golds. All I can say on the matter of dates is that Xanthe and the other Allies have not suffered some unknown educational calamity and lost whole years from their lives, it's simply the author being slow. So please may I avail myself of arch-stickler Peter Dowden's offer of leniency and plead for the use of 'Narnian time'?

Mentioning Peter Dowden makes me want to begin thanking all the people who have helped Xanthe and I through rather a difficult writing period, but first I have an important disclaimer to make. There *is* a gloriously scarlet light vessel moored in the Tollesbury Saltings and she *does* provide outdoor adventure for many young people every year. Her name is *Trinity* and she is managed by FACT (the Fellowship Afloat Charitable Trust). Initially I made contact with Andrew Eastham, the

Principal of FACT. He was ready to be welcoming – but I didn't visit. At that early point in the story I had no idea whether Dominic and Martha and the *Godwyn* Companions would turn out to be helpful or not to Xanthe. I certainly didn't want to muddle up my fictional characters with real people who are doing unambiguously good work. So I admired *Trinity* from the other side of the creek and allowed poor *Godwyn* to suffer difficulties and disasters as the fictional events unfolded.

I kept *Jenny Marx*, an elderly Skipper dinghy, in Tollesbury marina whilst writing this book. I didn't manage to sail as much as I'd liked (does one ever?) but she and I appreciated the friendly attitude of the marina management and so did *Peter Duck*, who spent a few days there after encountering a violent summer storm round the top end of Osea Island. I'm very grateful to Francis's cousin Nigina Römer, a member of the Swiss sailing team, for her invaluable tips on sailing Laser Radial dinghies.

The Blackwater is a lovely river and so is the Colne. I was lucky to meet Richard Haward, doyen of Mersea oysters, one bright January day on the Bradwell shore. I also benefited from helpful advice and information from the Maldon Oyster Company and enjoyed a memorable walk in the company of children's literature aficionado, Elizabeth Williams, to investigate their racks. Recently I've been visiting the Pioneer Sailing Trust at Brightlingsea. This has made me more deeply aware of the past and present history of the area. It was unexpectedly thrilling to discover that Felicity Lees, their operations manager, shared my (and Xanthe's) feeling for the transformative power of Tollesbury. *Trinity*, the real *Godwyn*, had been central to her sailing education and she even admitted to running across the saltings, leaping pools and channels, just as Xanthe does.

Members of my family – Ned, Ruth, Bertie, Frank – came sailing with me and all of my family have enjoyed Janet and Allan Ahlberg's classic *Ha Ha Bonk Book* as much as Nelson would. Frank, Georgeanna, Francis, Peter Willis, Peter Dowden, David Cooper, Lesley Simpson, Claudia Myatt, Megan Trudell, read, proof-read and commented on earlier drafts of this novel. And of those kindly souls it was the two I have never met in person – David Cooper and Peter Dowden – who were indefatigable in late night emailing or Facebook messaging to help me make sense of my story. Thank you both.

I'd like to thank Amanda Craig for suggesting a Dunkirk story – though I imagine this may not be what she had in mind. Voice actress Anna Bentinck's advice on developing a character's distinctive speech has been invaluable and I'll never forget the thrill of listening to her recording *The Salt-Stained Book*. Xanthe should be acknowledging her tutor at this point and I need to say, yet again, that many years ago Margery Allingham and *The Oaken Heart* changed the direction of my life. And so did Francis Wheen – in quite a different way.

Julia Jones, 2015

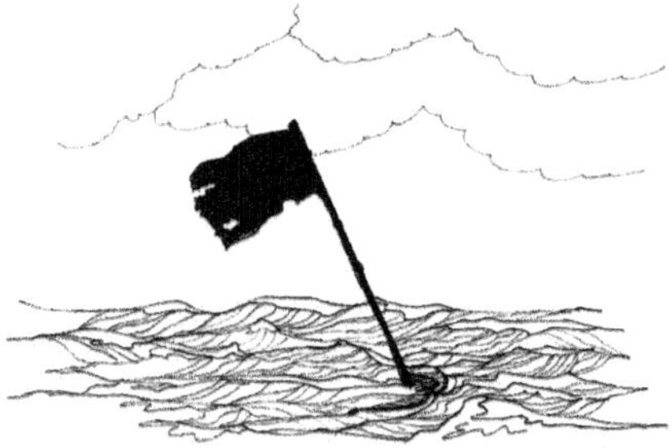

Maritime Titles from Golden Duck

The Strong Winds Series by Julia Jones (with illustrations by Claudia Myatt):

1 *The Salt-Stained Book* (available as an audiobook)
2 *A Ravelled Flag*
3 *Ghosting Home*
4 *The Lion of Sole Bay*
5 *Black Waters*
6 *Pebble*
7 *Voyage North* (forthcoming 2022)

The Yachtsman Volunteers Collection:

- *The Cruise of Naromis: August in the Baltic 1939*
  GA Jones (with an introduction & afterword by Julia Jones)
- *Man the Ropes: the Autobiography of Augustine Courtauld—Explorer, Naval Officer, Yachtsman*
  Augustine Courtauld (with an introduction by Susie Hamilton)
- *From Pole to Pole: the Life of Quintin Riley*
  Jonathon Riley (with a foreword by Noël Riley)
- *Maid Matelot: Adventures of a Wren Stoker in World War Two*
  Rozelle Raynes (with a foreword by Hugh Matheson and an appreciation by Richard Woodman)
- *We Fought Them in Gunboats* (HMS *Beehive* edition) (forthcoming)
  Robert Hichens

You may also be interested in *Uncommon Courage: The Yachtsman Volunteers of World War II* by Julia Jones, published by Adlard Coles, additionally available as an audiobook.

Books by Claudia Myatt:

- *Anglo-Saxon Inspirations: Designs to Colour and Create*
- *Keeping a Sketchbook Diary* (new edition forthcoming 2023)
- *One Line at a Time: Why Drawing Is Good for You and How to Do It*
- *Sketchbook Sailor*

We hold most titles in Claudia Myatt's RYA *Go Sailing!* series.

The East Coast:

- *The Deben* (biannual magazine)
  River Deben Association
- *Waldringfield: A Suffolk Village beside the River Deben*
  Waldringfield History Group

We also sell Robert Simper's books on East Coast history, people, and boats.

For a full list of Golden Duck titles, including the Allingham family series, *Wild Wood* by Jan Needle and the *Please Tell Me* activity books for older people, see golden-duck.co.uk. Most are additionally available as ebooks.